I0589335

*BETWEEN TRUTH AND LIES*
PUBLISHED BY MATTIE DUNMAN
Copyright © 2016 by Mattie Dunman

All rights reserved. Except for use in any review, the reproduction or utilization of this work in whole or in part in any form by any electronic, mechanical or other means, now known or hereinafter invented, including xerography, photocopying and record-ing, or in any information storage or retrieval system, is forbidden without the written permission of the publisher.

This is a work of fiction. Names, characters, places and incidents are either the product of the author's imagination or are used fictitiously, and any resemblance to actual per-sons, living or dead, business establishments, events or locales is entirely coincidental.

Printed in the USA.

Cover Design and Interior Format

© THE KILLION GROUP INC.

# BETWEEN TRUTH AND LIES

## MATTIE DUNMAN

*For Mom and Dad, with all my love—*
*You never questioned my dream, only ever asked "how can we help?"*

# CHAPTER ONE

" I'M COMPLETELY DISHONEST. I'VE SWINDLED everyone I've ever done business with."

I grab my Mom's arm and smile apologetically at the guy in the business suit who sits across from us. Mom glances down at me, eyebrow lifted in inquiry. I shake my head. She nods and turns back to the slightly bemused man across the table.

"Well, this has been very enlightening. I will take your offer under consideration and let you know," she says, rising from her chair.

The man is startled for a moment but recovers smoothly, his voice oiled with charm as he bids us goodbye. We've played this particular scene many times before; Mom meets with a potential buyer or seller for her antiques business and then I stop by to introduce myself and hear whatever unwelcome truth the client is hiding. Rinse, lather, repeat.

I don't look back as we exit the coffee shop. A morning meeting with a potential client at Starbucks. How cliché can you get?

As we round the corner outside the building Mom puts an arm around me. "Are you sure, sweetie? He had some great pieces, and he wasn't being unreasonable."

"I'm sure. He was lying," I say, a weary note in my voice. People are always trying to screw someone over. It gets depressing after a while.

"Oh well. Better safe than sorry." She shrugs and gives me a quick hug. "Thanks for coming with me."

I shrug back at her. What else am I going to do? Let my mom potentially lose buckets of her hard-earned cash by buying fake antiques from someone we know nothing about? Hardly. She needs me. She's always been terrible at reading people.

I, on the other hand, am infallible.

"C'mon. Let's get something good out of this trip. How about a new outfit for school tomorrow? There are some cute shops downtown, I bet we can find something you'll like," Mom offers playfully as we reach the car. I survey my outfit. Jeans, an old Ramones t-shirt, a vintage smoking jacket, and scuffed sneakers. Maybe some new clothes wouldn't hurt.

"Yeah, that sounds good," I agree. Mom's eyes brighten and she shoves me into the passenger seat, as if further discussion might make me change my mind. In the past, there has never really been any need for me to worry about what I wear. When you're homeschooled by your mother your entire life, hitting the books in comfy sweats is the norm.

The thought of school the next day starts the churning in my stomach again. I begged Mom to let me go to public school this semester, my last shot at a normal high school experience. It took weeks to wear her down, and since I already qualified for graduation, and got early acceptance to a university, high school is probably unnecessary. But I'm going to be eighteen in five months. This is the last opportunity I'll get before throwing myself into the unfamiliar and slightly terrifying world of college. I need to test the waters.

"You know, you can still back out of this," Mom says knowingly. I ignore the whirlpool in my stomach and force a smile.

"No way. How else will I know if the *Vampire Diaries* accurately portrays the average high school experience?"

Mom rolls her eyes more expressively than I ever could. She also manages to swerve the car into the opposite lane.

"Geez, Mom, watch the road!" I gasp, grabbing the door handle. She scoffs and makes it back into the right lane just as another car whizzes by, blaring its horn.

"I was fine. You worry too much."

Ten thrilling minutes later we pull into the parking garage three blocks away from the main drag in Georgetown. A long stretch of trendy boutiques, designer shops, and overpriced bistros populated by a mixture of well-dressed business people and stylishly scruffy college kids, M Street is a popular destination on Sunday, despite the frigid early January temperature. I half-listen to Mom's litany on city traffic as I look around. Two months ago we moved to Harpers Ferry, a small town in West Virginia about an hour outside of D.C, but this is only my second trip into the Capitol, and my first visit to Georgetown. Since I'm starting college in the fall at Georgetown U., I am avidly interested in what the neighborhood has to offer.

We stroll down the street glancing at the different shop names, Mom excitedly pointing out where we might eat lunch, but I feel a familiar melancholy wash over me. All Mom sees are the elegant window displays and sale advertisements. I see past the cutesy lettering on the signs. I read what they really promise.

Mom calls it instinct. She believes that I have clearer first impressions than other people. An uncanny knack for sensing the truth where others can't.

But I know better. I'm a freak. I'm so weird and wrong that I've been separated from the rest of the world for as long as I can remember.

"Sweetie, do you see anything you like?"

I blink and look around me, realizing that I have zoned out completely. Mom is pointing to a window display in front of us with mannequins wearing faded t-shirts paired with short skirts and brightly colored scarves wound around the white plastic necks. I dart a look up at the sign over the door.

'Over-priced and Poorly Made' stretches across the sign until I blink. The words shimmer slightly and then I am reading what everyone else sees. Just like always.

"No. I don't see anything I like," I say, my previous jolt of excitement over shopping fading into a disenchanted resignation. It's hard never to be blissfully unaware of reality. The trendy window display just looks forced and falsely cheerful to me now.

"Oh, come on. We'll find something for you," Mom argues, grabbing my arm and dragging me through the frosted glass door. With a sigh I go along, knowing that it will please her to buy me something. She always feels guilty after she makes use of my "gift." I might as well make someone happy.

An hour later we emerge, Mom flushed with success, me trudging along behind her, clutching my one bag and feeling awkward. She picked out sweaters and skirts and carefully demolished jeans that she swore would help me blend in, but nothing looked right on me. She ended up buying the clothes meant for me herself, and I left the store with a pair of yellow ballet flats decorated by a cheerful white flower on top, my one concession to mom's determination to get me something. As we walk down the street, Mom chatting away obliviously, I worry that I've been needlessly stubborn about attending school. That I won't fit in.

I've never been to school. I've never gone to a party, or a dance, or a football game. I've never played on a sports team or been in detention.

I've never had a boyfriend.

I've never had a friend.

Mom told me that when I was little, she and my father put me in kindergarten before it became apparent that I was too "different" to be with normal people. I don't remember much, but there was another little girl with whom I used to share toys and play at recess. I guess no one really noticed the way I picked up on every little thing, the way I would blurt out what someone had been hiding after they spoke to me for the first time. Kids are forgiven a lot of tactless things when they're that little.

But most adults don't want you to tell the teacher that they're beating their child at home.

We were having a parent day, where everyone's mom or dad or whatever would come in and look at the macaroni pictures we'd made or the modeling clay lumps we proudly called sculptures. My playmate dragged a frayed looking woman with cold eyes over to meet me.

"Mommy, this is Derry," my friend had to say several times before the woman took notice.

I had smiled up at the woman, extending my small hand for her to shake as my father had shown me to do, feeling hurt when she didn't take it.

"I'm going to beat Chrissy with a belt when I get home for talking so much," the woman had finally said, whatever greeting she had really imparted lost in the truth she was hiding.

That's what happens with me. I'm not psychic, or clairvoyant, or even telepathic. I simply can't be lied to. No matter what someone says to me, the first thing I hear is the truth. Usually what they're thinking about or something related to the situation, whatever they are holding back in that moment.

Once that first statement is out of the way, I can get through the rest of a conversation without hearing the double-speak. Still, even if I can't hear the truth behind the words, if someone is lying I can always tell. Lies find their way under my skin like tiny insects clamoring for my attention, forcing me to see the uglier side of people. There's no way to get rid of that first impression. And it's always right.

Always.

So I ran straight over and told my teacher what I'd heard. Though she acted like I had misheard, I knew that she believed me, had probably already had suspicions anyway. I saw her go over to my friend's mother.

They argued and the woman left, dragging my friend behind even as the teacher hurried after them. That was the last time I saw her. When my teacher later mentioned to my mother what I had said, my parents removed me from kindergarten. That was the last time I ever had anything resembling a friend.

I shrug off the old memories. The last thing I need to be thinking of tonight is how woefully inadequate my experiences have been. All my knowledge of social interaction and school politics is based on *Gossip Girl*. I have serious doubts as to its accuracy.

But I can't help the impatient, fluttery feeling in my veins when I think about tomorrow. The whole thing could be a bust, of course, and yet I lose myself in the fantasy of sitting at a lunch table, surrounded by friends, talking about the big party coming up, and stealing kisses with my gorgeous, totally devoted boyfriend. As I slip into the car and Mom weaves her way through the brutal afternoon traffic, I can almost pretend that the fantasy is real, and I look out the window with a smile.

"Ok sweetheart, remember, if you want to come home, you just call me. I can be here in fifteen minutes," my mom says for the third time in the last five minutes. Her forehead is creased with worry and she's gripping the steering wheel too hard.

"I got it, Mom. I'll be fine," I protest, my hand on the door handle. Before I push the door open I hesitate and turn to look at her. "Do you really think it's going to be that bad?" I ask, unable to stop myself.

She pins me with her warm hazel gaze and then smiles, relaxing her shoulders. A knot inside me eases a little as she brushes a hair back from my face. "No, sweetie. I think it's going to be a little overwhelming at first, but I know you can handle it. Just…be careful. You know that when you first meet people, you seem a little…"

"Weird? Stupid? Psycho?"

Mom fixes me with a look. "No, and don't start that up again. You can seem a little distant sometimes while you're sorting things through. Relax and let people get to know you. You're going to be a hit," she promises and leans over to kiss my cheek.

"I hope so," I mutter under my breath and suck up my courage. I swing the door open and hop out onto the sidewalk, looking up at the

hulking brick structure that makes up John Brown High. A wave of nausea rolls over me and the urge to jump back in the car and beg Mom to
take me home is all consuming. Clenching my hands around the strap
of my bag, I steel myself, keeping the fantasy of friends and fun forefront
in my mind until my feet unglue themselves from the asphalt and I can
move forward. I glance around and wave goodbye to my mom. She taps
her horn lightly and pulls away, taking with her my last escape route.

With no other options left, I head toward the two flights of concrete
steps leading up to the front doors of the school. The building is totally
retro, probably built in the 1970s and never renovated. I bet the pipes are
ancient. Probably shouldn't drink the water.

I reach the top of the stairs and brace myself for my first step into the
school as a student. Mom and I came here three weeks ago to get registered, and I was given a tour and picked my schedule. But everything had
still been theoretical then. This was the real show.

The sign over the doors reads "John Brown High School." I don't see
anything else because there isn't any truth to conceal. The building is
exactly what is advertised, and my nerves calm their ragged dance slightly
at this reassurance. Taking a deep breath, I put my hand out and get ready
to open the door.

It swings open, nearly swatting me in the face, and I stagger back, almost tumbling down the stairs I just climbed. An angry looking boy in
a black wool pea-coat and dark jeans stalks past me, not even glancing
my way or noticing the way I'm cradling my arm where the door struck
it. I consider saying something, but the hard set of his shoulders prevents
me from forming words. I swallow my irritation and rub my forearm
until the stinging passes. The boy runs down the stairs and halts before he
crosses into the street. He glances around as though searching for something and then slowly pivots and locks his gaze on me.

My chest constricts and I can't breathe. An invisible hand is gripping
my throat and deliberately tightening until my head is no longer connected to the rest of my body. The inside of my mind burns like molten
lava being poured in my brain and my legs and hands start to shake uncontrollably until I almost cannot remain standing.

Just as suddenly it stops and the vise on my neck is released. My mind
clears with no residue of pain, as though the past few seconds never happened. I see the boy widen his eyes in surprise before he jerks abruptly
and turns his back to me, crossing the pick-up lane and turning the cor-

ner, out of my sight. I am left breathless and stiff with terror.

I don't know how, I don't know why, but I can't help feeling that somehow that boy just nearly killed me with a look.

I'm not sure how long I remain standing there, staring down the street where the boy vanished, but finally the door opens again and a familiar face peers out, voice strident in greeting.

"I want another Vicodin and I want a divorce," she says, unwittingly revealing a hidden truth instead of a simple 'hello.'

I shudder and refocus. I don't know who the boy was or what just happened, but he isn't here now and I have a major life change to get through. Mrs. Hayworth, the secretary I talked to when I registered, looks at me expectantly and I nod and force a smile.

I'm sorry, I didn't hear you," I say, wishing I didn't know how miserable the woman in front of me is.

"I said I wondered if you'd gotten here yet. Come on in, let's get you settled." She gestures for me to follow and I enter the school unceremoniously. There is no turning back now.

"Ok, so we've got your schedule finalized and I've got a map for you. I'm going to show you your locker and give you your books, and then you'll be on your own. Any questions?" Mrs. Hayworth asks briskly, her low-slung heels clicking emphatically on the linoleum. I shake my head and frown. In all the movies, new students get assigned mentors or helpers their first day. Usually a nerd or someone impossibly good-looking. Guess that's the first inconsistency between my research and reality.

I'm about a half-hour early, mainly because I thought there would be more orientation to get through and I didn't want to be late for my first class. But within a few minutes Mrs. Hayworth shows me my locker and gives me the combination, asks one last time if I need anything, and then disappears into her office, presumably to take another Vicodin. I stand next to my locker, reeling from the speed and indifference with which everything is happening. None of this matches my notions of what today would be like. Disappointment begins to bubble under my skin.

I shake it off and scold myself for being so sensitive. Did I really expect the whole school to shut down and people to line up waiting for me? Well, maybe a little, but that's not important now. At least I'll have a chance to figure out where my classes are while the halls are empty. So I stash the books I won't need until after lunch in the locker and hang a Georgetown University sticker on the inside of the door to personalize it. Once I see what everyone else puts in their lockers, I'll make some adjustments. With a frisson of excitement, I look at the map and try to figure out which of the circled rooms is my first class.

The school isn't big. Mrs. Hayworth said there were only about a hundred students in each grade, so it doesn't take me long to formulate a plan for the day. I glance at my watch. It's still only seven-forty. Most of the buses aren't due to arrive for another ten minutes. I chew on my bottom lip and begin to doubt that I have any idea what I've gotten myself into.

Needing to find something that fits my expectations, I take off in the direction of the journalism room, where my fourth period class is held. The day is broken into four periods, each an hour and a half with a forty-five minute lunch in the middle. Part of the reason I was able to convince Mom to let me undertake the great experiment was because of the opportunity to work on the school newspaper. Since my major is going to be print journalism, I argued that I needed the experience of working with other students on a paper.

I peek through the window of the room and see the teacher sitting at his desk, staring with a vacant expression at something on a laptop. He is younger than I expected, probably in his early thirties, and slim with tufty, non-descript brown hair. He has the furtive air of a mouse, with quick movements and eyes that never seem to stop roving. Screwing up my courage and reminding myself this is one thing I can feel confident about, I knock on the door. The teacher looks up and waves me in, closing the lid of his computer as he opens his mouth to speak.

"I look at porn while I'm in school."

I halt and stare at my feet in to hide my blush, thankful I have had so many years of practice schooling my features not to reflect my reaction to whatever unwelcome truths I have to hear on a daily basis.

"Can I help you?" the teacher says impatiently, probably repeating his original statement. I force myself to start walking again and to smile at him normally, like I don't know that he has naked pictures on his computer screen.

"Hi. Um, I'm Derry MacKenna. I'm new, and I'm signed up for your fourth period," I explain, rapidly beginning to rethink the wisdom of bringing myself to this man's attention. There is no mistaking the appreciative gleam in his eyes as he looks me over with more than professional interest. I am very aware of the dim lighting in the room and how silent the halls are as he stands and comes toward me, hand outstretched. Swallowing my unease, I shake his hand, noting with disgust that it is slightly damp.

"Derry, it's nice to meet you. I'm Mr. Shockey. What can I do for you?" he asks, perfectly naturally. Maybe I'm imagining things.

"I just wanted to introduce myself and talk to you about joining the paper," I say, shoving my misgivings aside, trying to focus on the task at hand.

He frowns and tilts his head. "Well, I don't usually let students on the paper until they've spent a semester in journalism, learning the basic rules and how we do things here. I don't really think I can let you skip that."

I clear my throat and lift up my chin. This is where I can make the right impression. "I understand, but I have a lot of experience writing freelance for newspapers. I just want to get the opportunity to work with other people, get a feel for how a newsroom operates," I reply, digging into my bag to pull out the portfolio I prepared. I hand it to him and he raises an eyebrow as he takes it, his eyes darting over me again. "These are a sample of some of the stories I've done."

I wait while he flips through the folder, his eyebrows rising higher with each page. Finally he closes the folder and looks at me with a different light in his eyes, one of bewildered respect.

"It looks like you have quite a lot of experience. I see stories for at least three different papers, all of them very professional. How long have you been doing this?" he asks with real interest. My smile is genuine now as I explain.

"Since I was fourteen. One of my mother's friends was a newspaper editor in our old town, and he let me work as an intern for a few months in the summer, and then I started writing little stories and it just kind of grew from there. One of my articles was picked up by the Associated Press this fall," I say, opening the folder and pointing to the page in question. Mr. Shockey nods and then laughs.

"I read this article. I remember being impressed that the reporter managed to get a city councilman to confess to selling utilities contracts to the lowest bidder for kickbacks. That was you?" He grins with a boyish amusement that makes me more comfortable.

"Yeah. He couldn't believe he was telling me either," I inform him, smiling at the memory of the councilman's shock when I changed the subject of our interview from his upcoming campaign to the corrupt practices he'd been covering up during his tenure. It's hard to hide something like that from me.

"This is fantastic. Yes, I think in your case we can definitely make an exception."

I begin to hear voices in the hallway, the first of the students going to their lockers and taking care of the business of morning. "Well, we can talk more in fourth period. Usually I divide up the class and have the students on the paper meet in the computer lab or work independently. My editor this year is Jake Wise. I'll get you started with a beat and he can show you the ropes, okay?"

I nod vigorously, thrilled to have something go the way I'd hoped. Mr. Shockey puts his hand on my shoulder and squeezes lightly. I tense and my smile dims.

"See you fourth period, Derry. I'm looking forward to it."

I smile nervously and back away, trying to head to the exit without looking like I'm running away. I can feel Shockey's eyes on me as I walk out the door.

The hallway is teeming when I emerge. For a moment, I am frozen in shock at the vibrant eddy of students that streams past me. Eyes glance up to meet mine and then flash away, lost in a sea of faces that have an alarming uniformity. Four hundred students may not seem like much for a high school, especially one near D.C., but the reality is overwhelming.

I shift the bag on my shoulder and enter the fray, finding it more difficult to locate my class now that the halls are filled with the clanging of lockers being slammed, bodies pushing past me uninterestedly, and the swelling din of voices that bounces off the white concrete walls and reverberates in my brain. The halls are nearly empty before I find the correct room, and I pause outside the door, drawing in a deep breath before the plunge.

"I'm terrified of everyone," a harsh female voice declares.

I swing around to see a girl with a pinched face staring at me with irritation. "Didn't you hear me? Go in or get out of the way," she barks, knocking past me.

"Oh, sorry," I mumble and step to the side to let her pass. She rolls her eyes and slips through the door. Not wanting to look stupid, I follow into the room. About half the students are there, most standing around their desks chatting, some sitting quietly in their chairs looking through textbooks. No one looks at me. The teacher is writing on the whiteboard, so I wait patiently by her desk, casting surreptitious glances at the rest of the room.

More students file in, calling out to others, unwittingly revealing their honest impressions as each voice strikes me for the first time. I have spent so many years tuning out accidental revelations from strangers that I am able to keep my concentration on appearing normal with relative ease. The students are clustering together and putting their heads close for whispered conferences. I worry that there won't be a chair left for me and wonder exactly how I planned to make friends with people who have probably been grouped together like this since childhood.

"I'm not really making a difference anymore."

I smile hesitantly, unsure of what the teacher actually said. "Hi, I'm Derry MacKenna. Mrs. Hayworth said to give you this to sign," I say, handing her the sheet of paper that will prove I am responsible enough to get to all of my classes and make myself known to the teachers. She gives me a friendly smile and takes the paper, signing it with a flourish as she looks me over.

"I heard you've been homeschooled up until now, so if you have any questions about the way we do things here, feel free to ask. You have your textbooks?" she asks kindly. I nod and glance down at the nameplate on her desk.

"Yes, Ms. Sullivan. Um, where should I sit?"

She looks out over the room and points to an empty desk near the back. "That should be fine for now. I usually start out the semester with free seating, but depending on behavior it may change later. Would you like me to introduce you?"

I bite back the immediate yes that springs to my lips and think it over. So far nothing has gone the way I expected it to. Maybe identifying my-self as the new girl in such an obvious way is *not* such a great idea.

"No, that's ok. I'll just take my seat," I say quietly and Ms. Sullivan nods.

"That's fine. See me after class if you have any questions."

I slip through the aisles to take my seat. A few curious glances are sent my way, but on the whole, I am ignored. To my left sits the pinched-face girl who was so rude at the door. She doesn't look at me. I might think it is because she is unapproachable or important if I hadn't heard the truth already. That she's as terrified as I am.

"Um, hi," I whisper and her head jerks slightly. "I'm sorry about be-ing in the way before. This is my first day, and I wasn't sure where I was going."

The girl's shoulders relax infinitesimally. Maybe she thought I was going to tell her off or something.

"It's ok," she whispers back, but doesn't turn around. My spirits sink a little. Fantasies of being the cool new girl that everyone wants to know are quickly disintegrating, and I'm left with a void that's both unnerving and a relief at the same time.

I lean back into my seat and pull out my notebook and text. One of the reasons Mom never put me back into school was because of my difficulty reading. If I had been in school, I probably would have been put in a class with learning disabled students, my odd ability mistaken for dyslexia or slowness. The first time I read something, like with the signs over the stores in Georgetown, I see the truth behind the statement. Reading fiction doesn't bother me, mainly because there is no true reality behind the words, just a perceived one the author creates. The same thing goes for movies and TV meant for entertainment value only.

But reading a textbook presents a challenge since the information is meant to be authentic and factual. People would be shocked to know how many lies their children are being taught, how inaccurate textbooks really are.

I look at the U.S. History book in my hands and sigh. History books are full of falsehoods. I just hope Ms. Sullivan doesn't ask her students to read out loud.

I hear the desk behind me shift as someone takes a seat and a tone sounds, like the warning on the Emergency Alert System. I glance around, but no one else seems surprised. As Ms. Sullivan rises from her chair and faces the class, I realize the tone must be the signal for classes to start. Guess they don't use bells anymore.

"Ok, everyone, quiet," Ms. Sullivan orders, her voice carrying to the corners of the room. After a few moments, the hubbub dies down and she welcomes us to her class and passes out a syllabus. She stops and talks to a few students as she passes, asking about their Christmas breaks, but most students eye her warily. I can't help but be relieved that I'm not the only one new to this class.

"Everyone here will be assigned a partner. You will complete class projects together, and if your partner misses class, you will be responsible for collecting their assignments."

Excitement stirs in me. This is more like it. I wonder who I'll be paired with and try to resist the urge to look around the room. I don't want to seem too eager.

Ms. Sullivan wanders around the room pairing people together. When she reaches me, she gestures to whoever is sitting behind me and smiles. "The two of you can work together," she directs before moving on.

There are a few grumbles as everyone shifts to greet their partners. My pulse picks up and I put a pleasant smile on my face as I turn to meet a clear green gaze. I feel my smile widen as I take in the boy I'm paired with. With dusty blond hair that grazes his cheeks and falls into moss-colored eyes, high cheekbones and a strong jaw, he is the living, breathing embodiment of the high school hero I've read about and watched on TV. I wonder if he's the captain of the football or basketball team.

"Hi, I'm Phillip Bennett. You're new here, right?" the hero asks, his voice low and pleasant. But I don't notice that.

I don't hear the truth.

I stare at him for a moment, baffled, resisting an urge to touch my ears and make sure that they're still attached. He watches me attentively and I struggle to find my way back to normalcy and answer.

"Um, hi. Yeah, today's my first day," I reply, absently clicking my jaw to try and pop my ears. "Oh, and my name is Derry."

He smiles and I flinch slightly at the dazzling gleam of teeth. He could be in an ad for toothpaste with that grin.

"Derry, that's an unusual name," he says, tilting his head slightly and letting his eyes travel over me.

My heart is pounding furiously and my skin itches. What's wrong with me? I always hear the truth when someone first speaks to me, always. I try to focus, not wanting to seem weird.

"Yeah, it was my grandmother's maiden name." My fingers are clenching and unclenching at my side and my stomach twists uncomfortably.

"Well, it's nice to meet you, Derry. Has anyone shown you around yet?"

I force myself to concentrate. I will figure out what's wrong with me later. "I had a tour when I registered a couple weeks ago," I answer.

Phillip gives me a pitying look. "With Mrs. Hayworth, right?" I nod. "Well, I'd be happy to give you a tour. One from a student's perspective," he offers, blinding me with that smile again.

My pulse picks up for an entirely different reason. "Yeah, that'd be great." Up front Ms. Sullivan calls the class to attention again.

"I'll show you to your next class," he whispers and I give him a quick smile and turn around, not really sure how I feel about that. It's odd. Earlier I would have been thrilled about a cute boy offering to walk me to class; it fits in perfectly with my daydreams. But I am completely off-balance. For as long as I can remember, the first thing anyone says to me is a hidden truth. I always have to ask people to repeat themselves, or guess at what they might have said. I've never heard just a regular introduction.

I rub my arms absently and then stop. The low-level buzz under my skin, like feathery wings beating against my veins, is fading, but it is unmistakable now that I'm paying attention. It's the buzzing that warns me when someone is lying, and it was sounding alarms the entire time I was talking to Phillip.

I look over my shoulder at him. He is reading the syllabus, tapping his fingers on the desk in a light, repetitive drumming. Sensing my scrutiny, he glances up and the corners of his mouth turn up slightly, but the smile doesn't reach his eyes. I turn around hurriedly and stare down at my hands. Something is wrong. First the boy outside the school looks at me and I feel like I'm dying and now I can't hear Phillip's truth, but my entire body screams that he's lying. I take a deep breath and try to slow my pulse. After a moment the hum under my skin is gone and I can focus.

With an effort I return my attention to Mrs. Sullivan's opening spiel. She goes over the syllabus and tells us her expectations. I'm a little surprised at how spread out the material is. Our first assignment is to read ten pages of the first chapter tonight. Much less than I'm used to. Studying with Mom, I've always had to cram a lot of info in a very short time. At our old store, I used to work every day and then spend a few hours in the evening doing school stuff with mom. I love her, but she can be kind of flighty sometimes, and having a steady schedule of homeschooling is not always her top priority, so I have gotten used to reading whole books in a day or several chapters in a night. Plus, I usually have to read them twice in order to get past the lies.

I open my text and look down at it glumly. Tiny, cramped print glares back at me. It's going to be an ugly semester.

"I'd like to get some perspective on what you already know. For the rest of the class, write an essay based on one of these questions." Ms. Sullivan gestures to the board. Three questions are written, and I sigh as I learn more about Ms. Sullivan without wanting to.

1. Every year teaching gets more difficult and the students are more ungrateful.
2. I'm going to default on my mortgage if I can't find a second job.
3. I'm so tired of looking out and seeing these apathetic faces.

I blink and the words reform themselves into the intended questions, asking about certain periods in American history. I close the text and prepare to write without it. I'll have to read ahead tonight so I can get through the rest of the week.

After a few moments I lose myself in the work and stop worrying about why I heard exactly what Phillip said and not some deep dark secret, the buzzing under my skin, or the boy who ran into me outside of school. For me, writing is cathartic, natural, and one of the rare times that I don't have to worry about honesty. Anything I write goes down exactly as I mean it. No matter what anyone says, you can't lie to yourself; not really. So I can read anything I've written with no problem. It's one of the reasons I first developed an interest in journalism. I can wield my uncanny talent to find out what people are hiding and then write the truth for everyone else to read.

The rest of the period passes quickly. Everyone is involved in their assignment and only the occasional whisper or snap of someone breaking pencil lead disrupts the peace. For a while I feel perfectly at ease, comfortable with this new world that I've entered, and the knot between my shoulders unwinds a bit.

"I'm not looking forward to reading these," Ms. Sullivan says and I jump in my seat. I'm back to hearing the truth again. What happened with Phillip must have been a fluke, a once in a lifetime mistake. As much as I sometimes hate always knowing the truth, as much as I wish I could be normal, it's part of me and always has been.

I glance around, wondering what Ms. Sullivan said, and my eyes meet with the pinched-faced girl. "What did she say?" I whisper and she hesitates before answering.

"I'm going to be all alone this semester."

I sigh inwardly. This is going to get really tedious.

"I'm sorry, I didn't catch that?"

The girl rolls her eyes and leans closer. "She *said* to pass the papers up front. Geez, open up your ears."

I'm beginning to understand why this girl is worried about being alone. Charm is not her middle name. I laugh awkwardly and lean back in my chair, putting my name on my paper and hand it to the girl in front of me. I smile at her, but she doesn't seem to notice.

Pinched-face girl is still looking at me. I smile tentatively and wait to see her reaction. Her lips turn up at the edges.

"You said you're new, right?" she asks quietly. The rest of the class is talking in low voices so I lean forward to answer.

"Yeah. I'm Derry."

"I'm Nicole. Sorry I was rude, I just…I hate the first day, you know?" she says, dropping her eyes.

I feel my heart twist in sympathy. "Yeah, I do. This is my first day of school. Ever," I admit, feeling a little foolish.

Nicole raises her eyebrows. "Ever? What does that mean?"

I lower my voice, not really wanting anyone else to hear. "I was home-schooled. I've never been to school."

Her eyes widen as she looks me over. "Really? I wouldn't have guessed. You look so…normal." She grimaces. "Sorry, that sounded bad. I just meant…"

"You meant that I don't dress like I'm in a cult or have weird hair. It's ok." Nicole blushes and I find myself warming to her. At least she says what she means. "I kind of figured people might think that."

"Yeah, well. Um, do you want to…" she breaks off as the tone sounds, signaling the end of class. Chairs scrape as students jump to their feet, and I stuff my book in my bag. Phillip steps up next to me and smiles, turning his back on Nicole, almost as if on purpose.

"Ready to go?" he asks. I glance over at Nicole, wondering what she was about to ask.

"See you later," she mumbles and hurries away, holding her book close to her chest. She reminds me of a frightened rabbit, always looking around for the next attack.

I shake my head and turn back to Phillip, realizing that once again, I heard what he really said the first time around. A light hum whispers under my skin. There's no doubting that there's something different about Phillip. It's like my talent goes haywire around him.

"Yeah. Thanks for doing this," I say, fighting the urge to shake all the confusion out of my head. He smiles, teeth flashing, and leads the way out of the room.

"So what class do you have next?"

I glance over my schedule again. "Biology with Mr. Keckley."

"Oh, I had him last semester. He can be a little…off-putting. Just don't sit too close to the front. He tends to spit," Phillip informs me conspiratorially.

"Oh. Thanks." My throat seems to be closing over. I'm not sure if my reaction to Phillip has something to do with my ability or if it's just because he's really cute. I decide to go with the latter for my own peace of mind.

"So where are you from?"

"Williamsburg, Virginia. I grew up there," I say, glad to get on solid ground.

"Oh, I've been there, when I was a kid. It's near Busch Gardens, right?"

I laugh. You can tell someone's age by how they identify Williamsburg. It's either the colonial town or that place near the amusement park. "Yeah, that's the place."

"That's nice," he says and we lapse into silence. In my mind, I am this great conversationalist, bubbly and vibrant, drawing people to me just by the sound of my voice. In reality, my tongue seems to have swollen up to twice its size and my brain is sputtering like a stalled engine.

We round a corner and Phillip points to a door. "Well, that's Mr. Keckley's room. Remember, stay in the back," he reminds me jokingly.

"Thanks for…um."

"No problem. Do you know how to get to the cafeteria from here?"

I wonder if I've really come off as that dense. "Yes."

"Good. Well, it was nice meeting you. If you need somewhere to sit at lunch, just look for me."

"Oh, thanks. I will." I scratch my arm, electricity surging beneath my skin.

"Ok. Good luck," Phillip says, tossing another brilliant smile over his shoulder. As he merges into the quickly moving mass of students my skin quiets, the buzzing dissipating until I'm not sure it was there to begin with. I square my shoulders and head into the room.

Mr. Keckley doesn't offer me any help or ask if I want to be introduced to the class. He signs my paper with a grunt and gestures broadly at the room. I take a desk near the back, following Phillip's advice. The last students to come in grumble as they take the front row seats. No one speaks to me. I barely rate a glance from the people sitting next to me.

This period moves slowly. Once Mr. Keckley is finished droning on about how his class is run, he puts in a mind-numbing National Geographic film about photosynthesis. Halfway through the movie I'm blinking rapidly to stay awake, letting the half-truths the narrator utters pass through my ears without really listening.

Someone taps me on the shoulder. Startled, I glance around and catch the eye of the girl behind me. She is holding out a folded piece of notebook paper to me with a bored expression on her face.

"I stole a hundred dollars from my brother," she whispers impatiently, shoving the paper into my hand. I close my fist around it and open my mouth to say something, but the girl stares studiously at the TV screen, obviously not interested in striking up an acquaintance.

I peer anxiously at Mr. Keckley, but he is looking at something on his computer and doesn't seem to notice that anything has happened. With a thrill of anticipation, I open the folded paper and read the note.

"You don't belong here. You're going to be miserable."

Tears sting my eyes as I stare down at the paper. The words flicker and reform into what the author meant me to see.

"Welcome to Harpers Ferry. You're going to have fun here."

I glance around, wondering who wrote the note. My eyes meet those of a girl two rows over. She winks at me and tosses gleaming blond hair over her shoulder. If I didn't know her true intention, I would think she was being friendly.

I smile weakly and return to the movie, biting my lower lip to keep from crying. This was a mistake.

# CHAPTER TWO

I STAND AT THE ENTRANCE TO the cafeteria, gripping the strap to my messenger bag so tightly my fingers are numb. My eyes dart around the room, searching for Phillip, since he is the only person to offer me a seat at lunch, but I don't see him right away. The cafeteria is larger than I'd expected, with round tables that seat eight crowded all the way to the windows at the back. I am amazed anyone ever finds a place to sit here and debate just finding a corner somewhere quiet to eat. I saw students sitting in groups on the floor outside the gym as I walked from class, and they seemed perfectly happy.

"I'm so tired of being alone," a familiar voice says behind me.

Unsure of what she said, I just smile hesitantly. "Oh…uh…I'm just looking for somewhere to sit."

Nicole shifts on her feet and glances around. "Well, you can sit with me if you want," she offers in a rush, looking regretful almost instantly.

"That would be great, if you don't mind," I reply honestly. She nods and motions for me to follow her. We end up sitting in a nook created by an entrance to a lecture room across from the gym, silently chewing on our respective lunches. I am glad I packed mine this morning. The thought of getting a tray and searching the cafeteria for a friendly spot is daunting. Everyone who is sitting out here in the hall is eating a packed lunch. I take stock of the students around us and decide that this must be where all the outcasts sit. So now I've identified myself as one too.

We finish eating and Nicole watches me apprehensively, once again reminding me of a rabbit quivering in the presence of a deadly predator. I suppress an impulse to laugh at this image of myself as dangerous. I spend so much of my time shielding myself from everyone around me and the never-ending onslaught of truth, that I've never viewed myself as anything but a victim. My opinion changes now as I look at Nicole. She screams victim with every breath.

"I want a friend so badly," Nicole says.

"Sorry, what?" I ask, turning my attention back to her.

"I said, where are you from? Do you have a hearing problem or something?"

I smile bitterly. "In a manner of speaking."

Nicole flushes and bites her lower lip. "Oh, I'm sorry, I didn't mean to…I was just kidding, I didn't really think…" she stutters, looking mortified. I hasten to reassure her.

"Don't worry about it. I just have trouble focusing sometimes," I explain vaguely, hoping she doesn't ask any more questions.

"I get it. Sorry," she mumbles. I can guess at her thoughts. Based on everything she's accidently revealed to me, I know her social circle is pretty limited, probably to the point of nonexistent, so there's no doubt she is kicking herself for insulting a potential friend. I find myself warming to Nicole, the only person apart from Phillip who has shown any interest in me at all.

"Seriously, forget about it. Thanks for letting me sit with you," I say, trying to change the subject. She studies me sharply before she relaxes and answers.

"You're welcome. Not that it will do much for your status. I'm pretty much persona non grata around here," she says, shrugging offhandedly with long practice at looking unconcerned. I decide right now that whatever else happens here, even if I end up quitting by the end of the week, I will befriend this girl. I don't know what has caused her to be so lonely, but the long isolation that her slumped posture and downcast eyes speak of calls to me, to that secret self that I keep tucked away, even from my mother. The part of me that knows I'm a freak, some weird abomination that should never have existed.

"Oddly enough, that sounds pretty appealing right now," I finally say, giving Nicole a weak smile. Her eyes brighten before she looks away. After this, we seem to grow easier around each other. I tell her about Williamsburg and my mom's antique store, how we moved because keeping a shop in the historic district had become too expensive, and mom's old high school friend had told her how much cheaper it was to live in West Virginia. Nicole tells me she's an only child and she's lived in Harpers Ferry her whole life. Since I've only been on a basic tour of the town and pretty much just gone back and forth between home and the store since arriving, she tentatively offers to show me around.

"That would be great. I've been up and down the street with all the shops, but that's about it."

"How long have you been in town?"

"Around two months."

She looks puzzled. "You didn't come to school last semester?"

I shake my head. "No, I didn't want to start at the end of a semester. Technically I already qualify for graduation. I just wanted to see what high school was like before it was too late," I say, a little too truthfully.

"Oh wow. That's the opposite of me. All I want is to get out of here."

"Yeah, but I've never been to school, remember? And at least this way, if it sucks completely, I'm only in it for a few months."

"A few months can be a long time here, trust me," she says cryptically. I frown at her and she shrugs. "You may have noticed that I'm not surrounded by a group of adoring fans."

"Yeah, but..." I break off, not sure what to say.

"Look you'll hear about it soon enough. I used to be fairly popular and everything, but something...happened, and the people I thought were friends ganged up on me. They were pretty cruel." Nicole's voice wavers and the shine of tears threatens to spill over.

"I'm really sorry." She just nods and we don't speak for a moment. "I've never had a friend," I say quietly, feeling like an idiot.

"Never?" she asks, her eyebrows creasing in pity. I shake my head. "I'm sorry, that's got to be hard. Look, not to get all after-school special on you, but I could use a friend right now...you know, if you're interested."

I give her a brilliant smile, touched by how difficult it must be for her to offer.

"Definitely."

Before we can say more, the tone sounds and we get to our feet.

"What classes do you have this afternoon?" Nicole asks as she swings her over-laden backpack over her shoulder and brushes a hank of dark brown hair back from her face.

"I've got English Lit next, and then Journalism."

"I've got calculus and gym. How did you get out of taking P.E. anyway? It's required."

I grin and pull my bag over my head. "Mom argued against it. She said since I was only going to be here for a semester, she wanted me to have all academics. The principal didn't really seem to care," I tell her, hiding part of the truth. The main reason was because my mom didn't think I could handle working in teams and playing sports with so many people. There wouldn't be enough full conversations, just people yelling things out randomly, and I would be too distracted. I had to agree with her on that one.

"Lucky," Nicole mutters and I laugh. For a fleeting moment, she grins unselfconsciously before her face closes down again and I feel like I've won a small victory.

"Do you know where your class is?"

I have an idea, but I figure it won't hurt to let Nicole show me. She seems determined to embrace the friend concept. "Kind of, but I could use an escort if you don't mind."

"No problem," she says and leads me into the teeming mess of students pouring out of the cafeteria. We head up a dilapidated-looking set of stairs to the second floor, and I try not to trip on the worn linoleum. We emerge into a hallway I haven't been down before and I almost walk past it before I halt and stare in surprise.

"What is this?" I ask, pointing to a locker that's covered in fake flowers and permanent marker with notes that say 'I'll miss you' and 'Be at peace' all over it. A picture of a smiling, pretty redhead is glued in the center.

Nicole's face shuts down completely and it takes her a moment to answer. "That's Miranda. She…died at the end of October. They've practically made a shrine to her," she says quietly. I glance over at Nicole and am startled by the fierce glow in her eyes. "They didn't even know her."

"And you did?" I ask, understanding.

She nods. "She was my best friend, since we were kids. Then she started dating Phillip and everything changed. He did something to her; I know he did. Someone doesn't just one-eighty their personality like that for no reason."

I am tempted to push for more, but Nicole turns away abruptly and I have no choice but to follow. We turn the corner and she pauses in front of a classroom door. "This is your stop," she says and then shifts on her feet awkwardly. I know she is trying to decide something, so I wait, giving her a moment to figure it out.

"Look, people might say stuff to you about me. It's not true, okay?"

I frown in confusion but nod. I'll know if someone is lying anyway. "Ok. Is your offer to show me around town still open?"

She is surprised for a moment and then smiles cautiously. "Yeah."

"Tomorrow after school?" I ask.

"Ok. I have a car, so if you want to catch a ride with me, we can leave from here," she says precisely, as though measuring every word.

"Sounds good. Let me give you my number." I program the number in her cell. "See you tomorrow." I wave goodbye and enter the room. Glancing back over my shoulder, I see she is smiling to herself, an incredulous expression on her face before she turns and walks away.

My English class goes smoothly. After my initial flash of sympathy at learning that the teacher, Ms. Harris, has breast cancer, I am able to relax and enjoy her lecture about Shakespeare's *Romeo and Juliet*. I read the passage over and over again in my text, letting the words slide through my mind like water on a parched throat. No hidden truths for me to decipher, just beautiful words and a tragic story of loss. By the time the period ends, I am sad to leave. I have had over an hour of peace, and I begin to rethink my earlier fear that coming to school is a mistake.

I find my way to the Journalism room without any help for the last class of the day. Shockey looks up and beams at me as I enter. I dread what I will hear him say.

Instead, he gestures for me to go to the smaller room at the back of the class. I hesitate and then go in, finding a small lab with six computers and a sliding door leading to an attached darkroom. I am the only one here, so I take a seat and wait, disliking the slight trembling in my hands. After a few moments, several students wander in, whispering quietly to one another. They break off when they see me and exchange unreadable looks before sitting down and continuing their discussion.

Shut out again.

I hear raised voices coming from the main classroom and the students across the room flinch and look at each other in confusion. One, a short, pixyish girl with shoulder-length blond hair, jumps up and hurries over to the door, ignoring my presence completely. I watch her raise her eyebrows and glance back over to her friend.

"I love watching other people be miserable," she says in a muted voice. The boy gasps. Another girl walks in, her eyes wide.

"Cathy, what's going on?" the pixie girl asks her.

"I am in love with Jake," the girl named Cathy whispers. The boy who remained seated now hops up and joins the girls, all of whom are oblivious to me listening in. I nearly growl in frustration, knowing I am missing half of the conversation.

"What did he say?" asks pixie.

"I have no idea," Cathy answers. "Shockey just called him up and said something and Jake completely freaked out."

"I want to bang the new girl," the boy says and the girls giggle. I jerk in my seat, aware no one else heard him say this, but feeling like a huge spotlight has been thrown on me nonetheless.

"Oh, whatever Shane, you know Jake would never quit. He thinks he's the boss here. Besides, Shockey knows that Jake would print a story about finding him downloading porn last year if he ever really pisses him off."

"Yeah, but look at him. His face is all red," Shane says and darts a look over at me. His glance is appraising and he grins widely. I smile back weakly, pretty sure that I'm not going to like him. "Guys, we're being rude. Hi, there. I haven't seen you before, are you new?" he asks me, perfectly affable. I swallow my initial discomfort and try to answer normally.

"Yeah, I just started," I say. "I'm Derry MacKenna."

The pixie girl snorts and covers her mouth. "Dairy? Like a dairy cow?" she asks snidely. I blink at the insult and stare at her uncomprehendingly. "Should we call you Bessie?"

"Shut up, Megan. Don't be a bitch," Shane says lazily and then gives me an apologetic look. "Don't worry about Megan; she can't stand it when someone is prettier than her."

Megan snarls, her face red, and I think he is probably right. Still, I'm kind of pleased she is jealous of me; it means that I'm at least attractive enough to function in high school, something I have been paranoid about all day.

"I was just kidding. God," she mutters, shooting me a poisonous look. I don't think I've made a friend there.

"Nice to meet you, Derry. I'm Cathy." The other girl sticks out a skinny arm and extends a hand for me to shake. She is tall and thin to the point of being scrawny, with a long face ending in a pointed chin. Her jaw looks sharp enough to cut a steak. Flat brown hair clings to her skull, hanging limply around her shoulders. Still, she has a pleasant smile on her face that brightens her skin, and I can feel that she is genuine.

"And I'm Shane, and obviously that's Megan. Not that I'm not glad to see you back here, but are you sure you're supposed to be in the lab? Shockey doesn't usually let new students on the paper, and this is where we meet." Shane is tall and bulky without being fat. He wears a tight polo shirt that strains against the ropy muscles in his arms in a way that screams weight-lifting. Dark brown hair is cut short, buzzed close to his scalp with almost military precision. Features slightly too heavy prevent him from being attractive, but based on the way the girls defer to him, I'm guessing it hasn't stopped him from getting his way.

Struggling to focus, I smile and nod. "Yes, I talked to Mr. Shockey this morning. I've worked on a paper before, so he was willing to let me join."

Shane's eyes gleam, and he looks me over again. "Cool. Welcome to *The Agitator.*"

I frown. "The what?"

Cathy laughs and waves her hands in protest. "I know, it's dumb. The paper's name is *The Agitator.* In John Brown's honor, you know." I had read about the abolitionist John Brown before moving here, knowing that his attempted slave insurrection before the Civil War was one of the most controversial events during that period. His name is everywhere in town. There's even a wax museum based on his exploits.

"Sounds like a wrestler's name, doesn't it?" Shane jokes, and I can't help a small smile.

"Maybe a little," I admit, still trying to ignore the death daggers Megan is flinging my way with her eyes.

The tone for the start of class sounds and my three companions tense up, looking back toward the door, waiting, I assume, for Jake. A shadow precedes him through the doorway and then a startlingly good-looking boy walks in. Chestnut hair is luminous beneath the fluorescent lights and falls into his eyes charmingly, shifting to reveal brilliant slate-blue eyes that are crisp with anger. High cheekbones and a clear cut jaw frame his features, as perfect as any star in the movies and TV shows I've glutted on for the past few weeks trying to learn proper high school etiquette. He is lean, but with his fists clenched in silent fury, I can see the hard line of muscle taut against his sleeves. No wonder Cathy is in love with him. I feel a bit breathless myself.

For a moment he just looks around the room, as though waiting for a challenge, and then his scowl lands on me. Something flickers in his eyes, and they take on an intense focus that is both intriguing and disquieting. I am frozen under his stare, trying to think of something to say that will make the hostile edge of his expression soften, to release me from the harsh power of his glare.

Finally the moment passes and he puts out a hand and smiles at me, teeth glinting in a manner that reminds me of a wolf baring fangs at its prey.

"I could kill you," he says.

I leap to my feet, staggering back away from him. He blinks in surprise, and I can feel the shock of the others in the room, but all I can see is the fierce glint in his eyes, all I can hear is the vehemence with which he promises to kill me.

"Are you ok?" he asks, brow clouding in bewilderment, and I take a deep breath, trying to slow the frantic pounding of my pulse. I take another step back, putting as much distance between us as possible. My eyes dart around frantically, searching for something I can use to explain my bizarre behavior. At last, I spot a quarter-sized spider hanging from the wall behind him and I blow out my breath in a huff.

I point to the offending arachnid and force myself to focus. "Sorry, there's a…a spider…" I whisper, my voice hoarse with fear. He whips around and sees it. His fingers unclench and he quickly grabs a piece of paper and collects the spider.

"Be right back," he says, baring his teeth at me again and slips out of the room. My entire body sags in relief, and I drop back into my chair. The others are watching me with bewildered expressions, and I smile to cover my embarrassment. Megan rolls her eyes.

"Man, you must really hate spiders," Shane finally breaks the silence. "You looked like you'd seen a ghost or something."

I laugh nervously and nod. "Yeah. Terrified of them," I lie. Spiders are okay.

Cathy gives me a sympathetic look and then shrugs. "I hate stink bugs. You'll see a bunch of them around here in the spring. They're everywhere," she says, and I am grateful to her for trying to make me feel less like an idiot. I hear Megan mumble something derogatory under her breath, but she doesn't push it.

Jake walks back into the room more controlled. He has smoothed his hair back from his face and I am struck again by the clarity of his features, the confidence in his posture. A shiver runs down my back and I have to force myself to stay still and not back into the corner furthest from him.

"It's gone. You okay?" he asks again, his voice less confrontational. I nod and try to work up some semblance of normalcy.

"Yes, thanks. Sorry about that, spiders just freak me out."

"No problem. So, who are you?" he asks, his tone still not completely friendly. He looks right and his tone is almost there, but I can still sense a veiled ferocity that makes me wary.

"I'm Derry. And you're Jake?"

I hear Megan snicker in the background but ignore it. "Yes, like I said." Irritation is just beneath his tone. I wonder what I've done in the thirty seconds I've known him to cause such hatred.

"Well, Derry, I hope you're as good as you think you are. I don't know what you did to charm Shockey so fast," he says, though his expression makes it clear exactly what he thinks I've done. "But we'll see soon enough if you can take the pressure."

I frown, not understanding what he's talking about. How can he be so upset that I'm on the paper?

Before I can reply, Shockey enters the room and closes the door behind him, cutting us off from the rest of the class. Jake steps toward him, his mouth opening, but the teacher gives him a quelling look and turns to address the rest of us.

"I want to see all of these girls naked," he says, and gestures to me with a welcoming smile. I have a sick feeling in my stomach, but I assume he is introducing me, so I wave. Megan's eyes roll so far back in her head it has to hurt.

"Derry has an impressive portfolio. She's worked on several different papers in the past couple years, so she should be able to give you all some insight on how journalists do things in the real world," he continues proudly, as though my success up until now is his doing. I can feel my cheeks flush as I take in the skeptical looks of my fellow classmates.

"Anything you want to add, Derry?" Shockey asks. My throat has closed up again, so I just shake my head. "Ok, Jake you show her the ropes, and the rest of you, I want to see story ideas by tomorrow." With another smile and a leisurely survey of the girls in the room, Shockey heads back out to the main classroom, leaving an uneasy hush in his wake.

After a moment, Jake, who does seem to be in charge, gives me a venomous look and turns to the others. "Megan, maybe you can check with the principal and see if he has any announcements to make. Shane, why don't you get the sports schedules for the semester, and find out if the coaches have anything for us. Cathy," he says in a slightly softer voice, "any idea what you want to work on?"

Cathy beams under his attention. "Um, I had thought maybe a spotlight on seniors? You know, each issue we could have interviews about their time here…sort of a last semester hurrah?" she suggests, her voice gaining strength as she continues. Jake smiles at her approvingly.

"Go for it. Anybody have anything else?" he asks, looking at the others. Megan elbows Shane and he sighs before he speaks.

"Yeah, we kind of thought…well, look man, don't get upset or anything, but we thought maybe we should do a story about Miranda. Maybe get some interviews about her. Kind of a memorial piece," he says, confidence trailing as he finishes.

Jake's face is carved stone as he stares back at Shane, who seems to shrink slightly, quite an achievement for someone his size.

"Or not…you know, whatever you think is best," Shane says quietly.

I look back and forth between the others, who are clearly uncomfortable, glancing around at everything but Jake. It takes me a moment to remember that Miranda is the girl whose locker has become a shrine, the one Nicole said died in October. Jake's wooden frame and inscrutable expression suggests that he knew her too.

After a moment, Jake's face loses its dangerous edge and he gives Shane a faint smile. "Yeah, that's probably a good idea. Do you mind taking care of it?"

Clearly relieved, Shane nods and gestures at Megan. "We've got it, man. No worries."

"Alright, let's get to work. I'm going to call our advertisers and make sure they're in for this semester." Jake finally turns to me, his cloudy blue eyes stark with anger. "Oh. Right. Derry, you're supposed to take the community beat."

I hear a collective intake of breath from the others and understand this is what has Jake so pissed.

"Okay," I say cautiously, gauging how close Jake is to beating me senseless.

He glowers at me, and the rest of the group skitters away to their various assignments. There is so much focused rage in Jake's expression that his first statement to me doesn't feel so far-fetched. His entire body radiates barely contained aggression, and all of it is directed at me. For a moment I consider fleeing out the door and never coming back, but just as quickly I feel my spine stiffen and meet him glare for glare. He may want to kill me, but it won't take me long to learn enough about him to give him pause. Just a few conversations and I'll know his most hidden desires and secrets. Not a bad bargaining chip.

"What does that involve?" I finally ask. He blinks and narrows his gaze. His eyes hold all the warmth of a glacier.

"You keep track of what's being covered by the town's newspaper and other local news sources. You look for stories in the community that affect the school. It used to be my beat, so if you have any questions, I'd be happy to help you." He bites off his words as though they taste bad, and my skin hums with his insincerity. Understanding filters in and I can see why he's so angry. Given Shockey's proclivities, Jake probably thinks I've been given his beat because I flirted with the teacher or something. So not only does he have a quick temper and homicidal tendencies, he's a chauvinist.

"I'm sure I can manage," I say sweetly, stepping out of his reach, just in case.

"Fine," he snaps, and turns away, switching on one of the computers and stiffening his back so much I could bounce a quarter off of it.

I glance around and take the computer no one is using and pull up a search engine. It takes me only a few moments to find out who the PR manager is at the local paper, the *Daily Holler*.

Jake is using the classroom's phone, so I dig out my cell and notice I've missed a text from Mom.

*I don't think you'll last the day.*

I blink and the words right themselves.

*Hope you're having a great day!*

I quickly send back a falsely cheerful message and then dial the number on the computer screen.

"I'm completely broke," a harried male voice answers. I assume I've reached the right person and continue, wondering what the greeting was meant to sound like.

"Hello, my name is Derry MacKenna. I'm with the high school's *Agitator* and have just been put on the community beat. I know you must be very busy right now, so I don't want to take up your time. I just wanted to introduce myself and see when a good time to contact you would be," I say as congenially as possible. There's a pause on the other end and then he answers.

"What happened to Jake?"

With the boy in question in the room and listening to me if his slightly turned head and frozen posture is any indication, I reply carefully. "Jake has been put onto a more pressing assignment for the moment, so I'm filling in." Jake's shoulders slacken minutely.

"Oh okay. Well, now's not a great time, but why don't you stop by the office Wednesday after school? Just ask for Derek at the front desk."

"Thank you so much. I appreciate your time," I say and we hang up. Jake spins around in his chair and spears me with a stare. I bat my eyes and smile innocently. Perhaps it's not wise to bait someone who has violent intentions toward me, but something about him makes my hackles rise and I can't seem to help myself. With a dark look, he turns back around and returns to his work. I hear Megan snicker next to me.

"I hate being short."

"Sorry, what?" I ask.

"I said nice try," she whispers. "Derek's his cousin. He's going to know Jake got replaced by this evening."

I shrug and start looking through the articles on the newspaper's website. Not satisfied by my reaction, Megan persists.

"What did you do to get that beat, anyway? Jake's had it since sophomore year and never gave it up, not even when he took over as editor last semester." She's genuinely curious, I can tell, so I decide to be honest.

"I've been writing for papers since I was fourteen. I started out as an intern, but I've been freelancing for the past two years. I do actually have some experience."

Megan runs her eyes over me doubtfully. "You sure it's not because you gave Shockey a blow job?"

I am shocked by her coarseness and feel the color rush to my cheeks. She smirks and starts to turn around.

"No. Is that how you got your position?" I ask ingenuously. Her own face reddens and she sneers unconvincingly. She can dish it, as they say, but she can't take it.

"Well, we must both be here based on our respective…talents." She ignores me and returns to her work. Fine with me.

I spend the rest of the period working quietly, trying to get a feel for the types of stories I might need to cover, and by the time the tone sounds, feel reasonably confident that I can come up with some ideas. Everyone gathers up their bags and gets ready to go. Jake stalks out the door without a glance in my direction, and despite my earlier resolve not to be scared, I am relieved to see the back of him.

Cathy gives me a quick smile and hurries after him. I wonder if they're dating. If so, he's not a very attentive boyfriend. Megan leaves, barely holding back a snarl as she passes. I hear laughter behind me and see Shane watching Megan with affectionate amusement. He turns and waves for me to go ahead of him.

"I'm a total hound," he says. I repress an urge to bang my head against the wall.

"Sorry, I didn't hear you."

"I said don't worry about her. She'll cool down eventually. She's been queen bee around here for so long, she can't stand any competition," he repeats and I smile despite myself.

"I'm not really looking to compete," I mumble.

"You don't really have to," Shane says, admiration clear in his voice. Despite his unconscious admission to being a player, I am flattered. At least someone here likes me.

"I hurt girls like you." Shockey's voice rings out through the classroom and I jerk to a halt. He is looking at me expectantly, but hot fingers of loathing clutch my throat. I know instinctively that he doesn't mean hurt emotionally.

"She did great, Mr. Shockey. Fits right in," Shane answers and I smile at him gratefully, even more thankful for his big, muscular male presence. I am absolutely certain I never want to be alone with Shockey.

"Well, great. See you tomorrow, guys." I wave half-heartedly and follow Shane out the door, feeling a huge sense of relief as soon as I'm out of Shockey's eye line.

"You okay?" Shane asks, worry darkening his features for the first time.

"Sure."

He glances back at the room and then puts his head close to mine. "Look I don't want to freak you out or anything, but everyone knows that Shockey's a perv. And let's face it, you're totally hot." A wolfish grin splits his face and I laugh. "Just…watch out for him, okay?" he warns, all seriousness back.

I can't help but wonder why the man is a teacher if everyone agrees that he's some sort of sexual deviant, but what do I know? This is my first experience in a public school, and I guess that kind of thing is hard to prove.

"Yeah. Thanks for the warning," I say, rethinking my earlier impression of Shane. He might have sex on the brain, but he is a teenage boy. He seems nice.

"No worries. See you tomorrow." He takes off, joining a group of guys who are wearing basketball uniforms and heading toward the gym. I knew he was a jock.

Mom is waiting for me in the long line of cars out front, and I hop into our faded yellow 1971 Gran Torino. It is louder than a twin engine airplane, but it runs well and is a tank when it comes to accidents. Mom once backed it into a telephone pole when she wasn't paying attention. The pole was chipped and mauled. The car didn't have a scratch.

"I want you to quit school and work at the shop," Mom says in greeting, leaning over to give me a quick kiss. I sigh, not in the mood for an argument we've already settled.

"Mom, I want to go to school. I need this if I'm going to be able to function at college," I say wearily. She looks chagrined and pulls away.

"Sorry, Sweetheart. I was just asking how it went. I've been worried all day."

I consider my first day as a whole, remembering the strange boy with the death glare this morning, the unexpected reaction I had to Phillip, the reluctant kindness of Nicole, Shockey's perversions, and finally the promise of murder from Jake. "It was different," I finally answer, not really wanting to go into detail. If Mom knew half the things I found out today, she'd never let me go back. And I find that I want to. There are too many unanswered questions and secrets buried in the school walls.

"Different good? Bad?" she presses. I shrug.

"A little of both. I'm going back tomorrow, Mom. Like we agreed," I say adamantly. She grumbles and pulls into the slow trickle of traffic that leads to the exit.

"Alright. If you really are going to keep this up, I'm going to have to hire someone at the store. I'm not used to running it by myself." I feel a pang of guilt about deserting her, but squelch it immediately. I've given most of my life to making things easier for her. It's my turn now.

The rest of the drive, she tells me about a customer who bought an eighteenth century snuffbox this afternoon, and I try to focus on the conversation, but my mind is spinning. I can't get Jake's face as he promised to kill me out of my head. I know he didn't mean to say it, and of course no one else knew he did, but the desire was so strong in him at that moment that it overrode any other truths he might have revealed. I've heard a lot of things with my gift, but I've never been personally threatened by them.

Harpers Ferry is built on the edge of a mountain, sloping gracefully down to a flat plain that separates the Potomac and Shenandoah rivers. Everything about the town blends with its environment; the alleys are paved with natural rock, the buildings seem to spring out of the ground, rock-hewn and comfortable enough to seem ancient. From my mother's shop on High Street, past a rusted, derelict train bridge, I can see the cliff face across the river in between the shadows of buildings that date back before the Civil War. Train tracks weave along the riverside, iron gleaming in rich veins echoed by the twist of water threaded with jutting rock and thin deltas. The sun is setting and the town is enveloped in a pink haze that feels warm despite the nearly frigid temperatures. The cobbled streets are bare of tourists this deep into winter, and most of the shops are closing early. My mother's antique store, *Time Honored*, is closing as well.

I glance contentedly down the narrow room that serves as the storefront. Mom rented the cellar below to store larger items. Every time I go down the weathered stone steps in the front of the building and stoop to enter a door built for someone about six inches shorter, I feel like I'm stepping into a cave. The cellar is all rock walls and the sound of gently dripping water; down there I'm alone, but instead of being terrified or claustrophobic, I feel like the land here has accepted me, and the isolation is peaceful. Even though we've only been here a few months, I feel like I was born there in the cool dark.

"You want to get some sandwiches for dinner?" Mom asks, continuing a conversation we've been having for the past few minutes. "We haven't tried the café across the street yet," she reminds me.

I glance over and see a black-clad waiter lounging at one of the iron bistro tables littering the stone paved patio. He lifts a cigarette to his mouth and the end flares as he inhales deeply.

"I don't know. I never see anyone over there. Do you think it's any good?"

"Only one way to tell, Sweetie, and I'm tired of pizza." She locks the cash register and turns the sign in the window to *Closed*. We had a grand total of five customers today.

"Yeah, ok. I'll go," I offer, hopping off the 1950's diner style barstool I've been sitting on. I grab some cash out of mom's purse and head across the street to the cafe, noting with amusement how eagerly the waiter leaps to his feet and puts out his cigarette. He must be bored.

He ducks inside as I approach and another guy in black slacks and a sweater emerges and leans casually against the wooden doorframe. I shudder to a standstill as I recognize him. He raises a dark eyebrow and stares at me so intently I feel transparent. It's the boy from this morning, the one whose glare made me think for a mad second that he was strangling me with a look.

I can see him more clearly from this distance, and am surprised to feel a tug of admiration. He is a study in angles and shadows, tall and lean with a wiry grace that makes me think of a cat stretching on a fence. Dark, almost black hair is swept back from his face, revealing features sharp without being brittle. Proud cheekbones and a high arched brow frame eyes too obscured to make out a color. His lips are the one incongruity in an otherwise ascetic face, full and now curving into a sardonic half-smile. With a start, I realize I have frozen in the middle of the street, my eyes locked with his.

I shake it off and spin on my heel, hurrying back to the shop while trying to look nonchalant. I know I am failing when I hear a soft chuckle drift across the street. I tighten my lips into a flat line and head inside to tell Mom we're having pizza after all.

# CHAPTER THREE

THE MOMENT I WALK THROUGH the door, I feel it; a creeping, insidious conviction that I am walking into a trap, that each step I take is leading me down a road from which I can never return. Students are hurrying by me, rushing to get to their lockers or meet their friends before classes start, but each time I try to move forward, trembling panic seizes my limbs and I remain frozen, feet cemented to the floor. Minutes pass by and I am still stuck just inside the door to the school, head spinning and lungs tightening. No one stops to ask if I am okay. It is as though I have become some concrete statue melded to the dirty tile floor, a tribute to adolescent terror.

"Your fear is sweet," a pleasant, smooth voice says behind me and I am released, my entire body sagging with relief and rubbery muscles. I spin around and take a step backward when I see who has spoken.

It is the same dark haired boy from yesterday, whose knowing laughter had followed me to my mother's store. He is watching me with one eyebrow raised, expectantly, but there is a lazy grace in his stance that makes me think he is waiting for something else. The door behind him swings open and a girl steps through, a familiar redhead with a welcoming smile directed at me. I open my mouth to say something, to warn her about the boy standing between us, but no words come out; just a thin keening that burns my ears. The boy's face splits into a piercing smile, both beautiful and repellent in its naked ferocity, and he reaches out a hand to encircle the redhead's neck.

"It tastes so good," he whispers and his hand tightens, squeezing the girl's neck until his fingers meet and her face turns a crimson hue. I try to reach out, to stop him, but my feet melt into the floor and I flail helplessly as the girl's friendly smile becomes a grimace of pain and dread. Her skin wastes away in front of me, as though a black hole has opened in her core and is draining away her essence until there is nothing left but a wisp of smoke that writhes and dances toward me, forcing its way into my lungs until I clutch my own throat in desperation, clawing at my neck to get it out.

"It tastes so good," the boy repeats. Eyes flash a luminous green as he takes a step toward me, hand outstretched.

"I want to go back to bed," my mother's voice says over me and I bolt upright, nearly knocking my head against her chin.

"What…what…" I stutter, gasping for air like I've been held underwater too long. Mom scoots away slightly on the bed and gives me a tired smile. Glancing around, I realize I am in my own bed, slim beams of moonlight leaking through the blinds and illuminating my mother's drawn face.

"You were having one hell of a nightmare, Sweetie. I heard you from my room and came to wake you, but you just lay there gasping. I thought I was going to have to dump a bucket of water on you or something." She laughs shakily and puts a hand on my forehead. "You're all hot and sweaty. Are you okay?"

I am covered in a thin film of sweat and my hands are shaking. "I think so. Oh man, that was bad," I croak. My throat is dry and crusty, all the moisture sucked out. I reach blindly for the bottle of water on my bedside table and guzzle it. Mom waits patiently, stroking my hair like she would pet a frightened kitten, and gradually my pulse slows and I can breathe normally.

"Feel better?" she asks. I nod and glance at my alarm clock. Three a.m. "What did you dream about?"

I frown and try to remember, but the details are slipping away. "I was at school and there was this guy there who was choking me…or someone else. I think it was the girl who died."

Mom's eyebrows skyrocket. "Girl who died? When was this?"

I wave my hand in dismissal and lean back against my pillows. "I don't know; some girl from the high school died in October. I heard about it yesterday."

"Oh. Why would you dream about her?"

I shrug and rub my eyes. "I don't know. I saw her locker; her picture was taped on it. I guess it just stuck in my head."

"I guess. Can you go back to sleep?"

"Yeah, I'm fine. Thanks for waking me, Mom."

She bends to kiss my forehead. "No problem. Night, Sweetie." She closes the door on her way out. I lie staring at the ceiling for a while, my mind strangely empty, until my eyelids drift closed and I fall into an uneasy sleep.

This morning, I step cautiously through the front doors of the school, my nightmare from last night playing like a silent film behind my eyes. I hesitate in the hall, but no one approaches me, and I am not gripped by unexplained panic, so I shake my head and go to my locker.

"I am completely empty inside," a high-pitched, snide voice says next to me, followed by feminine laughter.

"I mean, did you see that pic of her and Miranda? She totally looked like she was going to murder her. Probably some lesbian jealousy thing," I glance over and see the girl who passed me the note yesterday talking to a carbon copy of herself, both wearing smug expressions.

"I have no ideas of my own," the other girl titters and slams her locker shut.

"Nicole probably killed her when she wouldn't make out with her."

The back of my neck burns.

The note passer turns slightly and catches sight of me, her self-satisfied expression spreading as she looks me over as though she's taking notes for later. "Oh, hey. You're the new girl, right?"

I frown, but nod. Were they talking about the Nicole I knew?

"I'm Tasha, and this is Meredith. I saw you hanging out with Nicole Sharp yesterday. You might want to be careful," she says in a mock serious voice.

"What are you talking about?"

The girls exchange sly looks. "Well, she's a total lezzie. And psycho. She killed her best friend when she rejected her. You'd better watch out or she'll go all stalker on you, too," Tasha warns, her lips curling into an elegant sneer. My skin is on fire, though whether it's because of the blatant lies or my rising anger, I am not sure.

"I don't think we can be talking about the same Nicole," I grind out through gritted teeth. The girls giggle again, the sound grating on my nerves like metal dragged across dry asphalt.

"Oh, I don't know. Maybe you're like her. She might not have to kill you after all," Tasha says, and they both explode into laughter. My fist clenches at my side and for the first time in my life I feel like hitting someone.

I slam my locker shut and turn to face them straight on. "That's not the truth, and you know it. Why would you say that?" I demand, my voice nearly shaking with anger. Instead of looking chagrined, Tasha and Meredith just snicker.

"Oh my god, I was joking. Don't take yourself so seriously," Tasha remarks, her tone suddenly superior, as though reprimanding a small child. I narrow my eyes at her, but she shrugs and she and Meredith begin to walk away.

"Guess Nicole's found her new lover," Meredith says in a whisper loud enough to carry and both girls look over their shoulders to make sure I heard. The anger drains from me and I am left feeling confused and uncertain. I have seen this over and over on TV shows and in books; there are always a few mean girls who rule the school and make everyone else miserable. I thought for sure that was an exaggeration.

Guess not.

I find my way to my first class with more ease than the day before and take my seat after smiling timidly at Ms. Sullivan. Phillip slides into his chair behind me and taps me on the shoulder.

"Hey, I didn't see you at lunch yesterday. You find your way around okay?" he asks concernedly, and once again my skin starts up its uncomfortable hum, even as his words wash over me without revealing anything hidden about him. For a moment, I feel an eerie sense of emptiness, a gaping hole where some substance is meant to be, but it passes and I manage to smile at him, accepting for the moment that my talent has a glitch when it comes to Phillip.

"Yeah, thanks. I looked, but I didn't see you, and then Nicole offered to let me sit with her," I explain, glancing over at Nicole's chair. The tone for class to start sounds and she hasn't come yet.

"Oh, ok. Well, the offer still stands. I usually sit near the back, by the windows," he whispers and then Ms. Sullivan calls us to attention and I turn around, the buzz under my skin fading again. I feel a pang of anxiety as I look at Nicole's empty chair, but then shrug mentally. Maybe she's sick.

Class moves slowly. Evidently the essays we turned in yesterday didn't convince Ms. Sullivan we have even the most basic knowledge of American history, because she spends the first half hour lecturing us on civil responsibility and the importance of understanding our heritage. By the end of class, even I feel guilty, and I aced the history portion of the high school equivalency exam.

Phillip doesn't offer to walk me to class again. He just smiles and says he hopes to see me at lunch. I am not sure if he is sincere or not since my skin won't stop humming around him, but I decide to take him at his word. After all, if Nicole isn't here today, I won't have anyone to sit with.

By the time lunch rolls around, I am rethinking my options. Nicole is nowhere to be seen, and I stand at the entrance to the cafeteria with the same sense of being overwhelmed as yesterday. I wonder if I can just sit in Nicole's nook and eat by myself, or if that will brand me as being a loser. Shifting uncomfortably in my leggings and sweater dress, I start to retreat, but a hand grabs my arm to halt me.

"There you are," Phillip's voice sounds behind me. He gives me a smile, his gleaming teeth taking on a yellow tint in the glaring florescent lights.

"Oh, hey. I was…just looking for you," I say uncertainly, still unable to tell if he meant for me to join him or if he was just being friendly. Tiny wings quiver under my skin in reaction to his nearness.

"Great. C'mon, I'll show you where I sit," he offers, leading me by the arm through the crowded cafeteria like a stubborn dog being dragged along on a leash by its owner. I shake off the imagery and paste a smile on my face as he pulls out a chair for me at a table with four other boys and two girls, none of whom I recognize. I brace myself for an onslaught of unwanted information.

"Guys, this is Derry. She just started here yesterday. Derry, this is Seth, Aaron, David, Josh, Mary, and Ruth," he introduces, gesturing at each as he names them. I bite back a laugh in surprise at all the biblical names. What are the odds?

"I'm only here because I want to date Phillip," the girl named Ruth, who seems familiar, says, giving me a friendly wave. I smile back at her and nod at the others, who seem pleasant enough. They start up their conversation again and I hear a number of things about them, most pretty mundane, but the boy named David gives me pause. The first thing I hear him say is that he used Rohypnol on his girlfriend at a party over the weekend. I glance at the girl in question, Mary, and wonder if she knows.

This is the problem with knowing the truth all the time. Sometimes I could help people by telling them what someone else said, or by revealing a truth about themselves of which they might not be consciously aware. But no one would believe me. Or they would think I was weird, or eavesdropping. Or crazy.

Mary catches me staring at her and gives me a quizzical look. I turn away, hoping no one else noticed.

"So where are you from, Derry?" Ruth asks politely, shifting closer to me and by extension, Phillip, who sits to my left. He gives her a bland smile and then joins in a conversation about football. Ruth's face falls a bit, but she rallies and focuses on me with genuine interest. I tell her I'm from Williamsburg and that my mom owns the new antique store on High Street.

"Oh my god, I love that place! I was just in there last week," she exclaims.

"Right. I knew you looked familiar."

I smile, remembering. She hadn't bought anything, but gushed over an antique Tiffany lamp for nearly half an hour to her mom. We talk for a bit about nothing, just school and things to do in town, and it's not long before I am completely at ease, laughing and joining in with the rest of the group like I've been at the table for years. Lunch is almost over and although I've barely eaten, a happy glow surrounds me. This is exactly how I'd envisioned high school.

"Mary, don't. It's just mean," I hear Phillip say and turn to see what he's talking about. He is staring down at his phone with a blank expression while Mary giggles impishly.

"Oh, whatever. Like you care." She tosses perfectly straight blond hair over her shoulder and looks at him through slanted eyes.

"What is it?" Ruth asks, distracted. Phillip rolls his eyes but passes the phone to her. I catch a glimpse as she takes it.

It's a picture of Nicole and the girl who died, the girl from my nightmare. They have their arms around each other and Nicole's pinched face is bright with laughter in a way I haven't seen. Miranda is smiling too, but there's a hollow look about her, as though a strong gust of wind would blow her away. I remember the way she turned to smoke in my dream and suppress a shudder.

"Oh, not this again," Ruth says drearily, shaking her head as she looks at the screen. Mary laughs, a cruel bite in its sound, like crunching ice.

"Isn't that Nicole?" I ask, and everyone looks at me. Phillip nods in understanding.

"You were hanging out with her yesterday, that's right. Look, don't worry about it." He reaches out to take his phone back, shielding the screen from me as he stuffs it in his pocket. Irritation flares in my chest and I turn my attention to Ruth.

"Is there something wrong with her?"

Ruth hesitates and then shakes her head. "No, it's just people being mean. Tasha and her crew are posting nasty comments about her again. I thought that died down over break, but I guess they're back at it."

I frown in confusion. "Posting comments? Where?"

"On Facebook. Aren't you on?" she asks incredulously. I shake my head vehemently. I tried it once; Mom wanted to put up a page for the store and I had to create a personal account to do it. I knew after ten minutes that I could never use it again. The pages were filled with lies, and they were constantly updated, so I never really knew what I was meant to see. I told Mom to manage it herself and closed down my account.

"Oh. Well, pretty much everyone here is. And before break, back in November, people started posting things about her and…um…" she falters, glancing nervously at Phillip.

"Miranda. It's fine, Ruth. You don't need to stop mentioning her name," he says chidingly. Ruth blushes and fidgets with a ring on her thumb.

"Nicole said they were friends."

"Yeah, best friends. She took it really hard when Miranda died." Phillip's voice is quiet and thoughtful. "So did I."

"Oh, I'm so sorry, I didn't know…" I begin, but he waves away my apology.

"No, it's fine. You'll hear about it soon enough anyway. Miranda was my girlfriend." He smiles sadly at me, eyes slightly glassy.

"I'm sorry," I say again. "Can I ask what happened?"

Phillip hesitates and then nods. "She killed herself."

I suck in a breath and look at him with more sympathy. That had to be hard, to lose someone you cared for in that way. I rub my arms absently, getting tired of the electricity under my skin that makes it difficult to be around Phillip. I nearly put my hand out to cover his, but fear of the buzzing holds me back.

The tone sounds and everyone rises from the table. Ruth tells me we should get together and I happily accept, thinking as much as I like Nicole, it would be nice to have more than one friend.

"Can I walk you?" Phillip asks, his mouth suddenly close to my ear. The barely detectable scent of sharp, spicy cologne snakes it way through my sense. He moves very quickly.

"Sure, thanks." We gather up our bags and throw away our trash in silence. It is only when we are in the thick of the crowded hallway that he speaks again.

"Look, I don't want to seem pushy or anything, but I was wondering if you're seeing anyone," Phillip asks without meeting my eyes. I trip over nothing and nearly pitch forward, but Phillip yanks me back by the arm. My skin burns where he touched me.

"Sorry, I didn't mean to shock you," he says with some amusement. I laugh uncomfortably, unsure of how to respond. "So are you?"

"No, no I'm not seeing anybody," I finally answer, feeling suddenly queasy. It seems in bad taste to be discussing this immediately after finding out about his dead girlfriend.

"Oh. Good. Well, once you get settled in here, would you like to go out with me?" He still isn't looking at me directly, but his gaze darts back and forth through the crowd restlessly, the way I've seen cats do when they're searching for a mouse or a bug. When his eyes finally land on me, I feel trapped between claws, pinned with the promise of pain to come.

"Okay," I whisper and then clear my throat. "I mean, that would be nice." My answer sounds less than enthusiastic, even to me, but Phillip doesn't seem to notice.

"Great. Maybe this weekend I can show you around." He pauses at the base of the stairs up to the second floor. "See you later, Derry." A quick smile flits across his face and then he is gone.

As I climb the stairs, ignoring the hurried press of students surrounding me, I analyze my feelings, trying to figure out why I am so unsettled about Phillip's apparent interest in me. After all, he's got a ready-made group of friends for me to join, he's romance novel hero good-looking, people seem to like him, and he's been nothing but kind to me.

But the way my skin hums around him has me on edge. I've never felt the buzz so strongly before, and it is constant around him. Even now my arms feel like someone has been using them for a pincushion. If I could just understand what is different about Phillip, why my talent goes wonky around him, I think I could be more at ease. And the only thing that will fix that is spending more time with him. So I should be pleased.

I should be pleased.

I pass Miranda's locker. Her face seems so familiar to me now that I have to repress an urge to go up and touch the picture. Unlike the photo I saw at lunch, this picture shows the redhead smiling with true warmth, as though someone has just told her the funniest joke and she can't hold back a laugh. Looking at this photo, I wish I had gotten a chance to know her, and I can't help wondering what happened to drain all that joy from her face.

And wondering why the thought of dating her boyfriend makes every inch of my skin crawl.

# CHAPTER FOUR

" I CHEATED ON MY MATH QUIZ," a booming male voice shouts in greeting as I walk through the door to the computer lab. Shane sits on a rolling chair, spinning back and forth inattentively as he looks up at me with a huge grin.

"Hey," I say, giving him a milder version of a smile. He jumps up to his feet and drifts over to me, his eyes taking a leisurely survey. I glance down and frown at my outfit. I am wearing tight black leggings tucked into faded leather ankle boots and a form fitting sweater dress circa 1972, rescued from one of mom's client's attics.

"You look mighty fine today, Derry. Mighty fine," Shane says in a fake cowboy accent. I attempt to give him a stern look, but a chuckle escapes me. Subtle he is not.

"I wish I looked like her," Megan grumbles as she comes through the door. I glance over at her, startled by her unwitting admission. She passes by me without looking, her shoulders set in an aloof stance. Even though she is at least a foot shorter than me and probably only weighs a hundred pounds, she seems to take up the entire room with her presence. Shane's eyes follow her with unmasked admiration as she goes by, apparently an equal opportunist when it comes to ogling.

"Stick your eyeballs back in their sockets, Shane. It's never gonna happen," Megan declares, but I can see the pleased tilt of her lips as she turns away. Shane clasps a hand to his chest and moans.

"Crushed again. I guess I'll just have to find comfort with Derry. Perhaps she will mend my broken heart." He mock-staggers over to me and collapses in the chair next to mine. I laugh at him and pat his shoulder. I can't believe that my first impression of Shane was so negative; granted, he's an outrageous flirt, but at least he's good-humored about it. There is something very open and guileless about him that appeals to me.

"My girlfriend found my porn stash," Shockey says as he joins us in the lab. My shoulders jerk involuntarily. His eyes drift over the room and land on me, once again reminding me of the cagey movements of a rodent. I have downgraded him from mouse to rat now that I know his proclivities.

"How's it going, Derry? Any story ideas yet?" he asks, his voice holding just the right amount of interest for a teacher, but he leans toward me slightly, a little too close for comfort. I can smell the slightly astringent note of his deodorant.

"Not yet, but I'm supposed to meet with the contact for the local paper tomorrow after school. I'm hoping to get some ideas then. I did see an article on a health inspection for a school in Shenandoah County that found asbestos in the gym. Maybe I could look into the latest inspection results here and see what comes up," I say, reminding myself that outwardly, this man has done nothing wrong.

Shockey nods thoughtfully. "That might be interesting. Let me know what you turn up. We'll have to run it by the principal before it's printed. He's a bit of a stickler when it comes to how this school is portrayed," he warns me.

I smile perfunctorily and return my attention to starting up my computer. He lingers for a moment and then moves on to talk to the other students. Cathy and Jake walk in together, deep in muttered conversation that breaks up when they spot me. Cathy gives me a cautious smile, but Jake's gaze is as hostile as yesterday. I wonder what I will hear him say today.

By the time the tone sounds, Shane and Megan are both out tracking down stories, and I am continuing my research on the local happenings in Harpers Ferry. Cathy and Jake whisper together, but are so quiet that I can't make anything out. About a half hour into the period, Cathy rises and puts her backpack on, collecting a camera from the shelf in the corner.

"My parents are getting a divorce," she says and gives me a quick wave. I feel a stab of sympathy as I watch her hunched form slip out the door. It takes me a moment to realize that I am alone with Jake in this small, isolated room. There are no windows to the main classroom, only the wooden door which is now swinging shut with an ominous click.

The silence expands into something almost tangible. The sound of my foot tapping against the desk leg is deafening. I force myself still, practically holding my breath in anticipation of the storm I sense brewing across the room. After a few moments I hear a defeated sigh and the squeal of the chair as it rolls over toward me. I stiffen my arms so my fists don't clench in response to my pounding pulse, so loud it drowns out the muffled lecture from the other room.

"I have a dangerous temper," Jake says quietly next to me. I shift warily to face him, braced for the hatred in his eyes, but he only looks tired.

"Sorry?" I say, leaning away from him imperceptibly. He sighs again and looks at me with more focus.

"I said I'm sorry I was rude yesterday. I'm sure you didn't know you were stealing my beat," he repeats, though he doesn't sound convinced. I chew on the inside of my lip and watch him. His hand twitches, and I have a mental image of him wrapping that hand around my throat.

"Oh. Um. It's okay," I roll my chair back just a bit. Jake notices and scowls.

"I'm not going to attack you. Just calm down," he growls.

Easy for him to say.

"Right. I know," I say, laughing awkwardly, like the idea of him throttling me and dumping me in the river never crossed my mind. He bares his teeth in what he fondly believes is a smile and then he rolls back over to his station. My breath releases in a soundless sigh. We work quietly, if uneasily, for the next hour. It helps that he is on the phone with advertisers most of the time, and we carefully ignore one another, even though I track every move he makes.

After a while, I accept that he's not going to kill me in the near future and I become engrossed in my research.

Without making a conscious decision to do so, I click on an article dated October 20th about Miranda's unexpected death. I hold my gaze steady so that I can read the truth before it fades away.

## LOCAL GIRL POSSIBLY MURDERED
## OR COMMITTED SUICIDE

I couldn't get a real answer out of anyone, but from what the cops on the scene said, it looks like the girl hit her head and drowned. The back of her head is cut so deep her skull is visible. They said it looks like a rock did it, but all they'll let me print is that it was a drowning. I'm pretty sure there was foul play, but I doubt they'll find any evidence. Looks like everything washed away. No one is saying much, but it seems like the girl was emotionally disturbed. Her friend is convinced she wouldn't kill herself. She thinks Miranda was murdered.

I blink and the words bleed into a new article, one that cleverly hides all the author's suspicions. A picture of Miranda, the same one pasted on her locker, is juxtaposed next to a blurry shot of people in uniforms wading in the water around a big stone tower of some sort, the rusty old train bridge hovering over them like an iron cloud.

### LOCAL HIGH SCHOOL STUDENT FOUND DROWNED
Authorities report that Miranda Oglesby, a popular student at John Brown High School, was found dead yesterday morning at the base of the old bridge supports above the fork of the rivers. Cause is yet undetermined, but sources at the coroner's office claim that accidental drowning is likely. Ms. Oglesby was an only child, beloved of her parents and friends, and was an honor roll student. Her parents were unavailable for comment, but close friend Nicole Sharp was on the scene shortly after the body was found and said "Miranda didn't do this. She would never do this on purpose."

My chair is wrenched away from the computer and spun around so violently I nearly fall off. Jake's face is so close to mine I can smell the peppermint on his breath and feel the malice vibrating from him like heat from a furnace. I shrink into my chair to try to escape, but he plants both hands behind me on the desk, trapping me between his arms. His eyes scorch me with barely contained rage as he moves forward slightly, his knees pressing against mine. Terror floods through me and I stop breathing. For a second I am reminded of the mind-numbing panic I felt in my nightmare, and my entire body freezes up, immobile until he releases me.

"I want to strangle you."

Jake's voice is unrecognizable in this low growl, like some primal beast issuing a warning. Whatever he is really saying is lost in the chilling knowledge that deep down, my pain is on his mind.

"You understand? This is none of your business. She's dead. She killed herself. End of story."

I try to nod, to say something, but my tongue is stuck to the roof of my mouth and my arms just tremble.

His face descends a touch, and his mouth is nearly brushing mine. Electricity flashes through me and my lips part slightly as I draw an unsteady breath. His eyes flicker and become uncertain before he pushes away, stumbling a little as he shoves the chair back with his foot. The back of the chair bumps against the desk, stirring me from my petrified state.

He is lying.

Jake runs a hand over his face and turns away, gripping his own chair with white knuckles. I have an odd impulse to put my arms around him and ease the rigid tension in his shoulders, but feeling rushes back into my limbs and along with my ability to think, a sudden blast of anger follows. I'm not a combative person by nature, but if you corner any animal, even one so harmless as a hamster, it will bite. Leaping to my feet, I grab a notebook from the desk and launch it at him with as much force as I can muster. It strikes the back of his head with a satisfying thwack, and he spins around, hand to his head, a comical expression of surprise replacing his earlier fury.

"What the hell is wrong with you!" I shout, fighting my own urge to choke the breath from him. He blinks at me and takes a step forward.

"Stop right there. You take one more step toward me and I'm going to scream and tell everyone how you think it's fine to threaten a girl you've just met."

Jake's face flushes red and he balls his fists at his side. "I didn't threaten you," he says, affronted.

"You physically intimidated me while telling me something wasn't my business. I could press assault charges," I inform him, working hard to keep my bravado going.

"I didn't touch you!" he protests, anger replacing confusion.

"Your knees did. And it counts anyway, because you pinned me to the chair and practically put your mouth on mine...you know what? It doesn't matter. You can go right ahead and try to explain how what you just did wasn't assault to the principal. I don't see any reason to cut you a break," I spit out, angrier than I've ever been with a relative stranger. Fear is driving most of my outburst, but I hate being pushed. Hit me hard enough and I'll hit back.

I stomp toward the door, fully intending to go out and tell my pervert teacher what just happened, but Jake grabs my elbow and yanks me back so hard my arm feels like it's ripping from the socket. I gasp in pain and he releases me almost instantly, but I can feel that I will bruise. Tears sting my eyes and I glare up at him, ignoring the softening in his expression as he sees how upset I am.

"Don't ever touch me again," I growl, holding onto my pride with grasping fingers. I am humiliated he can see how much he has frightened me. "You probably killed Miranda. That's why you don't want anyone looking into her death. What'd she do? Threaten to tell someone you're an abusive asshole?"

Jake stumbles away from me drunkenly, the livid red draining from his face until he is so pallid I worry for a second he might pass out. With the distance between us, I begin to feel the immediate threat dissipate and strengthen my grip on my emotions. He stares at me unseeing for a moment and then sinks to his chair.

"I'm sorry," he whispers. "I'm so sorry. I don't know what got into me. I just get so angry sometimes…"

The violence of the moment before has faded, but I still keep a safe distance between us. "Look, I'm sorry. I didn't mean what I said. You just really freaked me out, you know?" I am not sure why I am apologizing to this boy who a moment ago radiated brutality by just breathing, but the stricken look he wears makes me feel awkward and somehow at fault.

"No, you're right. I may as well have killed her." Jake sighs wearily and rubs his forehead as though he has a headache.

I glance around the room, totally unprepared to deal with this abrupt transformation. "I don't understand," I say warily. He laughs bitterly and looks up at me.

"I can't believe I just said that to you. It doesn't matter, okay? I'm sorry I frightened you. It won't happen again."

The tone for the end of class sounds and Jake grabs his bag and breezes past me without a second glance. I stand watching after him for a full minute before I get my own bag and start shutting down the computers since Jake neglected to turn his off. My back is to the door when I hear someone clear his throat.

"I want to touch you," Shockey says. I swing around to face him. He is only inches from me.

"Sorry, what?" I stammer, my stomach shifting queasily.

"I said I heard raised voices a bit ago. Is everything alright?"

"Oh. Um, yeah. Everything's fine. Just a little…journalists' tiff," I answer, surreptitiously taking a step back. I am up to here with psycho guys getting in my face today.

Shockey's face twists into an awkward smile. "Glad to hear it. Are you settling in?" His voice practically drips with fatherly concern. He stands between me and the door.

"Yeah, everybody's been great." I shift slightly to the left. He tracks me with his eyes, a hard glint hiding behind the mask of normalcy. I repress a shudder of revulsion.

"Well, if you need anything, come to me. I'll be happy to help," he says, lingering over the word *help* as though savoring the taste on his tongue.

I manage a weak, insincere smile. "Thanks." I gesture toward the door. "Well, I gotta get going."

He shifts slightly and waves for me to go. I slip past him, cringing away from his touch, but my shoulder brushes his arm. I can't be sure, but I think he sniffs my hair as I pass.

"See you tomorrow, Derry."

"Yeah, see you," I stammer and take off down the hallway like my feet are on fire. If I go the rest of my life without being within fifty feet of that man again, I will die happy.

I make it to the loop where parents wait to pick up their kids before I realize what a mistake I've made. I told Mom this morning that she didn't need to pick me up since Nicole was going to give me the grand tour. She is no doubt at the store now, not waiting patiently in the line of cars.

"Damn it!" I grumble, stamping my foot. I dig out my phone and call her, but her voicemail comes on.

"I probably won't return your call," her recorded voice cheerfully pierces my ears and I hit end, knowing it's useless to keep trying. She's got her phone turned off, probably sitting in her purse back in the storeroom. I try the store number, and after ten rings she picks up.

"I'm going to overcharge this guy," she says brightly and I bite back a smile. Mom has the shopkeeper's innate ability to sense which customers will pay more than something is worth and those who know how to spot a price hike.

"Hey, Mom. Nicole wasn't at school today, so I don't have a ride."

There is a pause and I hear the cash register slam shut. "It's a little busy here. Can you hang out for a bit? Or maybe get a ride with someone else?"

I sigh and look around. Most of the cars in the student lot have cleared out, and I don't recognize any of the people still milling about. The sound of my mom's voice is muffled as she talks to a customer, her bubbly laugh suddenly grating on my nerves.

"You know what? Don't worry about it. I'll be there in a bit."

"Okay, Sweetie. Call me if you need me," she says distractedly and hangs up. I stare down at my phone and fight the burn of tears behind my eyes. I just want to go home. I don't want to have to walk to the store; it's at least four miles into town from the school.

A loud rumbling intrudes into my moment of despair and I glance up. A glossy black motorcycle roars past me, swinging to a halt in front of the double doors to my left, where the last students of the day are exiting to the parking lot. I tense as Jake emerges and catches sight of the helmeted rider waiting at the curb. He strides forward and waves his arms angrily, pointing past the school in a clear message for the rider to go away. The guy on the bike abruptly straightens and turns his helmeted head around until he faces me, his gaze powerful even across the distance. I look away quickly, but my eyes are drawn back to the strange pair in time to see Jake glaring in my direction and then shaking his head at the rider. With a jerk of his head that seems almost dismissive, the rider revs the bike and does a quick turn, leaving Jake behind to wave exhaust out of his face as he heads toward a battered looking truck.

I shake off whatever fascination I felt and concentrate on the fact that I must now walk home. Before I can turn to head down the sidewalk leading to the road into town, the outrageous growl of the bike surrounds me.

Glancing up, I see the rider has stopped beside me and is looking me over from behind the shaded visor of his helmet. I smile hesitantly, unsure of what he wants, and without meaning to I return his appraising study. He is wearing a familiar looking black pea-coat that outlines broad shoulders and a narrow waist. Lean denim-clad legs hug the sides of the bike, and I watch as they shift to throw the kickstand and the rider swings his other leg over. My heart is pounding frantically now, and an overwhelming urge to run sweeps over me, my entire body screaming flight.

He removes the helmet and shakes his head, dark hair falling into his eyes, a midnight blue dark enough to drown in. I gasp and take a step backward. It is he, the boy from my nightmare, watching me with the same amused intelligence in his eyes, the same feline grace to his stance.

"I am fear," he says, his voice delicious and deep, like dark coffee. I just stare at him, his truth too close to what he said in my dream. Even as dread drips down my spine like melting ice, it is impossible to ignore this guy's dangerously appealing edge; the sharp angles that slash his features into a fierce beauty no artist could even hope to sculpt. I take another step back. There is so much peril here I can't think straight.

His mouth tilts up into a crooked smile. "Can you speak? Or do you just stare and back away?" he asks wryly. I shake my head and take another step back, noting with embarrassment that my hands are shaking. He glances at them and laughs outright. My skin is vibrating.

"I'm guessing you need a ride," he says, glancing around at the departing cars. Out of the corner of my eye I see Jake standing next to his truck, watching us from across the lot.

Like an idiot I say nothing, but stare down at my feet, hoping if I just continue to ignore what's happening I'll look up and see my mom waiting for me.

"You're afraid of me, aren't you?" he says quietly and I look up despite myself. He is still exuding laughing confidence, but there is something in his eyes that is wounded, a crack in the perfect veneer. It gives me the courage to answer.

"Maybe a bit. You know you hit me with the door yesterday," I finally answer, yanking my coat sleeve up to display my bruised arm. His lips twitch and he obligingly looks at the miniscule spot on my forearm. After a moment he reaches out and takes my arm, fingers gingerly pushing the edges of my sleeve back. I am startled by the warmth that scores my skin at his touch until I see the already forming bruises he has exposed higher up on my arm. His entire countenance darkens as he interprets the marks left from Jake's rough handling. I jerk my arm away and take another step back. My heart slams against my ribcage so hard it hurts.

"Who did that?" he demands, his voice a stern threat. Inadvertently my eyes dart over to where Jake is still standing by his truck and then I look my interrogator in the eyes.

"It was an accident."

He looks at Jake over his shoulder, his scowl deepening, jaw clenched in a punishing line. Jake jumps into his truck as the boy in front of me shifts his gaze back, softening his expression and loosening his lips into smile. I am mesmerized by the way his mouth moves, like liquid marble, hard and fluid all at once.

"Hop on, I'll give you a ride," he says, swinging back onto the bike and handing his helmet to me. I take it without thinking and then laugh jerkily.

"What? No way. I don't even know you," I protest, holding out the helmet. He ignores it and laughs low, the sound brushing my ears like a feather.

"You're right. I'm Cole. I work at the restaurant across from your store. What's your name?"

"Derry," I answer without thinking.

"Now you know me. Hop on." When I resist he sighs and points over his shoulder. "Look, it's either me or Jake the Ripper over there. Trust me; I'm a much safer bet."

With a start, I follow his gesture and see that Jake's truck is idling at the end of the sidewalk. The window is rolling down. I know beyond a shadow of a doubt that I do not want to get into a car with Jake. I look Cole over again and watch as his grin stretches, lightening his features into something more approachable, less severely beautiful. Still, this is the boy who starred in my nightmares last night, whose face was burned into my brain all day as the very image of fear.

"We need to talk anyway," he says, interrupting my train of thought. "That's why I came here today. I know what you are."

I look at him sharply, forgetting my uncertainty as I taste the truth in his words. My skin doesn't tingle a bit, and I know he is being honest. The fear that has been ruling my decisions today takes a backseat to curiosity as I grit my teeth, pull the helmet on, and climb behind Cole.

"Hold tight," he says quietly, taking my hands and placing them on his stomach. Even through the thick barrier of his coat, I feel the muscles in his abdomen contract as I touch him and something deep in my core flares into burning life. Without another word, Cole kicks the ignition and we fly forward, careening down the road and leaving my doubts in the dust.

# CHAPTER FIVE

THE FRIGID AIR HITS MY face like a wall even through the visor of the helmet and I squeeze my eyes shut so they don't freeze. Wind whips through the lining of my coat, fusing my bones with a deep, aching cold that makes me tighten my arms around the warm body in front of me. It's my first time riding on a motorcycle, and with an incredibly hot guy, but all I can think about is what kind of maniac rides a cycle in the dead of winter?

"Let's make a pit stop," Cole shouts over his shoulder and picks up speed, darting through the light traffic punctuating our descent into town. The high school perches on a flattened hilltop with a curving, steep incline of a road trailing down from it with the same twisting unpredictability of a river. Each time I dare to open my eyes a bit, I immediately slam them shut as the trees and houses blur past me with nauseating speed.

"Can you slow down?" I beg, not even a little ashamed of the panic in my voice. No sane person would be anything but terrified in this situation.

Cole scoffs, but gradually drops his speed until I feel safe enough to open my eyes again. Though everything we pass still seems to be sprinting in the opposite direction, it's not with the same breakneck pace.

"Thanks," I say sincerely. He takes a hand off the handle bars and grabs my arm, pulling it tighter around his waist.

"Don't loosen your grip too much. There's no seatbelt holding you on," he warns, and I strengthen my hold on him until my entire body is pressed into the scratchy wool on his back. He laughs again even as my skin hums a signal that he's stretching the truth. Realizing he is just messing with me so I'll hold him tighter, I pull away slightly and look around as we make the last curve into town.

Heavy clouds hang over the mountains like a scowl and the scent of snow is on the air, a crisp, biting taste that burns my throat pleasantly. The town is huddled against the hills as though seeking shelter from the coming storm, the eroded brick buildings pressed close together in defense. For a moment, I forget the upheavals of the day and let the charged breeze caress me, the rapidly cooling air no longer painful but alive, stinging my skin into wakefulness. I feel the steady thrum of the engine beneath me and the accelerated pulse of the boy in my arms and throw my head back in sudden exhilaration, a wild grin stretching my mouth.

Cole pulls the bike to a stop and cuts the engine, the quiet almost oppressive after the riot of noise. I release him and pull off the helmet, shaking my hair free. He turns, opening his mouth to speak, when he pauses, his breath catching and eyes darkening in an expression I don't recognize. I realize I am still grinning, probably looking like a crazy person with my hair all disheveled, and I drop the smile and paw self-consciously at the tangles. Cole gives his head a slight shake and the familiar sardonic smile catches his lips.

"I think you're beautiful," he says and my heart swells and stutters before resuming its flow.

"Sorry, what?"

"Your first time?" he asks in a voice that would leer if it could.

I roll my eyes and prepare some scathing remark, but honesty compels me to answer without sarcasm. "Yeah. That was amazing," I laugh, unable to pretend differently. A light sparks in the shadowy blue of Cole's eyes and for a moment we smile at each other in perfect understanding.

The cough of an abused engine startles me and I am rigid with alarm as Jake's truck materializes around the corner. Belatedly, I realize we are not in front of my mom's shop, but down the hill on the street that runs adjacent to the train tracks. A small café advertising hot apple cider and pie waits to my left and I remember Cole mentioning a pit stop. A door slams and I flinch involuntarily. Cole emits a jaded sigh as Jake strides toward us, a thunderous expression on his face. The bruises on my arm throb in response to the anger that seems to precede his every step.

"Calm down, Jake. We're just going in for some cider," Cole calls, jumping off the bike, nearly dislodging me in his haste. He moves to stand between me and the swiftly approaching Jake.

"I'm barely in control," Jake barks, with a glance at me. Cole puts out a hand to prevent Jake from getting any closer.

Noticing the gesture, Jake's expression darkens, fury pouring off him in waves. "I told you to leave her alone," he growls, pointing at me. I am stunned by his reaction and completely at a loss as to the reason for it. At the same time, I am more than a little exasperated by the overtly masculine standoff playing out in front of me. Two overdramatic boys hyped up on testosterone.

"Hey, standing right here," I interrupt sharply, and both boys shift their attention to me. Seeing them stand next to each other, I can't help but notice some similarities in their appearance; a curve of the jaw, the shape of the nose, a way of holding themselves.

"You stay out of this," Jake snarls before returning to Cole. My knees are nearly knocking at the ferocity in his voice, but I draw in a breath and get ready to ream him up one side and down the other. Cole beats me to it.

"Don't talk to her like that! If you're pissed, be pissed with me. But back the hell off." Cole fills his voice with a hardness I haven't heard before. Jake narrows his eyes, his body taut with hostility. I take a step back and he glances at me again. Seeing me move closer to Cole, his expression falls and he presses his fists into his head like he's trying to push through to the other side.

"Damn it!" Jake yells and spins around, leaping back into his truck and slamming the door with a reverberating crash. A moment later the engine guns and the truck spins the gravel of the parking lot as it tears away, the angry motor soon just a distant echo. My shoulders sag in relief and I realize just how exhausted I am by the entire day. Too many unexpected difficulties and challenging people. I think I might skip going to the store and go home instead. A nap sounds pretty good right now.

"I'm sorry about that, Derry. Jake can be a little...out of control sometimes," Cole is saying, his voice gentle and concerned, totally clashing with the bad boy, rebel without a cause look he's sporting. I can't understand him at all, and I definitely can't comprehend what it is about me that has Jake so worked up.

"I really don't like him," I say vehemently. Cole lifts the corners of his lips in another of those mercuric smiles that make his austere face so engaging.

"Oh, he can be alright. He's just got a stick up his ass."

I frown at Cole, recalling my earlier impression of similarities with Jake. "How do you know him?"

With a wry twist to his smile, Cole takes the helmet from me. "He's

my brother," he answers simply. Though I am a little taken aback, his dec-
laration isn't a complete surprise to me.

"Oh. Sorry," I say, not sure what I'm apologizing for, but feeling it is
somehow necessary.

Cole laughs shortly and holds out a hand to me. I hesitate for a moment, but then place my hand in his, trying to ignore the thrill that races
up my spine when his fingers close around mine. "Don't worry about
it. Believe me, I know what he's like." He leads me to the door of the
café and then pauses. "He doesn't mean to scare you, you know. But you
should be careful around him. He's not always…safe," Cole says enigmat-
ically, and pushes open the door.

The warmth of the interior is welcome after our chilly plunge down
the hill and any protest I might have made about being dragged here by
Cole is swallowed up in bliss when the waiter puts down two mugs of hot
cider in front of us. The heady scent of apple and cinnamon fills my senses
and I am instantly at ease. A song that was popular five years ago plays on
a jukebox in the corner, the singer's voice raspier than natural through
the blown out speakers. There is something comforting about the lazi-
ness of the man at the cash register, who leans back in his chair reading a
tattered paperback, the slow but efficient movements of the single waiter
as he goes back and forth between the three occupied tables, smiling and
calling each customer by name, knowing their orders before they even
speak. I experience a sudden sense of belonging, as though my life in
Williamsburg was only a stopping off point until I found my way here,
to this town that can't make up its mind about which era it belongs to.

"What are you thinking?" Cole asks, interrupting my train of thought.
I look at him with more focus and feel my heart sputter just a bit as I
take in the tender expression in his eyes, the soft curve of his lips as they
hover over his drink.

"I like it here," I reply honestly, at the same time wondering what it
is about Cole that makes me feel safe now, when yesterday his glance
paralyzed me with fear. Being so close to him, I can feel a fragile thread
connecting us, an unexpected magnetism, two polar opposites suddenly
switched and now drawn inexorably together.

"So what is your talent?" he asks, apropos of nothing, and I am startled
back into suspicion.

"What do you mean?"

Cole rolls his eyes and gives me an exasperated look. "I told you already, I know you're different, gifted. So what can you do?"

"Look, I don't know what you're talking about," I say, my earlier peace rapidly draining away. Now that I am thinking more clearly, I wonder what on earth possessed me to come with Cole, why I am not leaping out the door and running to the safety of my mom's shop.

"Ok, fine. I'll go first," he says, not appearing to care about my equivocation. "The first time you saw me, at the school, you were terrified. You felt like you couldn't breathe, the pain in your head was excruciating, and you were petrified with fear, isn't that right?"

My mouth drops open as I hear him calmly describe one of the worst moments of my life.

"That was me. I made you feel that." Even as the logical part of my mind rejects what he is saying, some inner wisdom nods with satisfaction at this confirmation. "I can impose fear on other people, in different levels. You got a high dose, unfortunately. I can give people severe panic attacks, or even just a vague sense of unease. I'm sorry about that, by the way," he continues, seemingly unaware of my stupefied response of stuttered breathing. "It was an accident, but I should have been in better control. When I'm angry, it's hard to contain my ability, and I was really pissed off yesterday morning. I didn't realize you were there until too late, and you got caught in sort of a radial blast."

"You're crazy, aren't you?" I beg, my throat dry. Cole shakes his head at me disapprovingly.

"Come on, don't do that. You know there's something different about me. You can sense it, the way I could sense you."

I stare at him while my thoughts flit around too quick to catch. Yes, I did know there was something out of the ordinary about Cole, I felt it from that first moment, but it had never occurred to me that there might be someone else out there with unexplainable abilities like me. Now that I think about it, I am struck by how self-centered I have been. Of course I couldn't be the only person in the world who is "special," and it should have been obvious before now.

"I know the truth," I whisper, the words escaping before I can take them back. Cole's eyes widen, but he waits for my explanation. With a sense of recklessness, I give in.

"Whenever someone speaks to me for the first time, I don't hear what they're saying, I hear what they're hiding, what they don't want the world to know. Whenever I read something, the first thing I see is the truth. And anytime someone lies to me, I know. I get this buzzing under my skin, stronger when it's a bigger lie, just a hum when someone sidesteps the truth a bit." A nervous giggle bubbles up in my throat as my whole being screams that I'm an idiot, that revealing my ability for the first time to a complete stranger who made me nearly pass out from terror the first time I saw him is a mistake I won't live long enough to regret.

But Cole's face splits into a heart-stopping smile, as though a blazing light has burst into life within, and he reaches out to take my hands in a crushing grip.

"I knew it! I knew I was right about you! You have no idea how long…I've looked for you my whole life," he exclaims, a startling passion in his voice that is both frightening and tempting. "I knew, I knew there had to be someone else out there like me. And then I found…Jake…but he's in denial, he can't admit what he is, but you! You've got control over it, I can tell." He continues rambling, his eyes gleaming with possibilities, but the shock of what I've just done hits me like a bat to the head and I stop listening.

Cole seems to realize I'm not paying attention and pauses in his outburst. "What is it? Are you sorry you told me?" His voice is uncharacteristically uncertain and once again I am struck by the set of contradictions he represents. He is gorgeous and sarcastic one moment, solicitous and sweet the next, and yet underlying it all, he is a walking vessel of fear.

"No, of course not." I pause, thinking it through. "Okay, maybe a little. I've never told anyone about me." Cole nods his understanding, but hurt flickers in his still brilliant eyes. I look down at my hands, still encased in his, the calloused palms scratching against my skin. "Did you say that Jake is like you? I mean…us?"

A cloud passes over his expression at my question, and I wonder if he really meant to tell me about Jake or if he just got carried away. "He is and he isn't. I'm not even completely sure about what he can do, but I can feel that he's talented. It's something to do with emotion, particularly anger. And strength. I know that." His expression is grim, and I get the feeling he has experienced the power of Jake's anger for himself.

I pull my hands away and take a sip of my cider, drawing back in disappointment at its now lukewarm temperature. If what Cole says is true, and I have no doubt it is since my skin is quiet, Jake's violence toward me makes a little more sense, even if I still resent it.

"Why didn't he want you to give me a ride?" I ask.

Cole sighs, leaning back in his seat. "Jake feels responsible for every-one." I frown and start to ask more, but Cole doesn't seem to notice. "I'm guessing you and he had some kind of argument earlier?" I nod. "Well, he probably felt guilty over that and when he realized I was interested in you, he felt like he had to intervene. I have kind of a bad reputation," he says a little sheepishly, looking up at me through thick, dark lashes.

I raise an eyebrow skeptically. "Shocking," I respond, keeping my voice dry and even. Cole chuckles softly and then leans forward, keeping his voice quiet.

"Yeah, I know. I ride a motorcycle, I wear black, I'm devilishly hand-some." He winks at me, and even though I know he's kidding my heart skips a beat. "I used to have trouble controlling my gift; or actually, I didn't bother to control it, and it made some bad things happen around me. People started avoiding me, even if they didn't understand why. Then when my mom died…" His voice breaks, and there is such devastation in his eyes that I reach out for his hand and squeeze.

"Don't. You don't have to talk about it if you don't want to," I assure him. He smiles sadly and shakes his head.

"No, I want to tell you. I want you to know about me." He is so earnest that I don't protest anymore, but give his hand an encouraging squeeze and wait for him to continue.

"Mom never really got what was wrong with me, but she always had my back. I did some really stupid stuff, just mean things because I was angry all the time, and I got into a lot of fights. She never yelled at me; she would just look hurt, disappointed. Eventually I started working on my control. And I got better. Mom was so much happier not having to cover for me all the time. But then she was out jogging one evening and our neighbor was driving home drunk and hit her. It took her three days to die, and she was in pain the entire time."

His voice is shaking slightly and he pauses to take a few deep breaths. My throat is tight and tears burn my eyes as I think of how hard it would be to watch my mother die slowly and painfully, unable to do anything to help. A tear snakes its way down my cheek and Cole watches it with sad fascination, reaching up to brush it from my jaw, as though he wants to collect it before it's too late. My skin is singed where his finger touches.

"I was angry." Cole's voice is quiet and hard, and his eyes trap mine with their intensity. "Really, really angry when she died, and I lost con-trol. I broke into the neighbor's house the night of her funeral and found him sprawled out on his couch, empty beer bottles all around him. He was drunk, and he stank, and I couldn't stop thinking about how sweet my mom was, how endlessly patient with me and that waste of flesh was the reason she wasn't there anymore, and I killed him."

My breath catches in my throat and I feel dizzy. He is telling the truth. His eyes bore into mine, pleading, begging me to understand.

"I didn't mean to. But I was so out of control that I pushed fear on him as hard as I could. I wanted to hurt him, to scare him, but he starting shaking and fell over on the floor, and when I tried to wake him up, I knew he was dead. He had a heart attack. It was my fault."

There is so much unexpressed agony in his voice as he tells me what he's done that I feel my initial shock being replaced by sympathy.

"You didn't mean to, Cole. That counts for something," I say, needing to comfort him in some way.

He just shakes his head. "Maybe I didn't go there planning to kill him, but I knew what I was doing. I could have controlled myself. Mom would have been so mad at me." He blows out a shaky breath and blinks rapidly. I realize he is mastering strong emotion and I reach out to take his hand again. He waves me away without taking it, and I pull back, rebuffed.

"Anyway, once she was gone, I had to come here, to live with my father."

"Were your parents divorced?"

He laughs bitterly. "No, they would've had to have been married for that."

I can feel the blush in my cheeks and bite my lip. "Sorry, I didn't mean to…"

"No, don't worry about it. It's a long, complicated story. I don't want to get into it now; it's not important." With a sigh he seems to refocus, but the hard edge I noticed the first time I saw him is back, making the harsh, beautiful lines of his face cold and rigid where moments before they were warm with sentiment. It is like looking at a different person.

"I wasn't happy about living here, and my father and I… don't exactly see eye to eye. So I got into trouble again. Stupid stuff. At the end of last semester, a teacher was trying to break up a fight between me and David Sharp and I accidently hit her. I was expelled." He wears a sarcastic smile now, reminding me forcefully of his attitude in my dream. I can't help feeling disappointed.

"So that's why Jake doesn't want me around you? Seems like an over-reaction. I don't get why he cares. He hates me, that's pretty obvious," I wonder out loud.

"Yeah, well. He's weird like that," Cole says dismissively, clearly finished with the subject. His mood has changed so abruptly that I am beginning to wonder if I imagined the heartbroken, desperate boy who talked about his mother a moment ago.

"Hang on, David Sharp? Is he related to Nicole?" I ask, suddenly registering the name. Cole cocks an eyebrow and nods.

"Yeah, he's her cousin. Why, do you know her?"

"Kind of. We ate lunch together yesterday and she offered to show me around town, but I haven't seen her today." Remembering the fleeting hope in her eyes when we made our plans, I am again puzzled as to why she didn't come to school today.

Cole is watching me carefully. "You know what happened with her, right?"

"Um, yeah. Her friend died and everyone started a bunch of rumors about her, right?"

"Basically. She was nice. One of the only people who didn't walk around on eggshells around me. She's the reason David and I fought."

"Really? Why is that?"

"You know, I've never talked this much about myself to anyone," Cole says unexpectedly, looking at me with a calculated expression. "You seem to inspire confidences. Does this happen to you often? People telling you their deep dark secrets?"

"Well, yeah. But I guess I've learned to ask the right questions. It's easy when you know if someone's lying or not," I answer casually, thinking that should be obvious.

"I don't know, I think it's more than that. This is really pretty unusual for me." His eyes regain a little of their earlier excitement. "Have you considered that it might be part of your gift? Maybe people are compelled to share their secrets with you, tell you things they wouldn't with other people?"

I stare at him dumbly, my mind immediately rejecting any suggestion that I'm even more of a freak than I thought. Abruptly, the whole conversation is just too much for me on top of an upsetting day. I stand up and throw my bag over my shoulder, digging for my wallet.

"Look, I've got to go. Mom's expecting me at the store. Thanks for the ride. And for…for," I stammer, unsure of how to address the intimacy we've shared. The friendly interest drains from his expression and it hardens into the cool mask of my nightmare.

"Oh sure, don't mention it," he says dryly, lips pulled tight. "Don't bother, my treat." He closes my fist around the money I am holding out, fingers a rough caress on my hand. "We should meet again. There's a lot to talk about."

Maybe when I get my head on straight.

"That would be great," I say with mixed feelings. The hard smile dissolves and there is another flash of the sweetness I saw before.

"See you soon," he says, releasing my hand, his fingers lingering a moment too long. Before I can do anything else stupid, I spin around and head out the door, forcing myself not to look back. His quiet laughter follows me as I exit into the bitter evening air.

Snow is falling thick and fast outside my window. My homework is spread out on my bed in front of me, but I watch the white glitter cling to the glass, shrinking into beads of water that slink down and disappear into the dark. A heavy feeling rests in my chest, as though all my blood has solidified and is too heavy for my heart to support. My mind is running through all the events of the day, but foremost is the image of the murdered girl. There is no good reason for it, I didn't know her, and I don't even know all the details, but that smiling face surrounded by a cloud of flame-colored hair keeps pushing its way into my thoughts.

Giving up, I shove my homework to one side and turn on my computer. Thinking there have to be follow-up stories on Miranda's death, I pull up the local paper's archive website. It takes me nearly ten minutes to find what I'm looking for, but eventually one article stands out.

## HIGH SCHOOL STUDENTS QUESTIONED ABOUT OGLESBY DEATH

My source at the station told me that they have been questioning several of Miranda's friends at school about her state of mind in the past few months. He wouldn't tell me what they found out, so I interviewed her best friend and her boyfriend. The boyfriend seemed pretty upset, but it was hard to get him

alone, since he was surrounded by sympathetic friends perpet-
ually. He told me Miranda had been depressed lately because
her ex had been stalking her. The best friend didn't confirm
this, but accused the boyfriend of being unfeeling and coming
between them. She seemed to think the boyfriend might know
more than he was telling. I tried to get in touch with the ex,
but he won't comment. The coroner is going with accidental
drowning, probably due to a suicidal leap off the bridge. There
is evidence pointing to a second presence at the scene, but the
police don't want to push the matter.

The words reform into what was actually printed and I am struck yet
again by the deviation between what the journalist perceived as truth and
what he actually printed. The article is brief and simply states that police
interviewed Miranda's friends to check on her mental state, but doesn't
share the results. It goes on to explain the final ruling on the death as an
accidental drowning, implying suicide without actually stating it.

My stomach is queasy as I look at the now familiar picture of Miranda that seems to be everywhere. The same bone-deep instinct that tells
me when someone is lying trembles in my veins as I stare at the round,
smiling face in the photo. There is something hidden there, some truth
that has never been spoken, but is still dwelling deep in someone's mind,
waiting for me to ask the right question. With a frustrated growl, I jump
up and begin pacing my room, my hand on the phone, itching to call
Nicole and get some answers from her. But I subside, remembering that
I don't have her number, and she hasn't called me to explain her absence.

There is a knock at my door and I halt, realizing I have been muttering to myself for the past ten minutes. Tossing my phone on the bed, I
open the door to admit my mother.

"I want you to quit school and work at the store every day," she says,
giving me her usual cheerful, ingratiating smile.

With a sigh, I flop down on my bed and give her a stern look. "Mom,
we've talked about this. I'm going to be gone in the fall anyway, so it's
better for you to start getting used to having me at the store less. What
happened to hiring someone else part-time?"

Her lips tighten in irritation as she sucks in her cheeks the way she
always does when she's trying not to say what she really thinks. "What did
I say?" she asks finally, her voice impatient.

"That you want me to quit school to work full-time. Again."

She passes a hand over her face and takes a seat next to me. "I just meant to ask how your day was. I'm sorry, I guess I was hassled at the store today and thinking how much easier it would have been if you were there." Mom puts an arm around me and gives me a squeeze. I hold stiff for a moment and then relax, resting my head on her shoulder.

"Sorry," I say, guilt washing over me before firm resolve takes its place. She knows how important going to school is to me right now, and my sympathy dwindles as I consider her selfishness. My entire life I have used my talent to make sure she gets a good deal, to help her outthink her competition. I have even wielded it against my father for her.

And lost him.

"You know what? I'm not sorry. You agreed to this, and for once you could just let me do what I want. It's not like I've asked for much," I say roughly, jerking out of her embrace. "Anything else you want?"

Bewilderment lines her face and I waver for a moment; she stares at me with childlike confusion, arms still open from holding me. Then her face clears and she rolls her eyes.

"You are so melodramatic. I wasn't going to say anything, but you asked. Don't ask if you don't like the answer. Goodnight." She stands and brushes invisible lint from her sweater, carefully avoiding my eyes.

My anger deflates and I sigh, wanting to be left alone. "Mom, wait. I didn't mean it. I'm just tired." She nods stiffly and gives me a peck on the cheek before she shuts the door behind her.

I drop back down on my bed and pull the laptop to rest on my legs, looking over the article again while I consider what I learned from its more revealing first impression. There seemed to be some question about her death, but it could just be the difference between suicide and an accident. Or maybe the evidence suggests someone else was there, someone who pushed her off the bridge.

"This is stupid," I say out loud, trying to push the conjecture out of my head. But the mention of her ex stalking her resurfaces and I wonder who he is. Phillip was obviously the boyfriend referred to, and Nicole the best friend, but there is still no indication of who could be the ex. Maybe someone whose stalking could have pushed her to the brink.

Or just pushed her.

I force myself to shut down the computer and work on my homework. But as I am drifting to sleep later, the steady, shining fall of snow outside my window hypnotizing me into unconsciousness, Miranda's face still fills my thoughts.

I am standing on the bridge, the entire world outside of the iron skeleton and the swiftly moving water beneath it dark and bleak as a void. Sound is muffled, as though a glass jar has been dropped over my head, and a rushing fills my ears, accompanied by frantic drumming I recognize as my pulse. Soft laughter rasps behind me and I spin around, only to freeze in terror, my breath choked into a white cloud before my face. Cole stands before me, the same wicked grin stretching his face that I saw this afternoon. His eyes are glittering chips of emerald, swallowing the dark surrounding us like an empty vessel.

"Jump, Miranda," he whispers, the sound of his voice dragging across my skin with claws. I try to tell him I'm not Miranda, he's made a mistake, but no air fills my lungs and the edges of my world are growing dim.

"Jump, Miranda," he whispers again, stepping forward until his face is a breath away from mine, the flash of green light in his eyes boring into my brain with indescribable pain. He opens his mouth, teeth white as a shark's, and blows a kiss at me. The world drops from under me and I am falling, falling, and everything is cold and dark, and I see him above me, still smiling, his green eyes vivid against the black cloud that hovers like a dark halo above his head. A quiet gasp escapes me, but I feel it inside like a primal scream, the sound of my heart stopping.

I jerk awake, my heart racing so fast I cannot breathe, the scream still caught in my throat. For a moment, my body is rigid with the terror of the dream, as though Cole is somewhere nearby, pouring panic into my veins. Gradually my pulse slows and my limbs loosen into rest. The muscles in my legs ache as though I've run a marathon.

The clock reads four-fifteen. With a groan, I sit up and rub my eyes. Two nightmares featuring Cole in two nights. I am beginning to think that no matter how hot and charming he is, how much we have in common, he may not be good for my mental health.

I get a glass of water and return to bed, telling myself I am overreacting because I'm worried about sharing my secret with Cole. I'm not very convincing. By the time I am calm enough to fall asleep something strikes me as odd about my nightmares. In both dreams, I distinctly remember Cole glaring at me with vivid green eyes.

Cole doesn't have green eyes.

# CHAPTER SIX

"WHERE WERE YOU YESTERDAY?" I demand as soon as Nicole comes into view. I have been waiting for her outside the classroom since I got to school. She looks up at me with red-rimmed eyes and splotchy skin, limp brown hair hanging over her face like a ragged curtain.

"I don't want to live," she whispers, pushing past me. Guilt burns in my throat as I follow her, realizing I have been thinking about how her absence affected me, not what was wrong with her.

Hastily I take my seat next to her. "I'm sorry, Nicole. I wasn't thinking. Are you okay?"

She gives me a weak smile. "Don't worry about it. Look, it's probably better if you don't hang out with me."

My chest tightens with unexpected disappointment. "I said I was sorry," I mumble.

Nicole frowns at me and finally allows a smile to soften her face. For a second, I glimpse the bright-eyed, carefree girl in the photo Phillip had on his phone yesterday, but she fades as quickly as she came.

"No, that's not it. Look, you've probably heard about how...unpopular I am by now." She looks at me expectantly and I nod, knowing there is no point in denying it.

"Yeah, I'm sorry about that."

"Not your fault. Anyway, looks like the campaign to make me miserable is starting up again," she says, her voice breaking slightly. "If you hang around me, you'll just get caught up in it too."

There is such defeat in her tone that I want to take Tasha's neck and throttle it. Nicole has done nothing to deserve such treatment. She lost her best friend and instead of being embraced in sympathy by the world around her, she is outcast, tormented by the very people she once called friends. I remember how dismissive everyone was at the lunch table yesterday. Even though Phillip and Ruth said it was mean, they still looked at the posting and didn't try to set the record straight.

The bags under Nicole's eyes are so dark she could be bruised, and I think deep down she is. I wonder if the injury that has been done to her can ever be healed.

"Screw them, Nicole. I'm your friend now, and I don't care what anybody says. The truth is all that matters to me," I whisper fervently and then Ms. Sullivan calls the class to attention.

Nicole stares at me blankly for a moment and then an unguarded smile creases her face, tears shining in her eyes. I hold her gaze for a moment more and she nods, wiping her cheeks with her sleeve. Her eyes shift behind me and something hard enters her expression before she turns to face the front of the class. I glance around and see Phillip watching Nicole with a thoughtful expression, his moss-green eyes narrowed. There is something so cold, so detached in the way he looks at her that a chill settles around my shoulders. After a moment he senses my scrutiny and turns to me, mouth stretching in its trademark blinding smile. My lips twitch in response and I face forward, my skin humming almost painfully.

Class cannot move quickly enough for me, and I am out of my chair before the tone sounds, turning to Nicole eagerly. Before I can say anything, Phillip takes my arm, his fingers pressing on the bruises Jake left yesterday. I flinch and his grip tightens slightly before he releases me.

"Can I walk you to class?" he asks, completely ignoring Nicole as she watches us with a concerned expression.

"Oh, thanks, but I need to catch up with Nicole. I'll see you later." I smile at him and grab my bag, feeling his eyes on me as I gather my things. He is still standing there when I glance up again, his lips pulled tight, pupils constricted to a pinprick.

"Yeah, *Phil*," Nicole adds, a sharp edge to her voice. "Not trying to steal away another of my friends, are you?"

He jerks his head to spear her with a stare so quickly I'm surprised I don't hear his neck crack. Nicole pales under his glare, but holds his eyes, exchanging some silent conversation that doesn't look new.

With a smile that doesn't extend to his eyes, Phillip turns back to me. "Nicole still thinks Miranda stopped hanging out with her because of me. Is it my fault that we were so crazy about each other?" His face sobers and he looks down at his hands. "I miss her too, Nicole."

Nicole's cheeks redden but she doesn't reply. My skin is buzzing so hard it hurts, like I've stuck my finger in an electrical socket. Everything about Phillip is screaming 'liar' at me, but I have yet to get any sense of the truth from him the way I would with anyone else. I am more unsettled than I'd like to admit.

When neither of us responds, he sighs heavily and slings his bag over his shoulder. "Well, see you later Derry. I'll look for you at lunch."

I smile at him noncommittally. He has been nothing but pleasant and thoughtful to me, but I am having trouble ignoring my instincts about him, however misplaced they might be. I begin to hope he forgets about asking me out again, because in the pit of my stomach something revolts at the thought of him touching me.

He disappears through the door and I turn to say something to Nicole. She is trembling and ashen, as though she was holding off some intense reaction while Phillip was there and only now succumbed.

"Nicole? Are you okay?" I reach out to touch her arm. Her skin is clammy and covered in goose bumps.

"Yes I'm fine," she lies. I hesitate and then dive right in.

"No you're not. C'mon. Let's go find somewhere to talk." She resists for a moment and then nods, following me submissively as we merge into the foot traffic of the hallway. "Is there anywhere we can go?"

She rouses and glances around. "Yeah. The library."

She doesn't elaborate so I simply force my way through the crowd, maneuvering through the maze of hallways until we reach the door that leads to the media lab and library. As we enter, I am overwhelmed by the smell of bleach, the inside of my nose tingling and bringing tears to my eyes.

"What the hell is that?" I whisper, looking around for some kind of puddle of the noxious stuff, but am greeted by gleaming countertops and the neatest library I've ever been in.

There's something about a place that houses books that needs a little comfortable chaos, the sense you could turn the corner and find the story you've been looking for waiting for you on the arm of a sunken armchair. There is a scent to books that is almost tangible, the flavor of all the hands that have touched them, the minds that have devoured their words; and no library should be without the solid sense that someone has been here before, has dropped their coat and gotten lost for a while.

This library is sterile and cold. The temperature is too low here, especially for the dead of winter. The rest of the building is comfortable, maybe even a little on the toasty side, but this cavernous room has sucked all the warmth from the air and I shiver involuntarily, wishing I hadn't left my coat in my locker. There is no sign of even a single book being off the shelf, no papers lying loose on the counter, and the fluorescent lights are bright enough to cause a glare off the white concrete walls.

"Oh, yeah. It's the librarian. She's OCD." Nicole shrugs, but she's looking a little less frail. "There's a reading room in the back. No one is ever there." She leads me through the stacks, while I marvel at how even the spines of the books are. Not a one is out of place. I wonder if anyone is actually allowed to check any out, or if the entire library is illusion, like the fake food and TVs that furniture stores always put out to make their layouts seem real. Everything is 'look, but don't touch.'

We turn into a small enclosure at the back of the room where several stiff-looking armchairs and a couch are scattered around conversationally. Still unnerved by the surreal atmosphere, I sit down cautiously, half expecting the chair to be made of cardboard.

Nicole slumps down in the chair opposite me, dropping her bag to the floor and burying her head in her hands. I am unsure of what to do, whether I should say something or pat her shoulder in comfort, but she looks up at me before I can do anything.

"Has Phillip asked you out?" she asks abruptly. I blink in surprise and then nod slowly, frowning. "I thought he might have. Don't do it. Don't go out with him," she orders, her tone uncompromising.

I bristle slightly. I don't like being told what to do, even by someone as damaged as Nicole. "I wasn't really planning on it, but that's my decision," I reply frostily.

"No, look, I'm not trying to tell you what to do, but…" She pauses and frowns, looking at the floor as though it will answer for her. Finally, she gives a resigned sigh and looks at me with renewed purpose in her eyes.

"I'm going to tell you some stuff, but you've got to promise to keep it quiet."

"Sure," I promise, leaning forward in avid curiosity.

She studies me for a moment, gauging my sincerity and then nods. "Ok. I think…no, I know Miranda didn't kill herself. I think it was Phillip."

I stare at her for a moment, more surprised at my lack of shock than her theory. "That's a pretty serious accusation. Why do you think that?" I ask cautiously, wanting to know but still skeptical.

Reassured by my interest, Nicole leans forward and speaks in a whisper, even though I haven't heard anything to indicate we're not alone in this strange, sanitized room.

"Miranda and I were friends since fifth grade. We told each other everything, did everything together. We were like sisters. A few weeks after she started dating Phillip, she stopped talking to me."

"At all?"

Nicole shakes her head, memory etched into her face. "Not completely, but she wouldn't say anything about Phillip, kept me away from him. It wasn't like her. When she was dating Jake, she told me stuff all the time…"

"Wait," I interjected, a piece of the puzzle falling into place. "Miranda and Jake were a couple?"

"Oh yeah. Since freshman year. Then…something happened between them last summer. He shoved her into a pool."

"Shoved her as in play, or shoved her as in trying to hurt her?" I ask, desperately interested in her answer.

"As in he was pissed off and shoved her so hard she had bruises on her chest."

A clear picture of Jake sinking to his chair, pale and shocked after I had accused him of killing Miranda, floats through my head like a stray photograph.

"So she broke up with him?"

"Yeah. It was pretty bad for a while. He called all the time and would show up outside her house, dropped flowers off and stuff. He always seemed to be around, wherever we went, begging her to take him back, saying how sorry he was. But Miranda said that if he hurt her once, he'd do it again. And I agreed with her."

So Jake was the mysterious stalker-ex mentioned in the true version of the article I read. I had no doubt that he did shove Miranda; he had amply demonstrated his capacity for violence and strangely obsessive behavior already. The dark purple smudges on my arm could attest to that.

"So what does this have to do with Phillip?" I ask, trying to get back on track.

"He asked Miranda out on the first day of school, as soon as word got around that she and Jake weren't together anymore. I think she was too surprised to say no."

"Why is that?"

"Well, Phillip hadn't ever dated anyone from school. Or anyone that I ever heard. No one thought he was gay or anything; he just never seemed interested. He told Miranda that he'd been waiting for her. She thought it was so romantic."

Nicole leans back against the chair, the slick vinyl fabric squeaking dissonantly.

"She just stopped after that. For a few weeks she was all giddy, telling me about the attention he lavished on her, the presents, the dates, and then one day she just…dried up. She started sitting with him and his friends at lunch, and suddenly I wasn't allowed. He stole her from me. She was never the same after they started dating. And she lost weight. She looked tired all the time. She was skittish, always looking over her shoulder and flinching when you touched her. She was afraid, and she wouldn't tell me why."

Nicole's voice is so quiet I can barely hear her, and slender tracks of tears wind down her face as she remembers her dead friend. Unable to stop myself, I reach out and put my hand on hers. She glances up suspiciously and then gives me a troubled smile, patting my hand before pulling away.

"I'm okay. It's just hard to think about, you know? I got mad at her for how she was acting, and she didn't come to me for help." She closes her eyes, drifting for a moment, and then straightens, eyes piercing me with a fierce intensity.

"She didn't kill herself. I don't care how depressed she was, or what was going on, Miranda would never have killed herself. She wasn't like that. She would have fought back eventually. And Phillip knew it. He couldn't let it happen. So he pushed her off that bridge."

Nicole sounds so certain, and I believe that she is telling me what she thinks is true, but a light hum under my skin contradicts her. I think about earlier when she unknowingly confessed that she didn't want to live. Wasn't it possible that Miranda had felt that way too? Even just briefly enough to make a terrible mistake?

"But why are you so sure it was Phillip? Jake sounds like a more likely candidate."

She scoffs and rolls her eyes. "Jake wouldn't have done it. He might have hurt her in the heat of the moment, once, but he wouldn't have killed her. He was crazy about Miranda."

"But he shoved her into a pool. Maybe he was on the bridge with her. It could have been an accident," I say thoughtfully. Although Phillip puts me on edge, Jake's violent nature makes him a far more conceivable murderer.

"She called the night she died. She was hysterical, said she had to tell me about Phillip. They found her body the next morning."

For a moment I am shocked into silence, thinking how of all the experiences I had expected to have at high school, knowing a potential murderer hadn't even been on the list.

"Well, what was it? Didn't she tell you?"

Nicole shakes her head, regret clear on her pinched features. "It was a message on my voicemail. I saw that she was calling, but I was so pissed at her for shutting me out that I ignored her call. She was dead by morning, Derry. He must have found out and killed her. And I could have stopped it, if I had just answered the damn phone."

Nicole's tenuous hold on her emotions shatters completely and she sags, shoulders trembling as deep, wrenching sobs rack her body. I jump off my chair and put my arms around her, murmuring soothing nonsense, and she slumps into me, her whole being shaking with misery. It is several minutes before she winds down, and by the time she pulls away to wipe her face, I am worried she might act on that unwitting confession from earlier. The guilt she has been carrying around is too heavy a burden for anyone to bear alone.

"Nicole, it's not your fault. You didn't know." I hesitate, taking in her bowed shoulders and the defeated expression on her tear-stained face. "You wouldn't try to follow her, would you? Hurt yourself?"

She glances up at me sharply, eyes wide with shock. "What? You mean…would I kill myself?" I nod awkwardly, uncomfortable asking such a personal question, but worry outweighs my sense of propriety.

"Never," she whispers furiously, her voice resonant with the truth. My skin doesn't have the slightest tremor, and I believe her. "I've been really upset, and I'll admit, I was pretty down when I came to school today because of that stupid Facebook page, but I wouldn't do that. It would destroy my parents."

I nod sympathetically, relief easing like a warm blanket around my shoulders. There is not a trace of doubt in her, and I know she is not in danger of following her friend to the river.

"Besides. I'm going to nail Phillip if it's the last thing I do. I know he did this to her, and I'm going to prove it. That's why everybody hates me, you know. After Miranda died I freaked out and accused Phillip in front of everybody at lunch. They had to drag me away from him kicking and screaming, and I missed a week of school while I 'calmed down.' When I came back, all these rumors had started about Miranda and me, and it just snowballed from there. No one talks to me now." Her voice is tinged with despair and rejection and once again I feel anger boiling in me on her behalf.

"They'll let it go eventually, Nicole. Especially when you start carrying on with your life." She just nods absently. I can tell she doesn't believe me, and given my lack of experience with people my own age, I may be wrong.

"I can't believe I just told you all that," she says wonderingly, looking at me with a quizzical expression. "I mean, you're really nice, and I'm glad we're going to be friends, but I still can't believe I laid all that on you. I'm sorry." She withdraws from me slightly, and I can see the fear in her eyes that she has gone too far. I ignore the twinge of uneasiness that slices through me as I realize what she has just said. Cole's words slither through my mind, trailing uncertainty and guilt. Before I let myself consider the possibility that my ability has something to do with her candidness, I hasten to reassure her.

"Don't worry about it. I'm glad you told me. It seems like you needed to talk about it anyway." She still seems uncertain, and I rack my brain for something to say. "You're not the only one, you know, who tells me stuff. I had a drink with Cole yesterday, and he told me more than he meant to. I guess I just have one of those faces." I cringe at the untruth, but I can see that my confession immediately makes her feel better.

"Cole Durant?" she asks, eyes brightening slightly.

"I guess. He never told me his last name. Tall, dark-haired?"

Nicole rolls her eyes. "Ridiculously hot? Yeah, that's Cole. He's a nice guy. How did you meet him? He was expelled last semester."

"Oh, uh, he works at the café across from my mom's store. We just sort of ran into each other," I answer awkwardly, feeling oddly resentful that Nicole knew him before me. Chiding myself for being neurotic, I smile at her. "He mentioned that you stuck up for him."

A blush softens Nicole's expression and she avoids my eyes. "Yeah, well. He was one of the only people who didn't give me a hard time about the postings. He actually stood up for me too, to my asshat cousin

David."

"Oh, yeah, I met him. He seemed…"

"Like an evil, soulless frat monkey? Yeah, he is. I try to avoid admitting the family connection whenever possible." She laughs and some of the tension that had lined her face evaporates. I can see that she is feeling better, having shared her concerns with me. "Thanks, Derry. I still can't believe I told you all that, but I'm glad someone else knows."

"No problem. Anytime." We look at each other in contented silence for a moment, and hope blossoms in my chest as I realize I really am making a friend, the first I've ever had. For a moment, it is hard to breathe.

We talk until the tone sounds, signaling the end of the period, and as we gather up our bags and sneak through the stark landscape of the library, happiness is burning in my throat like I've just downed a shot of my mom's not so cleverly hidden whiskey. I giggle helplessly when Nicole plasters herself against the wall and pretends to peer around the corner for imaginary assailants. Her laugh comes easily now, and satisfaction shoots through me, knowing that I have helped this girl, have brought the smile back to her face. Her features are no longer pinched, but relaxed and open, giving her a wholesome, sweet look. It's hard to reconcile this Nicole with the girl who was initially so rude to me, but there's no doubt that our meeting has benefited both of us.

We spend lunch together, not even venturing into the cafeteria. The thought of sitting with Phillip now is too discomfiting to contemplate. Nicole tells me more about Miranda, growing up together, and even as I laugh with her, I am struck with envy. I never got to have that; someone who finishes your sentences and has your back; someone to gossip with about boys, and raid each other's closets. Just having someone with whom to share all the mundane and extraordinary details of your life.

I have a feeling given time, Nicole and I might have that.

It is with an extra bounce in my step that I enter the computer lab fourth period, relieved to see that Shockey is too busy talking to another student to pay any attention to me. Remembering what he inadvertently said yesterday, I am in no hurry to attract his notice. Shane is once again already in the room, laughing at something Megan has just said, and Cathy is sitting at her computer, a hangdog look on her long face. After hesitating for a moment, I take the seat next to her with a friendly smile. She returns it weakly.

"Jake turned me down," she says, voice falsely cheerful. I feel a pang of sympathy for her. Her infatuation with Jake has been blatantly obvious since the moment I saw her, so I can imagine how painful a rejection from him would be.

"Um, I wondered if you would take a look at my story? Let me know if it fits with the *Agitator's* vibe?" I ask, trying to give her some kind of ego boost to counter the despondency written all over her.

Her smile gains some strength and she looks at me with more focus. "Oh, sure! No problem! Though Jake usually does this kind of thing," she wavers uncertainly.

Grimacing, I lean closer and lower my voice. "I don't want to bother him. He's still a little sore over Shockey giving me the community beat. It would feel like rubbing his face in it if I asked him, you know?"

She nods her understanding and a wistful expression clouds her eyes. "Jake took it pretty hard. That's been his beat forever. But he'll get over it. Jake is the sweetest guy…" she trails off, eyes watering. "Sorry, I'm just…"

"Are you okay?" I ask, knowing exactly what's bothering her.

"Oh it's nothing," she whispers, voice thick with unshed tears. She glances up at me and sighs, a wry smile twisting her mouth. "It's stupid. I should have known it was too soon, that he couldn't…"

I peer over at Shane and Megan, relieved to see that they are still deep in conversation. "I didn't mean to pry."

"No, it's fine. I asked Jake out and he said no. We've been spending so much time together since Miranda…died, and I thought we had bonded or something. He was really nice about it…he just said he didn't think of me that way." A single tear escapes and glides unheeded down her cheek. Although I think she's probably better off not being in a relationship with someone as conflicted and aggressive as Jake, she has obviously seen a different side of him.

"That sucks. But you know, it's obvious that he cares about you; even I can tell that and I've only been around a few days," I assure her, uncertain of how to comfort her. This is outside my experience. I've never even had a crush on a guy, much less asked one out.

"Really?" Cathy's expression is hopeful and she gives me a hesitant smile.

"Yeah," I say, beginning to wonder about the wisdom of encouraging her. "Look, I don't have much experience with guys…well, any experience…so I don't know how accurate my observations are. But it does seem like he cares about you, and you two have a special relationship."

Cathy's eyes mist over as her cheeks flush. "Yeah, we do. I guess I need to give him more time. It's only been a few months after all."

"Right." I frown, still puzzled over Jake's role in Miranda's death. "So he dated Miranda? But I thought she was with Phillip when she died," I say, hoping that Cathy can give me some insight on the strange dynamics between the three.

She glances around and drops her voice to a hush. "She was dating Phillip, but Jake was still all about her. He's been so torn up about it."

Cathy draws in a sharp breath, as though shocked at herself and pulls away, returning to her computer, cheeks flaming. Glancing over my shoulder I see a shadow stalk ahead of Jake through the door. His cloudy-blue eyes are luminous as he surveys the room, pausing momentarily on Cathy and then settling on me. Almost instantly their color seems to deepen, a cold sky above gathering clouds, and I am struck by dual urges to curl up into a ball and hide even as I begin to lean forward, closer to him. Catching myself, I break contact and swing back around to boot up the computer, trying to ignore the way my pulse is racing and the heat creeping down my neck. I can still feel his eyes on me, even as the quiet tap of his steps leads to the opposite side of the room.

"So you wanted me to look at your story?" Cathy asks quietly, her soft voice breaking whatever strange spell I was under. I can actually feel when Jake's gaze shifts, as though someone has removed a needle from under my skin I hadn't known was there.

"Yeah, thanks." I log on and pull up my file, opening the partially written story I had worked on yesterday. "It's not finished, but if you could tell me if I've got the tone right…"

Cathy scoots her chair over and I roll mine back, giving her room. Carefully avoiding Jake's corner of the room, I glance around, meeting up with Megan's frosty glare. She is watching me with hostile attentiveness, as though waiting for me to mess up or say something dumb so she can pounce. It is at moments like these I realize precisely how much I don't understand about social dynamics. Somehow I have gotten on Megan's bad side even though we've only had a few conversations, and I don't know how to fix it, or if I should even bother.

With a sigh, I lean back and close my eyes, tuning out the chatter around me. After a moment, I feel the heat of someone's presence beside me. Even without looking I know it is Jake. I can feel frustration rolling from him in waves, like the stuttering engine of his truck. Hoping he wants to talk to Cathy, I keep my eyes shut and pretend I don't know he's there.

He clears his throat and his voice sounds low and hesitant, suddenly too close. "I can't stop thinking about you."

I jerk away, my eyes flying open. Jake stands close enough to me that the bottom of his dark green sweater brushes against my shoulder. He is watching me with a cautious expression, as though waiting to be refused something.

"Sorry, what? I must have dozed off," I say, covering my reaction.

His eyes flash, but his answer is innocent enough. "I asked if I could talk to you for a minute."

I glance over at Cathy, whose back has stiffened, obviously listening in on our exchange. With an internal groan I get up and Jake moves back, but still remains closer than I'm comfortable with.

"Uh, sure. What's this about?"

His eyes narrow slightly in irritation, but I am in no hurry to go anywhere with him.

"Just come with me," he replies quietly, but I can hear the thread of purpose under his seemingly pleasant tone. Realizing I can't refuse without making a scene, I follow him out of the room and into the hallway. He waves at Shockey from the door as he closes it behind us. The silence of the usually exuberant hallway has an ominous quality as I walk just behind Jake, wondering where he's taking me.

Despite my unease, I cannot help but admire the view. Jake's lean figure, accentuated by the tight knit of his sweater and trim cut of his jeans, is disturbingly distracting. Furious with myself for feeling even a reluctant attraction to someone who is on my list of murder suspects, I force my eyes just above his head. When we turn down yet another empty hallway, I come to a halt.

"Where are we going?" I demand, determined not to take a step further. We've had ample time for a brief private discussion, and I am becoming more and more certain I don't want to hear what he has to say.

Jake spins around and clenches his fists at his side. Not thinking, I take a step back. He catches the movement and his face falls, hands loosening and his whole posture slumping with defeat.

"I'm not going to hurt you, Derry. I just want to talk." His voice is quiet and non-threatening now, reminding me of the injured tone he had when I accused him of abusing Miranda. A finger of remorse claws my stomach.

"What's wrong with right here?" I ask, not willing to give in to irrational bouts of guilt. I have a lot of practice with that from my mother.

Glancing around, Jake shrugs. "Nothing I guess. I just don't want to be interrupted. Would you feel more comfortable here?"

Startled by his sudden concern for my feelings, I just stare at him. His behavior is not tracking with what I've come to expect.

"There's a classroom that's not being used this period just down there," he says, pointing to the end of the hall. "But we can talk here if you'd rather."

I hesitate, but something in his expression tells me that he really isn't intending to lay into me again. There is actually a trace of shame in the way he ducks his head slightly and doesn't quite meet my eyes.

"No, it's fine. Lead on," I say, biting back my reservations. We're still at school, a public place. He won't dare to attack me here.

A faint smile tugs at his lips and my pulse flutters. Without a word, I follow him into the dimly lit classroom and take a seat by the window, figuring that if he does start flipping out, I can scream and get someone's attention.

He sits down opposite me, starting to scoot his chair closer until I give him a pointed look. Abashed, he moves back and finally looks me in the eye, his expression rueful.

"Derry, I just wanted to apologize. I have been really rude to you since the moment we met, and I want to explain." I nod slowly. Encouraged by my reaction, he leans his elbows on his knees and fixes me with an earnest gaze. "I'm really not like this normally, but I was pretty angry that Shockey gave you my beat, and I took it out on you. I know it wasn't your fault, you didn't ask for it, and I should have given you the benefit of the doubt. I let my anger get out of hand, and I'm afraid I've made you… nervous around me."

I serve him a skeptical look. My skin has picked up a low-level hum, indicating that he is not telling me everything. "Yeah, you did. But that doesn't really explain the level of your anger. Seems a little out of whack to me," I say, reining in my own irritation and keeping my tone even.

Jake's eyes flash again, and I could swear that for a moment the slate-blue of his eyes is swallowed by black. "It's not all about you, I just… projected or something," he says, some of the contrition draining from his tone. The hum under my skin picks up to a buzz.

"I don't think that's true. It certainly doesn't explain this," I say, jerking up my sleeve to uncover the bruises from the day before, which have darkened to a black-tinged purple now. His eyes lock on the marks and something akin to despair pulls down his features.

"I'm so sorry," he whispers, unable to remove his gaze from the bruises. Uncomfortable with the intensity in his eyes, I pull the sleeve back down and rub my arm. "I don't...I didn't mean to do that."

The buzz stops, and I know he is telling the truth. I soften slightly, remembering how Cole had mentioned Jake has some kind of ability linked to rage. It's possible he is not aware of how dangerous he is, but I am still wary of anyone who can snap so quickly.

I sigh. "I believe you." Relief widens his eyes and some of the tightness leaves his posture. "But I don't understand what I've done to get you so angry. And yesterday with Cole...you were pretty scary," I say honestly, unable to forget the blaze of fury in his eyes when Cole stepped between us.

Jake slumps and drags a hand over his face. "I know. I just get so angry and I don't know how to shut it off." His voice is so weary and hopeless I have to stop myself from reaching out to take his hand. With a sigh he straightens and locks his eyes with mine. "But that's no excuse. I should never have acted like that around you, and I don't want you to be scared of me."

His words have the harmony of the truth, sinking into my mind with no resistance. Curiosity takes the place of my initial doubt and I move my chair closer to him slightly. His eyes drink in the movement and he watches me with the vigilance of a hunter approaching a wounded animal.

"I don't want to be scared of you either, but I still don't understand what I've done to get you so angry. You don't even know me."

Color rushes his cheeks and he looks away. "I don't know," he lies. I fix him with a critical look.

"That's not true, I can tell."

"It wasn't you I was angry with, it was Cole," he counters. My skin amplifies its telltale vibration, and I know he's still not telling the whole truth.

"Look, Jake. I'm pretty good at knowing when someone's lying, and there's something you're not telling me. If you want me to be comfortable around you, you've got to be honest. Why are you so angry with me?"

For a moment, his whole body tenses and I am sure he is going to either lunge at me or flee, but he remains seated and looks at me with undimmed ferocity in his eyes.

"Fine. I'm angry because the moment I saw you I wanted you, and I hate you for it," he growls, and this time I can clearly see his pupils expand, blackening his gaze completely.

I twitch back in surprise, my heart pounding with a blend of terror and fascination. The black fades from his eyes and he looks almost as astonished as I am.

"Why…why did I just say that? I'm sorry, I don't know why I just…"

But I do. It's strange that I've never really considered before just how easily people confess things to me. Like the time I got that city councilman to tell me about his underhanded dealings with contractors for the city's utilities, the news story with which I made my name. I had known from the start he was hiding something, and pumped him with leading questions, but even I had been shocked at how freely he gave up the dirty details. Almost as though he couldn't help himself.

I think about yesterday, how much of himself Cole had revealed to me, so much more than he had planned. And today, Nicole shared her secrets and insecurities with me. Even Cathy succumbed to my questions with little resistance, and we've had precisely two conversations.

With a sick, dizzy feeling, as though the world slipped off its axis for a moment, I am forced to accept that there is more to my gift than I knew. Not only do I see and hear the truth when I first encounter someone's words, not only can I sense with my entire body when someone is lying, it seems the more I want to know something, the more others are compelled to reveal to me.

The danger of this ability astounds me for an instant, and I almost forget Jake's presence, feeling ashamed on so deep a level that my bones ache. The unfairness of my situation staggers me. Every question I have ever asked, ever will ask is morally unacceptable. If people have no choice but to answer me, how can I ever ask for the truth again?

"I have to go," I say abruptly, jumping to my feet, and reel unseeing toward the door, bumping into desks as I try to escape from the suffocating guilt that grips me. I am nearly to the door when Jake grabs my arm, his fingers falling almost precisely on the bruises he has already given me, swinging me around to face him, pulling me so close we are barely an inch apart. He glares down at me with fevered intensity, such fervor in his expression that I quiver with unexpected pleasure, nearly drowning in the sensation, almost wishing he would pull me under.

"Don't walk away from me," he growls and his lips are suddenly crushing mine, savaging my mouth with all the unspent fury of the moment before. His body is huge, towering, as he crushes me against the wall with enough force to knock out my breath, and for a moment I can do nothing but tremble beneath him, every nerve ending screaming for me to run even as a dark heat spreads through me, settling in my core almost painfully. My knees give way, and it is only the pressure of his body against mine that keeps me upright. His hands tangle my hair as he deepens his kiss, and everything about him is as hard and unyielding as the wall behind me.

Dark spots float before my eyes and I tear my lips from his, gasping for air. He gives me only a moment's reprieve before he renews his assault, and I can taste the anger and passion on his tongue like burnt cinnamon. With my breath returns sanity and I begin to struggle, shoving against his immovable chest with the panicked flailing of a trapped bird. When he doesn't release me, but thrusts his tongue into my mouth, I fight in earnest and land a kick on his shin.

With a shuddering gasp he lets me free, breathing heavily, his eyes black with arousal. I ram as hard as I can against his chest and he staggers back enough for me to break away. My mouth is throbbing from the harshness of his kiss and as I fling myself through the door, not daring to look back or to stop, I hear him give a hoarse cry.

My heart is pounding so hard it hurts as I run at top speed down the hall and slam my way out the door to the student parking lot, whipped into lucidity by the frigid air that blasts into me with the force of a physical blow. I stumble over to the wall and lean against it, sinking to the ground, sucking in the cold air as though my life depends on it.

I am too stunned to do anything but drink the air in great gulps, trying to slow my heartbeat down to something other than a rib-shattering pace. Several minutes pass before I am able to think straight, and as feeling returns, pain springs up all over my body. My arm aches, the bruises imprinted deeper in my skin from Jake's grip. A spot on my shoulder-blade begins to complain from being struck against the wall, and my mouth is a raw wound, even the edges of my lips pulsing cruelly from the force of Jake's onslaught.

I put my fingers over my mouth and am startled by wetness. Pulling them away, I look down in horror at a plump drop of red resting on my fingertip and lick my lip, tasting the coppery bitterness of my own blood.

Tears stream down my face, burning my skin in contrast to the iciness of the wind lashing against me, and I hug myself against the wall, trembling from the cold and the crash of adrenaline.

The squeal of a door startles me and I freeze. Jake rounds the corner, his face aghast as he takes me in. Panic and rage fight for dominance in my chest and I rise shakily to my feet, forcing myself to meet his eyes. He takes a step forward, his arm outstretched, but I dart out of his reach, relieved to find that rage is winning the day.

"Derry, I…"

"Don't. Don't speak to me. Don't touch me. Don't even look at me," I hiss, my voice a threat. "Don't ever come near me again, do you understand? I don't exist for you."

Pain is etched on his face and for a moment I almost relent, but I taste the blood on my lips and firm my resolution.

"Please, Derry. I'm so sorry…" he begs, taking another step toward me. I hold my ground, but I can feel my pulse picking up again, knowing only too well that it doesn't take much for his remorse to turn to mania.

"Stop it. Or I'll scream," I promise, and he halts, his entire body limp from the rejection. "Sorry doesn't cut it, Jake. Don't come near me again. I mean it. I want nothing to do with you."

Finally recognizing the sincerity in my voice, Jake just nods and turns away, limping faintly from my well-placed kick. He pauses at the door and looks at me pleadingly over his shoulder, but I keep my expression stony, and he nods again and disappears into the building.

The moment he is gone, I sag to the ground and shake uncontrollably. It is nearly ten minutes before I am able to drag myself to my feet and contemplate returning to class. Underneath the slowly fading terror and anger is a deep well of confusion. I cannot understand what has just happened, how someone so much a stranger to me could act like that, could possess me so completely even for a moment; and even more baffling is how I let it happen. And why it took me so long to fight back.

And how, for just a moment, it felt better than anything I've ever known.

# CHAPTER SEVEN

WHEN I FINALLY REENTER THE journalism lab, Jake hasn't returned. It took me nearly fifteen minutes to get myself looking presentable again and stop my lip from bleeding. It is swollen and my eyes are still puffy from crying, so I pull my hair over my face as much as possible and keep my head down as I make a beeline for my computer. The room is dead silent for a moment, and then a snicker explodes behind me. I am pretty sure it's Megan, but I don't turn around to confirm, instead keeping my eyes locked on the computer screen as though my life depends on it. After a minute a hand rests lightly on my shoulder and I am forced to look around.

Shane is looking down at me with his usually impish expression clouded by concern. His eyes survey my face, pausing on my split lip, and his lips press together tightly.

"My dad abused my mom."

I just blink at him and he frowns.

"C'mon, Derry. What happened?" he demands quietly but firmly.

I just shake my head and try to turn back around, but he tightens his grip on my shoulder. His thumb presses into a nascent bruise and I wince. Immediately he releases me, but a discerning look is in his eyes.

"That son of a bitch," he whispers and spins around, headed for the door. Acting on instinct, I lunge and grab his t-shirt, dragging him back. With a sigh, he halts and drops to one knee next to me. "What happened?" he asks in a gentler tone.

I just shake my head, knowing beyond a doubt that Shane is the kind of guy who will confront someone he thinks has hurt a woman, which is a wonderful quality, but one that might get him really hurt with someone like Jake. Recalling how Cole mentioned a link between Jake's rage and increased strength, I am convinced that if Shane goes looking for him now, he may get more than he bargains for.

"Nothing," I lie. "I…tripped. Don't worry about it." I try to put some real conviction in my voice, but I know I am failing.

"Derry, please. It was Jake wasn't it?" His voice is a sibilant whisper, full of menace, and I realize with blinding certainty that Shane knows that Jake hurt Miranda.

"It was an accident, Shane. I promise. He didn't hit me. Just let it go." Technically this is true, if not a complete picture of what happened. Shane reads my eyes for sincerity and is apparently somewhat satisfied.

"Look, I know everyone worships the ground he walks on, and most of the time he's a decent guy. But I've seen him when he's angry and I know what he's like. If he does anything like this again, you tell me. I'll look out for you," he promises and unbidden tears spring to my eyes at his willingness to protect someone he barely knows.

"Thanks, Shane. But why? You just met me," I ask, curious.

Shane rolls his eyes and a little of his usual humor makes an appearance. "Well, first, you're hot and I want to get in your pants." He wiggles his eyebrows lasciviously and I can't help the snort of laughter that escapes me. A grin stretches his wide mouth before his expression grows serious. "And anyway, I don't like seeing girls getting roughed up. Period."

I just nod and give him a weak smile, trying not to wince when my lip protests. The door swings open to my left and I look up with a sense of dread, expecting Jake, and it's not exactly a relief when Shockey saunters in, his gaze instantly fastening on my swollen mouth. His tongue darts out to moisten his lower lip and a frantic gleam touches his eyes before he clears his expression.

"Seeing you injured is a turn on," he says, voice filled with concern. Nausea digs at my insides and the back of my tongue burns with bile.

"She just tripped, Mr. Shockey. She'll be alright."

I am grateful Shane answers since I am too busy trying to hold back blistering revulsion. Shockey just nods, his eyes lingering on me before he turns to address the others.

"I need your stories by the end of class tomorrow so we can go to press Friday. Make sure Jake gets a chance to look them over first. Any questions?"

Megan raises her hand and he strides over to her, his hand clenching and unclenching restlessly. I am stunned that this man has been let anywhere near children, finding it hard to believe that no one else notices his deviant behavior. While they are busy talking I force myself to smile at Cathy.

"Did you get a chance to look over my story?" I ask, pleased to note that my voice has regained its normal tone.

"I hate you," she says quietly and I blink in surprise. Her normally sweet expression is petulant and sharp as she glares at me.

"Sorry?" I say, stunned by her unconscious admission.

"I think it's fine. But you should get Jake to look at it, since you two get along so well." There is no missing the edge in her tone and it occurs to me that she must believe Jake and I snuck away for some kind of romantic rendezvous. Right after she told me he turned her down. Irritation flares at her incredibly off-base assumption, but I keep my voice steady as I answer.

"I don't think that will work. Jake and I…I don't think we'll be working together much."

Cathy's eyes narrow, but she doesn't answer, just shrugs and spins back around to her computer, presenting me with a cold shoulder. I sigh, abruptly worn out with trying to get along with everyone, particularly when no one but me is interested in the truth.

Shane stands up and pats me on the shoulder, giving me a sympathetic look. My heart swells with gratitude, glad to know that at least one person doesn't hate me.

By the time the tone signals the end of the school day, I am hard pressed to remember why I wanted to come here in the first place, thinking maybe my mom was right about me dropping out and just working with her until college. Only the thought of my budding friendship with Nicole prevents me from stopping by the main office to get the paperwork.

I get into my mom's clunker of a car feeling like I've been given a stay of execution. When she asks, I try to answer her questions about my appearance reasonably. Since most of the time Mom isn't terribly concerned with how I'm feeling apart from if I'm capable of working or not, she accepts with aplomb my lame explanation about getting hit in the face with the locker door. Instead she fills our conversation with talk about the vintage flapper dress she sold to a buyer from D.C. this afternoon, and how the woman promised to return over the weekend with her other well-to-do friends. I am happy for Mom, but there is too much on my mind to settle on something so trivial just now.

She drops me off at the newspaper office, which sits at the top of the hill all the shops and restaurants are on. The *Daily Holler* office is small and cramped, one open room with a receptionist's desk and a bevy of shoddily constructed cubicles. I greet the receptionist, telling her I have an appointment with Derek, and she points back toward the left without taking her eyes off the computer screen or opening her mouth. I swallow my nervousness like a too-large vitamin and head in the right direction, glancing in each haphazard cubicle until I find a plaque on one reading *Derek Wise, Community.*

"Hi, I'm Derry MacKenna, from the high school. You told me to drop by today," I say, and the man in the cubicle swings around on his swivel chair with a grim smile. I have to school myself not to take a step back, he looks so much like Jake. I give him a shaky smile and take his outstretched hand.

"I'm going to give you a hard time," he says pleasantly, and I repress a sigh. I could really stand to have the rest of the day go without any other challenges or difficulties.

"Is now a good time?" I ask, hoping he didn't say anything that required a different response.

He shrugs and gives me a quick once-over. I return the favor, noting that while he looks similar to Jake at first glance, his face is longer, his jaw more pronounced, and he's about fifteen years older and thirty pounds heavier. Something inside me relaxes as I notice the dissimilarities.

"As good as any. Jake told me about you. You're some kind of hot-shot, right?" His crooked brow indicates he believes otherwise.

With a struggle, I smother all my other worries for the moment and focus on my newest adversary. "I think that's an exaggeration. I've been fortunate enough to freelance for several papers in Virginia over the past few years. One of my stories was picked up by the AP." I dig through my bag and hand him the portfolio I've been carrying around for days. He takes it with a skeptical look and glances through it perfunctorily. I can tell he isn't reading any of the material. He's going to be tricky to work with.

We talk for another five minutes, while he gives me a rundown of what's happening in the community, limiting his information to church bake sales and the closing of the "Old Tyme Christmas Festival." I take notes, all the while thinking that I'm going to have to find a more forthcoming source if I want to get any good stories. Derek's phone rings and he doesn't even glance at the caller ID before he tells me he has to take it, and to email him if I have any questions. Biting back a snippy retort, I smile and thank him for his time.

Instead of walking back the way I came, I round the corner of cubicles and stroll down the next aisle, looking for someone more affable to connect with. I halt by the third cubicle down, recognizing the name plaque as the same byline from the story about Miranda.

"Mr. Householder?" I query the slouched figure of the older man in front of an outdated computer.

He jerks slightly, and spins around to greet me.

"I'm undervalued here and tired of it," he says gruffly, his bushy snow-white brows drawn together. Householder looks to be in his sixties, with thick white hair topped by a round bald spot that reminds me of a monk's. He brushes crumbs from a well-worn green plaid shirt hanging loose over wrinkled khakis and squints muddy brown eyes at me before he puts on the glasses that hang on a chain around his neck. He is comfortably overweight, a man who enjoys his donuts in the morning and his fried chicken in the evening, and his clothes are sloppy; but there is a canny look in his eyes, and I have a feeling he is good at seeking out the truth too.

"Hello, sir. I'm Derry MacKenna, from the high school newspaper. I just took over the community beat and wanted to acquaint myself with the town's paper. I've read several of your stories and really enjoyed them."

He narrows his eyes at me and then his thin lips twist into a grudging smile. "Oh you did, did you? Well, you'd be the only one."

It doesn't take a rocket scientist to figure out that this is a discontented journalist who just needs someone to ask him the right questions.

My specialty.

"Is there any advice you can give me on covering the news in Harpers Ferry? I could really use a professional's perspective," I ask, pulling out my notebook, pen poised as though prepared to take down every word.

Householder laughs, a deep guttural sound that makes me think of cigars. "You're a sharp one, aren't you? Playing on my ego. Alright, Miss…"

"Derry."

"Derry. You can call me Simon. What do you want to know?" he asks jovially, clearly amused by me. I'm not entirely sure why, but I do know not to look a gift horse in the mouth.

"I just wanted to find out about some of the major news events in town. In particular, I heard that a girl from the school died last semester.

I'm new here, but I believe you covered it?"

His smile fades and he sighs, looking off to the side. "Yes I did. Sad thing. Everybody thinks she killed herself."

I catch his revealing choice of words and pursue them. "Thinks she did? You don't agree?"

Simon trains a shrewd expression on me, as though considering my mettle before he answers. Finally he turns around to shut down his computer and gives me a half-smile. "Buy me a cup of coffee and we'll talk," he offers.

"Absolutely," I return, my answering smile delighted.

Ten minutes later we are comfortably situated in a booth at the same café to which Cole brought me. Steaming mugs sit in front of us, mine filled with apple cider, Simon's with black coffee.

"So what do you really want to know?" he asks, and I can't help a small chuckle. It's kind of refreshing to have someone else be able to see to the heart of the matter.

"I'm interested in the circumstances of her death. From what I've heard, there was some evidence that she may not have been alone on the bridge."

Simon looks at me with more attention, his gaze calculating. "Not many people know that, young lady."

I give him an enigmatic smile. "I have my sources."

He snorts and takes a drink of his coffee. "Quite the little reporter, aren't you?"

"This is my first time working on a high school paper. I'm used to freelancing," I explain and when he asks for details I hand him the ever present portfolio. He looks through it with interest, and I can see by the quirk in his lips that he is both impressed and entertained. Finally he slaps it down on the table and gives me a sharp look.

"Alright, young lady, you've proved your point. There was quite a bit of dirt on the bridge where the girl jumped. And there were two sets of footprints. One the same size and shape of the girl's, and one larger set that could've been male. A couple people were questioned, namely the boyfriend and the ex, but neither was charged."

I process this information in silence, listening to the thrumming in my bones telling me once again that there is more to Miranda's death than meets the eye. "Is that all?" I ask, leaning forward.

Simon chuckles and shakes his head. "You're inquisitive aren't you? Well none of this is confidential, just unsubstantiated stuff I wasn't allowed to print. There were peri-mortem bruises on the girl's arms, like someone had gripped her too tight."

This news disturbs me on a number of levels. My eyes drift to my arm, where the bruises Jake gave me seem to come alive in response to what I have just heard. "Someone gave her bruises before she went over," I mumble, lost in thought. Simon nods, his eyes brightening with shared interest.

"That's right. And there was evidence of self-inflicted wounds on the inside of her upper left arm."

I drew in a sharp breath. "She was a cutter?"

"Looks like. Coroner said the oldest mark was only a few weeks. She started pretty recently." Simon frowns and I have a feeling he's wondering precisely why he's being so forthcoming with me. I now know better than to wonder myself.

"Then doesn't that support the suicide theory?" I ask, not willing to give in to the uncomfortable prick of guilt in my chest. After my encounter with Jake earlier, finding out if Miranda was murdered is a matter of survival.

With a shake of his head, Simon takes a swig of coffee. "Not necessarily. If she was cutting because someone was abusing her, then he may have helped her off the bridge too." He waves his hands dismissively and drains the last of his coffee. "But all this is immaterial now. Half the reason they wouldn't let me print this stuff was because the cops ruled it a suicide and closed the case."

"What was the other half?" I ask pointedly.

He gives me a disapproving look. "You're too curious for your own good, you know. This is a bit deep for a high school reporter."

I roll my eyes and lean forward, my voice unwavering. "I'm not your average high school reporter. I can read between the lines, and you left quite a bit out of your stories. Who didn't want those details printed?"

Simon throws up his hands, as though giving up. "Fine. It's your funeral. The police were looking pretty hard at the ex-boyfriend. Apparently there were some rumors floating that he may have gotten physical with her. Boy certainly seemed pretty unstable when I saw him." He stares off in the distance, remembering.

"And?" I prompt, deeply invested in the answer.

"And do you know who his father is? Mayor Geoffrey Wise. The evidence was circumstantial anyway, and you don't print speculation about the mayor's son in a small town, girl."

I examine my reflection with a sense of bewilderment. I've watched enough TV and movies to know that I'm not hideous, but I've never had an opportunity or reason to qualify how attractive I am. An antique store is rarely a place where teenagers go to shop, so exposure to people my age has been incredibly limited. Without regular comparison to my peers, or being out anywhere that guys might hit on me, I have no idea where I fit in. Mom has always told me that I'm beautiful, but I'm her kid and she has to say that.

I'm not skinny, but I'm tall and mom says I have an hourglass figure and should be proud of it. My hair is long, just below my shoulders, and wavy; a curious shade, not quite blond, but not quite red either. When I was very little, my dad said it was like spun gold. My face is heart-shaped accentuated by a widow's peak on my forehead, and my eyes are a clear, dark grey. My skin has an olive tint thanks to Dad's Spanish roots and my own addiction to sunshine, and my complexion is generally clear, excluding the occasional raging pimple that plagues everyone. But I do have a spray of freckles across my nose and cheeks that no amount of makeup ever seems to cover up. I can thank my mom's Celtic heritage for that I suppose.

What I don't see in my reflection is the reason for Jake's frenzied attraction to me. It's obvious after what happened today that he's more than casually interested, but I can't understand it, or comprehend why it's made him so angry. What frightens me more is the flash of exhilaration I felt when his lips first crashed into mine. Developing a crush on Jake is a really, really bad idea.

With a sudden wave of dizziness I realize Jake has given me my first kiss. At the thought, tears stream down my face and a choked sob escapes me. I feel like my chest is caving in, as though Jake actually beat me senseless. In all my imaginings, all those lonely afternoons at the store, watching happy couples window shopping, seeing thoughtful men coming in to buy their fiancés antique jewelry, dreaming of the day my own moment would come, being assaulted and ending up with a bloody lip wasn't part of the fantasy.

There is a bitter tang on my tongue as I realize how Jake has stolen this from me, has poisoned a desire I have cherished for so long, one of the hopes I wanted to fulfill when I came to school. It's gone now, and I can't get it back.

A clinking noise at my window startles me from my depression and I turn, frowning. When it comes again, it sounds like pebbles being tossed at the glass, but that can't be it. I can't imagine anything more stereotypical, so it can't be possible.

The tapping comes again, so I hastily wipe my face and trip over to the window, my heart pounding uncomfortably. For a moment I can't see anything outside. Twilight has come and gone and our miniscule yard is blanketed in shadows. As my eyes adjust to the darkness I can make out a man-like shape and panic clutches at my chest. A small glow flickers into life and the man's features are thrown into relief, revealing Cole, holding a lighter, smiling as he looks up at me.

My heart skips a beat, but it's not from fear this time. An answering smile creases my face and when he waves for me to come down, I have to force myself not to run down the stairs.

Mom is still sitting in the living room, curled up on our circa 1980's green sofa, a thick flannel blanket tucked around her feet. She glances up at me with a sleepy smile as I enter. I look around the cozy room, smaller than at our old house, but more comfortable somehow. When we moved, we had to downgrade our style of living a bit to cover the moving costs and the new store. Our old house had three bedrooms; but now we are down to two, and a bathroom we have to share. The rooms are a bit more cramped in this house, a pre-fab built sometime in the eighties, and it has a lot less character than our old historic home, but we've adjusted surprisingly well. I think part of it is the thrill of starting over, of finding this town where we have no ties, no previous obligations.

It's also the fact we are on our own. When we left Virginia, Mom drew up an agreement releasing my father from any further financial obligations. He'd been paying alimony and child support since he left when I was eight, but she let it slip that she wanted to cut all ties when we moved, including him. I respect her for it, and have tried not to make any unreasonable demands when it comes to money, hoping to make the transition easier.

I hate the idea of being indebted to my father as much as she does.

"I miss having a man in my life," she says, giving me a finger wave. I blink, surprised to hear that she's thinking of dating again. She only had one boyfriend since Dad left, a year-long affair with a perennially imma-ture artist who ended up cheating on her. She's been gun-shy since.

"Been watching romantic comedies again?" I tease. She widens her eyes and then blushes, realizing what I have heard.

"Caught me. I just met a really nice man in the shop this afternoon. He was looking for a vintage cigarette case. Very cute."

I grin at her. "Go for it. You're still totally hot," I say, ducking out of the way as she swats at me. "Speaking of cute guys, there's one waiting for me outside. Mind if we go for a walk?"

"Bring him to the door to meet me first," she stipulates and I groan. "I just want to see what Harpers Ferry has to offer!" She puts up her hands as though warding off an attack. I almost argue, but this playful exchange makes me hesitate. It's the friendliest we've been with each other lately and I don't want to ruin it.

"Fine. Hang on." I stomp to the door, making sure she notes that I'm doing this under protest. Cole is sitting on the porch steps and jumps to his feet, grinning wickedly.

"Hey," I say, grinning.

"I'm drawn to you," he says, and my heart slams against my chest in one great thrust. He watches me curiously, and I can see him wondering what he's revealed about himself. I clear my throat and forge ahead.

"So, my mom wants to meet you. Do you mind?" I ask, suddenly self-conscious, wondering if he'll read something into my request.

"Not at all. Mothers love me," he promises, his smile widening.

I blow out a breath in relief and wave him in, noticing with appreci-ation the tight cut of his jeans and his confident stride. It's impossible not to compare him to Jake, and I find myself wishing that my first kiss had been with Cole. It's funny how his overtly bad boy image is so misleading, how Jake, the golden boy, is really the dangerous one.

"Mrs. MacKenna, it's nice to meet you. I'm Cole Durant. I know your daughter from school," he lies smoothly, giving me a subtle wink. A smile twitches my lips as the faint hum of the falsehood dances under my skin. I have no intention of correcting him, since I doubt my mom would be thrilled about me meeting him on his motorcycle.

"I'm so glad Derry is making friends already. Between you, Nicole, and Jake, she really seems to be fitting in."

I nearly choke at her statement, and Cole's smile loses some of its zest. "How did you know about Jake, Mom?" I finally spit out. She glances at me, confused by the shock in my voice.

"Oh, I guess I didn't mention. The man who came in the shop today is his father, Geoffrey Wise. He told me Jake mentioned you. He said you two are in journalism together."

Cole cuts a glance my way, and I could swear there is an accusing look in his eyes. I swallow my initial response and force a smile. "Yeah, that's right. We are. We haven't really talked much though," I mumble, noticing the keenness in Cole's expression as he surveys my face, his eyes locking on my split lip.

"Well, it's still nice. Ok you two, have fun. Be back by ten," she says, waving us off. Cole shakes her hand and says something complimentary that makes her laugh before he puts a hand to my back and propels me out the door. He waits until we are at the edge of the yard before he swings around and takes my chin gently in his hand. Even though I know he is only doing it to get a closer look at my lip, my skin tingles under his fingertips.

"What did he do?" Cole demands fiercely, eyes narrowed in anger. An insidious finger of dread strokes the back of my neck and I shiver. Cole closes his eyes and immediately the feeling dissipates. He opens his eyes and gives me a sheepish look. "Sorry. Lost control for a second there. Are you okay?"

I mean to tell him I'm fine, not to worry, but the contrast between his momentary loss of control and Jake's strikes me hard and I gasp, tears welling up and preventing me from answering.

Cole's expression is stricken and he raises his other hand to tenderly trace my cheekbone soothingly, his eyes deep pools of remorse.

"Oh, Derry, I'm sorry. Please don't cry," he whispers forlornly. I shake my head and try to get control of myself, mortified I'm having this reaction. I draw in a steadying breath and attempt a smile.

"It's not you, Cole. I swear. It's just been a long day."

Relief softens his expression and he strokes my cheek with his thumb, moving slightly closer, the warm, spicy scent of oranges and cloves clinging to his skin. "I know Jake did something. How did you get a split lip?" he asks more calmly. I hesitate, wondering if I can get out of telling him, but the resolve in his gaze tells me I have no choice.

"We had…an argument. He was trying to apologize for yesterday, and

I asked him what it was about me that made him so angry and I kept pushing. He just…flipped out and shoved me into the wall and kissed me; it was rough, and he didn't let go at first."

Cole's expression is terrifying, and he drops his hands, clenching his fists so tight I can see the veins in his arms; he glares past me, eyes dark, no longer reflecting the light from the porch.

"He said he was sorry, and I know he was. I just…I guess I underestimated his strength. I shouldn't have pushed him."

Cole's attention snaps back to me and some of the anger fades. "Don't you dare blame yourself. He has issues with control, and yeah, it can be difficult. But he should never have even touched you, much less drawn blood. I'll kill him," he growls, the fury swelling again.

Tentatively I reach out and touch his arm. "It's over, Cole. I told him to leave me alone, and I think he will. Don't worry about it."

A rueful smile twists his lips and his shoulders relax. "I didn't mean that. But we are going to have a little brother-to-brother chat. I'll make it clear you're off limits. I'm staking my claim." There is a glint in his eyes that makes my pulse pick up.

Blood rushes to my cheeks and I bite my lip in confusion, wincing as I pull at the sensitive skin. "I don't…um…what?" I stammer, totally lost for words. I've watched people flirt for years thinking I was picking up technique, but now, faced with Cole's dark beauty and the brush of his skin against mine, my mind has gone empty and I'm left a blithering idiot.

"Well, at least it wasn't your first kiss, right?" he asks playfully, but I can hear the buried interest. My face falls and I look away. "It was?" His pitch rises with surprise, but I fix my gaze on a tree behind him, staring at it like it holds all the answers.

He places a finger on my chin and turns my head to face him again, his eyes a deep sapphire as they search mine. Compelled to answer honestly, I nod. Regret flashes across his face and then he draws me closer, his eyes trapping me in a moment that seems to last forever.

"Well, we can't have that, can we?" he whispers, mouth so close to mine I can feel his breath on my lips. Still incapable of speech, I just shake my head, my skin suddenly on fire, anticipation and hope thrilling through my veins. "Let me show you how it's done." His voice is little more than a sigh and suddenly there is no space between us.

His lips touch mine feather light, the disparity from what Jake did making me dizzy, the kind of head-spinning weightlessness I used to feel when I was a kid, twirling and twirling just to see the world fly by. He focuses on my lower lip, carefully avoiding the sore spot, and my mouth opens slightly, drinking in the heady, warm feeling that spreads through me as his lips part and press against mine with just enough force to make my knees weak. For a moment, he doesn't move, and I revel in the sensation of his lips, his breath mingling with mine.

He pulls back abruptly, eyes wide with surprise, and takes a step away from me. A chill settles over me and I miss his warmth, his closeness in a way that doesn't make sense, as though we have been pressed together much longer than a moment.

"I'm sorry, I don't know why I did that," he says and my heart drops to my stomach, my head turning hot and fuzzy.

"Oh...I...I'm sorry," I stutter, so humiliated I'm surprised I'm still standing. I back away, stumbling, wanting nothing more than to get away from Cole, from the disbelief on his face. "I'll just..."

I step on a fallen twig and the crack seems to wake him from his thoughts. I am avoiding his eyes, but he grabs my hand and I halt, so close to tears I don't dare speak.

"No, no...I didn't mean it like that. I just meant...that's not why I came here tonight. I wanted to continue our conversation from yesterday, but then you smiled like you were happy to see me and you were hurt... and I couldn't stand thinking Jake kissed you first." He speaks in a frantic rush, pulling me closer to him. I dig my feet in, searching for my lost dignity.

"You know what, Cole? I've had about all I can take of bipolar behavior today, so why don't you just get to the point or leave me alone?" I am shocked at how controlled I sound, since hurt is still roiling around my gut like broken needles.

"I can't believe this. I'm usually so smooth," he mutters, releasing me to run a hand over his head in apparent bafflement. I just glare at him and cross my arms over my chest to hide the fact that I am still trembling.

"I came here to talk, to start getting to know you better, and then I just wanted to kiss you, be near you. It's...unexpected." His eyes narrow for an instant and a thread of suspicion enters his voice. "You didn't forget to mention any other abilities did you?"

I crinkle my brow in confusion. "What are you talking about?"

"Do you maybe have some compulsion talent added in with the

whole honesty thing?" he asks casually.

I am speechless with my distress, and all the blood drains from my head, centering somewhere in my chest like a hot metal knot. The damn tears prick my eyes again, and I just start shaking my head, incapable of any other response. Cole's expression remains sharp for a moment and then he shakes himself and reaches for me.

"Sorry, Derry, I didn't mean that…" he begins, but I swallow my hurt and move away.

"Stay away from me. You and your psycho brother. I am done with this shit," I growl, turning to run back to the house, barely holding back the tears.

"Derry, wait. I'm sorry," Cole calls after me, grabbing at my arm.

I snatch it away and round on him. "You know, I have been pushed around my whole life by my mother. Don't you think that if I had the ability to make her do what I wanted I would've used it by now? Maybe I would have made Jake leave me alone?" I shake my head crossly and start toward the house, tossing one last comment over my shoulder. "You know what the first thing you said to me tonight was? You said you were drawn to me. I can't force that."

He calls after me and attempts to follow, but I hurry inside and rush up the stairs, ignoring my mother's startled exclamation. I slam my door shut and stomp around the room for a bit, trying to convert my humiliation and disappointment into righteous anger. It doesn't work.

I collapse on the bed and draw my quilt up around me, burying my face in my pillow. But the tears won't come now. After fighting them so long, I give a dry sob and feel my eyes burn, but there is no release. I don't even know what I am most upset about at this point, whether it's Jake or Cole or just life in general, but the inside of my skin throbs with the need to escape, to forget.

At the back of my mind, I am listening for the creak of the stairs, the sound of my mother coming to check on me. But the minutes pass by and there is no hesitant knock at the door, no whisper of fabric as she sits next to me. When I finally do hear her steps down the hall, she doesn't even pause at my door before she closes her own.

Then the tears come.

# CHAPTER EIGHT

I GRIN AS NICOLE COMES SKIPPING through the shop door, her hair blown in wild tangles and dotted with snowflakes. Her cheeks are red, her eyes bright, and there is no trace of the sullen, downtrodden girl I met my first day of school three weeks ago. After her first big confession about her fears over Miranda's death, she clammed up a bit, keeping herself distant for a few days, as though waiting for the other shoe to drop. But when I didn't call her crazy or start mocking her she made tentative gestures of friendship.

The day I told Tasha her boyfriend was cheating with her cousin, Nicole and I became best friends. Tasha had been posting nasty, unfounded comments about Nicole sleeping with old guys at the train station for crack money. Nicole was miserable, and I could see her drawing into herself like she did when we first met. Tasha was hanging all over her football player boyfriend, looking so smug, and then he opened his mouth. I don't know what he really said, but I heard about his little affair and for once I took vindictive pleasure in dishing out some unwelcome truth.

Tasha called me a freak, but she didn't target Nicole again. Every day after that Nicole's smile got wider, more natural. Every day she came further out of her shell. And for the first time in my life, I had someone that made me laugh, someone to talk to about my boy troubles.

It was heaven.

"I've got a secret you're not going to like," Nicole says, bouncing over to the counter where I sit unhappily with the cash register. I finish ringing up my customer, who purchases a beaded bag from the '20s. I give her my shopkeeper's smile and then sigh with satisfaction when the bell above the door announces her exit.

"Oh my god, do you ever stop working?" Nicole demands, climbing up onto the retro barstool next to the counter.

Rolling my eyes toward the back of the store where my mom is busy foisting her wares on an unsuspecting elderly couple, I heave a sigh. Mom has had me doing inventory all week, which means my newfound social life has taken a serious dip. If I thought it was really necessary, I wouldn't complain, but mom has revealed on several occasions that she doesn't want me to have friends or a social life. She just wants me to stay with her, working at the store, waiting to use my ability for her benefit.

"Oh, come on, you owe me dinner. And I'm hungry," Nicole pouts, extracting a reluctant chuckle from me.

With a grin to cover my trepidation over Nicole's unwitting admission, I call back to Mom, "Nicole's here. I'm leaving!" I jump down from my perch behind the counter and grab Nicole, dashing out the door before Mom has a chance to argue. We pause outside the store, trying to decide where to eat. Snow drifts down in soft clouds, dusting the cobblestone street, covering the old, muddied snow from last week like a balm over a bad memory.

"Ugh. No more pizza. I can't take it anymore," Nicole begs and I roll my eyes at her dramatics.

"Well, there aren't that many options. You've shot down all our usual choices."

She glances around impatiently and then her gaze settles on the café across the street, *The Stone Bistro*. Following her gaze, I shake my head violently. "Hell, no. No way. That's where Cole works," I remind her.

"Oh, come on. How long are you going to keep avoiding him?" Nicole sighs, repeating her oft-heard refrain. Since I couldn't really give her the whole story about my fight with Cole, I just told her he had kissed me and then regretted it. While she sympathized with me, she didn't understand the depth of my resentment.

Sometimes I didn't either.

Cole had come to the store the day after the big first kiss fiasco, full of contrition, but no explanation for what had happened between us. I told him I accepted his apology, and on some level I did, but the humiliation ran too deep to just let go. He stopped by almost every day and bugged me until I gave him my phone number, after which he called every night to talk, mostly about our abilities and what he thought we should do with them. Sometimes I answered, sometimes I didn't. He didn't bring up the kiss and neither did I.

But it hurt every time I saw him, and I'd been dodging him lately, too confused by my feelings and what our relationship really was.

"Forever," I finally answer.

"Fine, fine.  Pizza it is," Nicole capitulates, shrugging and looking wistfully toward the café. I ignore her and lead the way down the hill to the pizza parlor, not looking back.

"So, I have something to tell you," Nicole says, her voice hesitant.  I stuff the last of my crust in my mouth and look at her inquiringly.

When she doesn't continue, I lean forward, lowering my voice. "What is it? Are you okay?"

She nods and then looks out the window, watching the snow deepen, erasing the sidewalk in a streak of white. Finally she takes a deep breath and nods, as though making a decision.

"I think I know what Miranda found out about Phillip," she says, her voice barely above a whisper.

I freeze, startled by the sudden revelation. Nicole hasn't said anything else about her suspicions since the first day she told me, and I had let it go as well. The only time I see Phillip is in first period, and we've remained friendly, but I turned down his few attempts to ask me out. No matter what the truth is, I can't get over the unsettled feeling he gives me or the constant, uncomfortable buzz under my skin.

"What do you mean? I thought…you haven't said anything about this in a while," I ask, unsure of how to react.

"No, I just didn't want to say anything until I was sure. Hear me out, okay?" Nicole's voice is fragile and I know she is worried about how I'll react, but I can sense the truth from her and know that whatever she has to tell me she believes to be true.

"Of course," I say, maintaining eye contact until she relaxes and leans back in her seat.

"Okay. Let's pay and then go somewhere quiet."

Since it's my turn, I pay the bill and we head outside, shivering as the cold creeps through the openings on our jackets. "Where do you want to go?" I ask her.

"Let's walk down to the river," she answers, starting down the street before I can argue.    I'm not nuts about discussing her dead friend by the river she died in, but it's hard to change Nicole's mind when she's set it on something. I hurry to catch her, digging my hands into my pockets, trying to bury my unease.

"So what's with all the secrecy?"

Nicole gives me scathing look. "You're joking right? He probably killed Miranda because of what she found out and you want me to blurt it out in the middle of a restaurant?"

I put up my hands defensively. "Okay, okay. Yeesh."

She snorts and picks up the pace, reaching the bottom of the incline and turning to the right toward the overlook and the path to the old railroad bridge. "So has Jake given you any problems today?" she asks, changing the subject.

With a sigh I shrug. "Friendly as ever," I answer, uncomfortable with the turn in the conversation. Everything having to do with Jake makes me uncomfortable. While I have managed to avoid actually speaking to him about anything not related to the newspaper, it seems as though he is always there; waiting in the hall outside my classes, around the corner when I'm eating lunch, standing just behind me when I turn around, his slate eyes watching my every move with unnerving intensity.

"Not gonna say anything else about it, are you?" she asks, humor creeping in her voice. She can laugh. He doesn't threaten to either kiss her or kill her on a daily basis.

"Nope," I mutter, refusing to think about it. If I let thoughts of Jake intrude for too long, I'll drop out of school and move to a different town.

When we finally reach an acceptable spot alone in a corner on the overlook, Nicole drops her joking manner and turns serious eyes on me.

"So what is it? What did you find out about Phillip?" I ask, unable to contain my curiosity any longer.

Nicole sighs and gives me a wary look. "You're not going to laugh at me, are you?"

I roll my eyes so hard my head hurts. "No, Nicole. I think we've established by now that I won't laugh at your theories. If I wasn't willing to ride your crazy train, I would've gotten off weeks ago."

She punches me lightly in the shoulder and then drops all signs of humor. "Ok. Look, I don't have any solid proof yet, but I'm pretty sure that Phillip's a drug dealer."

I blink, thinking that compared to some of her other theories, dealing drugs seems kind of tame. "What makes you think that?" I ask, trying to be supportive.

"Miranda's mom called me yesterday and told me she was packing up some of Miranda's stuff to put in the attic. She wanted to give me the chance to pick out some of her things to keep." Nicole's eyes blur with memory for a moment and I feel a twinge of sympathetic pain on her behalf.

"That was nice," I comment, trying to encourage her to keep going, to not get caught up in the miasma of guilt and sadness that swarms her every time she mentions Miranda's death.

"Yeah. I haven't talked to her in a while, so I was surprised when she called. But Miranda and I were friends for a long time, so I guess she remembered me after a while." Nicole shakes her head and the focus re-enters her eyes. "Anyway, so I went, and I was looking through her stuff and I found her journal. It was hidden in the false floor in her window seat, where we used to hide our candy stashes and dirty books." Nicole laughs suddenly, warm sentiment written across her face.

"Dirty books, huh?" I tease, glad to see some of her grief has eased at the memory.

"Shut up. Anyway, I guess no one else thought to look there, because it obviously hadn't been disturbed. So I took it with the other stuff."

I frown at this news, wondering if what she has done is wise. "Was that a good idea? Maybe you should have given it to her mom, or the cops or something. For the investigation."

She just gives a dismissive toss of her head and pulls a dark brown leather journal from her purse. "There is no investigation, Derry. No one cares anymore but me. Even her mom is trying to forget her, packing up her stuff to tuck away like she was some visiting relative who forgot her suitcase. No one else wants this shit stirred up again, but I was right. Read this," she commands, flipping open to a page and shoving the notebook in my unwilling hands.

With serious trepidation I look down at the slanted script on the pages, the dark ink burning its message into my brain.

*I can't breathe, I can't think, I can't sleep. Food tastes like his spit and I can't get it out of my mouth. No one cares, I can't tell anyone. Phillip knows and told me I'm just a dirty slut who asked for it and if I tell anyone else he'll break up with me and make sure everyone at school knows what happened. Sometimes I don't care, I want everyone to find out so that he's punished, so that he can't do it to anyone else. But the shame...my mother would never understand and Jake...he'd hate me. I waited for so long, and I always thought it would happen with Jake, that we'd have our first time together and it would be perfect. But then Shockey took me and I can't get his scent out of my skin. Phillip says he can smell him on me. He wrinkles his nose every time he sees me like I'm rank, and I feel like I am, I feel like I'll never get clean.*

I gasp, tears burning my eyes, and put my hand to my mouth. The despair, the hopelessness that emanates from this page in a dead girl's journal is suffocating, her untold guilt and shame thick like smoke in my lungs.

"Right? That has to be what she found out!" Nicole exclaims triumphantly.

I glance up at her in shock before I remember whatever I just read is not what she saw. An overwhelming sadness settles on my shoulders as I realize that this poor girl's sense of degradation was so intense she lied even in her journal, something she never believed anyone else would see. With a heavy heart, I take another look at the passage, filing away the terrible knowledge that has just been forced on me.

*Today I found a mysterious brown paper bag in Phillip's glove box. When I asked him what was in it, he slammed the lid on my fingers and told me to shut up. I don't know what he's into, but it has to be illegal. He gets this expression on his face, this glee when he looks at it, the same expression he has when we walk around the halls together with everyone looking. He just likes to have things. I don't know why I don't just open the bag, why I don't tell him to go to hell. I just don't seem to have the energy anymore.*

"I don't know, Nicole. Why does this make you think he's a drug dealer?" I ask, trying to keep my voice steady. All I want to do is go home and lock myself away to weep for Miranda, for her deeply hidden anguish.

"Well what else would he keep hidden in a brown paper bag in his glove box and be so touchy about? That sick bastard, hurting her like that. I knew he was doing something to her. I just can't understand why she didn't leave him. She left Jake," Nicole muses, creasing her brow so deeply the lines are etched on her face.

"Is that the only part that makes you think that?" I ask, wondering if Nicole has any idea what really happened to her best friend.

"Yeah, and it's near the end. I got this journal for Miranda on her birthday at the end of September, so she only had it a few weeks before she died. Everything else is about how much she loves Phillip, how mad she is at Jake. There's one brief entry that seems weird, she mentions not being able to get clean, but it's really short. Here," she says, flipping back a chunk of pages and pointing to a half page entry. At first glance the handwriting is chaotic, frenzied, as though scrawled out painfully, against the writer's own will. With a sinking stomach I read what is truly written.

> *Shockey raped me. He took me in his car, he promised to take me home, but he locked the doors and drove to the river and he was so strong, so much stronger than I would have thought. He pushed me into the seat so hard it scraped against my skull. I can still feel it there, driving further and further through the bone, and my head hurts so badly. He covered my mouth so I couldn't scream and I couldn't breathe and he just poured himself into me, and I can't get him out, I can't get him out, I can't get him out…*

Tears are streaming down my face and I can feel a scream rise in my throat. I clench my hand into the fabric of my coat, digging in as hard as I can to keep myself from flinging the journal into the river, to get those words away from me.

"What is it? What do you think she was talking about?" Nicole asks, her expression concerned as she takes in my reaction. I am at a loss. How can I tell her what I know, what Miranda endured, without giving away my own secret? How can I burden her with this knowledge when she already carries so much guilt?

"I don't know," I finally whisper, so nauseous I can barely see straight. Nicole takes the journal back from me, staring down at the page as though it will reveal something new to her.

If she only knew.

"I wish she would have told me this. I would never have let Phillip do this to her if I had known. She thought she was all alone."

I just nod absently, still too raw to talk normally. Knowing the truth is too horrible sometimes.

Nicole closes the journal and I give a shudder of relief. I can't take any more revelations from that book today. She glances at her watch and jumps to her feet.

"I gotta go. I'm going to check some things out. I'll call you later," she promises, grabbing her things. I just nod again and then snap out of it when I register what she's said.

"Wait, check what out? You're not going to spy on Phillip or something are you?" I ask worriedly, thinking she is just determined enough to try something so ill-advised.

"No, I'm not going to spy on Phillip. I won't even see him tonight, I promise."

My skin is buzzing like crazy at the blatant lie. "Bullshit."

She gives me a startled look and a flush creeps up her neck. "Ok, fine. I called him and told him I wanted to talk. I just want to see what I can find out."

I shake my head violently. "Nicole, that's a terrible idea. You have nothing to go on." Nicole waves the journal at me but I just brush it aside. "That doesn't count. That's hearsay. It's an entry in a teenage girl's diary. That's less than nothing from a legal standpoint. What can you possibly use against him?"

Tears brighten Nicole's eyes and she pulls her lips in tight, as though sucking in all the words she really wants to say. A bevy of expressions flit across her face; fury, morphing into frustration and culminating in despair.

"But what can I do? I can't just let this go! He is responsible for her death, I know it."

The frantic gleam in her eyes makes me extremely nervous. It's the kind of look you see in the eyes of a cornered animal, one who is out of options and ready to strike out at the next thing that comes near, even a helping hand.

Leaning forward, I take her wrists in my hands, steadying the fine trembling fluttering over her arms. "I believe you, Nicole, I really do. But this is not the way. You have to stop taking all of this on yourself. It is not your fault. Miranda was troubled, there were other things going on in her life. You couldn't have prevented what happened," I say in a low, clear voice, pushing with all my willpower for her to accept what I'm telling her. Never before have I wished I could influence people in the way Cole insinuated, but now I hope he was right.

Nicole just shakes her head. "You're wrong, Derry. Miranda wouldn't be …gone if I had been there for her. And it makes me sick seeing Phillip walking around, smiling, laughing, hitting on you, acting like she never existed. I hate him!" She is drawing in huge breaths, sucking in air like a drowning person and for a moment an intense feeling of dread slams into me, a bone-deep certainty that something dangerous and insidious is clawing its way up between us; an iron fist dragging us apart inexorably.

"Nicole, I will do everything I can to help you find out what happened. Even though I never knew Miranda, I feel like I did because of you. And I want to see the truth about her death come out too. The truth is very, very important to me." I sigh, wishing she understood just how important the veracity about Miranda's death is becoming to me. "But this is not the way. Please, please promise me you won't meet with Phillip. Let me help you," I beg.

Nicole's face is wet with tears and I can feel the battle she is waging between her common sense and the need to assuage her guilt, but after a moment she nods. "You're right," she whispers, defeat clear in her tone. "I promise. I won't see him."

My skin is quiet and I breathe a sigh of relief, feeling as though I've dodged a bullet. "Thank you," I say, squeezing her wrists lightly before I let her go. I smile encouragingly and stand, abruptly realizing just how cold the stone bench has become. "Now can we go before a snowman forms on my head?"

Nicole laughs and brushes off the snow that has accumulated on her own coat. "Yeah. Thanks, Derry. I don't know what got into me."

"What are friends for?" I ask, bumping her with my shoulder. We walk back up the hill to the store in companionable silence, the swiftly falling snow washing away the heat of our tears.

We part ways at the store, Nicole heading for her Mom's waiting car up the street, me standing outside, fighting to gain control over the turmoil in my head.

That glimpse of Miranda's diary was like brushing up against a hot iron; it burned all the way through, and I had no doubt it would leave a scar. The thought of looking at those pages again leaves a sticky nausea in my gut, but part of me, the part always concerned with understanding the real story, commands me to take another look. I resist for a moment and then give in, knowing I won't be able to think of anything else.

"Nicole, hang on!" I call, running to catch up as she slides into the passenger seat. Her mom gives me a friendly wave as I reach them, her smile genuine.

"I'm so relieved Nicole finally has a new friend," she says pleasantly, her real greeting lost on me. I return her smile and mumble hello.

"What's up?" Nicole asks, her brows furrowing together.

"You've already read that book we were talking about earlier, right?"

I ask carefully, casting a pointed glance at her mother. Nicole catches on quickly and nods. "Can I take it for a bit? Maybe I can find something you missed."

Nicole takes the journal out of her bag, shielding it from her mother's view. Her fingers stroke the buttery leather binding hesitantly, and I know that she is loath to give up this tangible memory of her best friend.

"I'll be careful with it, I swear," I whisper solemnly. She glances up at me, a painful blend of fear and regret in her eyes.

"Okay," she yields, handing the journal over to me in a rough movement, as though she is afraid of changing her mind if she holds it a moment longer. I take the book from her and tuck it carefully in my own bag with a sense of foreboding. Nicole gives me a weary smile and finishes climbing into the car.

"I'll call you later," she says, and then I am alone on the street, watching the car disappear up the street and over the hill. A sudden wind whips around me, the cold biting sharply beneath my skin, settling low in my stomach, a frozen fist of ice that weighs me down all the way home.

# CHAPTER NINE

BY THE TIME I CRAWL into bed a little before midnight, Nicole still hasn't called. I check my phone a dozen times, some nagging feeling of disquiet tapping at my brain, but there are no messages. I call her twice and send several text messages, but nothing.

Miranda's journal lies unopened on my desk, the smooth leather cover gleaming dully in the moonlight that leaks through the blinds. It waits, disapproving, accusing, but even though I spent most of my evening staring at it, I hadn't the courage to crack the cover. I promise myself that I'll do it tomorrow, when I've rested, when I've recovered from what I've already learned.

I sink into sleep in stages, my mind drifting over my conversation with Nicole earlier, and it morphs into an entirely different discussion the way real life dissolves in a dream, the subconscious dragging up all sorts of details and nuances initially missed. The desperate light in Nicole's eyes takes on a feverish intensity in my dream, and her promise to me rings hollow. Her fingers are crossed in her lap, the tips lengthening until they form a stranglehold around my neck, choking off my protestations. A shrill keening comes from Nicole's throat, so piercing I try to clap my hands over my ears, but it only grows louder, more insistent.

I groan, coming slowly awake, realizing that the sound from my dream is coming from under my pillow. Rubbing my eyes groggily with one hand, I knock the pillow aside and look in surprise at my cell phone, wondering how on earth it got under there. Shaking my head, I glance at the clock, seeing it is a little past one. The caller ID announces Nicole. With a frown and increasing anxiety I pick up and hesitantly answer.

"Hello? Nicole?"

"I'm afraid I'm going to die!" Nicole's voice is a harsh whisper. I am immediately on the alert, my eyes opening wide, pulse pounding wakefulness through my veins.

"What's going on?"

"I was right, Derry. I was wrong about what he was doing, but God help me I was right," she pants, her breath coming in short gasps. I swing my legs over the side of the bed, throwing the blanket off me, prepared for action, whatever it may be.

"What are you talking about? Where are you calling from?" I demand, nearly frantic with worry.

"I'm over by the rafting center, down from the gas station across the Shenandoah Bridge. He tried to take the phone from me after I played Miranda's message," she explains, the sound of tears clear in the quaver of her voice.

Dread settles like lead in my belly. "Nicole, what did you do? What's going on?"

"You were right, and I know I promised, but when I told Phillip I didn't want to meet he said he had something to tell me. About Miranda. I couldn't help it, Derry, I had to see him."

My veins feel like ice. "Why didn't you call me? Damn it, Nicole, are you okay? Did he hurt you?"

"He was pissed, and he tried to grab me, but I ran. You've got to come get me, Derry. He's looking for me."

In a flash I am off my bed and shoving my feet in my shoes, not bothering to tie the laces or change my clothes. Every nerve ending is firing, propelling me out the door as though my body knows something I don't. "I'm coming right now. Where do I find you?"

"I'm going to move, I'm too visible here. Meet me at the river access, where the boats are loaded. I can hide down there." She gasps shortly and her voice is filled with urgency. "I gotta go now, I can hear him. Come get me, Derry." She draws a shaky breath. "I'm scared."

"I'm on my way," I whisper as I creep down the stairs, hoping my movements don't wake Mom.

"Hurry," Nicole whispers, and the line goes dead. I am frantic now, caution lost in the need to get to her as quickly as possible. I still don't understand what has happened, what made her break her promise to me, but I am absolutely positive time is a factor right now.

I swipe Mom's keys from her coat hanging on the outside of the closet door and slip out the front, closing the door softly behind me. I have a license, but Mom hardly ever lets me drive or have the car on my own, and despite the gravity of the situation, a thrill passes through me, adrenaline shot with excitement at breaking this long-standing rule.

It takes me an agonizing ten minutes to reach the place Nicole direct-ed, a narrow dirt road just past the bridge over the Shenandoah where one of the locally run rafting centers hides in the trees. Squinting through the snow that blankets the uneven gravel, I keep going until I find a slop-ing track between the trees used to take small rafts and kayaks down to the water. The Torino shudders and slips over the wet mess of the ground, but I go as fast as I can, my certainty that every second counts mounting. I don't realize I'm crying until my vision becomes so blurry I have to wipe my eyes.

Finally, I reach the bottom of the track, hurling the car into park and looking around. Nothing happens. Nicole doesn't come bounding out. Thinking she might be afraid I'm Phillip, I flash my lights three times, pause, and flash again. Even though we didn't agree on any signal, I can't imagine Phillip doing anything like it.

Silence meets my efforts. The wind has died down and the world is bathed in white, strangely luminescent, the snow reflecting the faint moonlight peeking through the heavy cloud cover, dappling the surface of the sluggish water with a radiant shimmer. It is like being trapped inside a snow globe, but there is no sense of wonder or magic. Just a pon-derous, unnatural quiet that fills me with misgiving.

I hesitate another moment and then get out of the car, immediately hunching over as the chill hits me. In my rush, I hadn't bothered to grab a coat or anything warm, so I am shivering in my thin pajamas, mentally cursing Nicole if she's playing some kind of bizarre prank.

But I know she's not.

"Nicole," I whisper, wondering if I'm being stupid, worrying about being quiet. But even my soft murmur seems to fill the space as though I'd shouted, the sound reflecting off the snow and water, hanging in the air like slowly drifting snowflakes. I call for her a few more times, and then trudge through the thickening snowfall, drops of melting ice slith-ering inside my shoes, encasing my feet in a freezing film.

I spend nearly five minutes searching for her before I realize some-thing unsettling. Mine are the only footprints. No one else has been to this spot, not since the snow began earlier today.

Nicole isn't here.

Unsure of what to do, I huddle in the car, clutching my phone in hand, waiting for it to light up and Nicole to tell me not to worry, she's home safe and sound, it's all been a terrible misunderstanding. We'll laugh about her failed espionage tomorrow, and she'll promise not to do anything so stupid again. Everything will go on as normal.

Another five minutes pass and there is nothing, and I must now face the possibility she hasn't made it to our rendezvous because Phillip caught up with her. Even knowing how certain Nicole is about his responsibility for Miranda's death, it's hard to believe he'd really hurt her. But she might be trapped in some heated argument with him, and things could get out of hand.

Feeling as though any decision I make is going to be the wrong one, I start the car and begin backing it up the hill, planning to look for her back at the rafting center where she called.

I make it halfway up when the slope becomes steeper and the car begins to protest, the wheels whining with effort against the slick ground. I gun it, hoping that the Torino's long history of being an indestructible tank will work in my favor, but the wheels find no purchase and the car begins a listless slide down the hill, toward the water. Acknowledging defeat, I swing the car sideways so it won't drift straight into the river, and it comes to a halt just before the bank. I slam it into park, pulling the emergency break and hang over the steering wheel, out of breath as though I have run a mile. Panic seizes me, and the cold is barely noticeable as I jump out of the car and begin the climb, feet skidding against the treacherous blend of snow and mud. It is like trying to ascend a stream of swiftly moving water, fighting the current the entire way.

By the time I make it up to the rafting center, I am soaked with a disgusting blend of mud and sweat. Despite the frigid air, I am burning up, my adrenaline pumping overtime. All I can think of is finding Nicole. There's no way she would have ditched me or skipped our meet.

Something has happened. I know it.

I waste precious minutes looking around for any sign of Nicole, but the snow has wiped everything clean and I know already, in my core, that she hasn't been here in a while.

Tucking my hands under my arms, bent over like an old woman against the chill, I drag myself up to the main road, planning to head for town. My teeth rattle inside my mouth and I suck the air in quick sips, my throat burning, face hot.

There is no one on the road, and I pause for a moment to tie my shoelaces. The last thing I need is to fall and injure myself before I can find help, or Nicole. My fingers are so frozen that the joints won't bend, and tying my shoes becomes a fierce battle of will. When they are finally no longer a danger to me, I begin to run, my cold limbs warming up, moving more loosely as I pick up the pace, fleeing back in the direction of town.

I have no idea how much time passes. The road goes on forever, the snow is pounding down on me, each flake heavy as iron, sticking to my unprotected skin until I feel as though I am made of frost, trapped in an endless circle, doomed to run with my terror and the cold forever. It is a shock when I emerge onto the bridge, the streetlights glaringly bright after the odd twilight I've been caught in. I stop, clutching my sides, gasping for air, the change in scenery waking me from whatever trance I've been in. I raise my hands to my face and realize with despair that is nearly incapacitating I have left my phone in the car.

I can't call anyone for help. I missed that window.

No cars are in sight, the landscape is silent, even the sound of the river moving beneath me muted, as though it is afraid of being noticed. Defying the lethargy creeping through me, the urge to curl up into the fetal position and wait for rescue, I force myself on, maneuvering through the concrete embankments that separate the road from the narrow pedestrian walk. Clinging to the safety rail along the side, my steps slipping on the icy sidewalk, I make it halfway across the bridge before I collapse, my lungs burning, the cold so intense, so deep that any further movement is impossible. I crouch there on the sidewalk, one hand on the railing, knowing that if I let go, I might not get back up.

The sound of the water fills me up. It is louder here out in the middle, suspended over the river. In my exhaustion, I feel as though I am balancing on a string, one false move enough to send me pitching over, down into the dark.

Nicole's terrified voice sounds in my head, her last command to 'hurry.' Gathering what little energy I have left around me as a barrier against the insidious cold, I lurch to my feet, hanging onto the railing like a lifeline. I stare down at the river, fighting for the strength to keep going, my eyes just drifting over the surface, too blurred with tears and fatigue to really take anything in. I start moving, pulling myself along with the rail, each step a monumental achievement. Even if I manage to find Nicole, I don't know what I'll be able to do for her in my condition.

I am nearly across the bridge when I see it.

Just below, caught on an outcropping of rock that slices into the path of the river, there is a dark smudge, strangely shaped. Why this has grabbed my attention among the dozens of other shadows I don't know, but now that I see it, I cannot tear my eyes away. Straining my eyes, I try to focus, to understand why this smudge seems so important, but it is too far and too dark.

A quick wind strikes me from behind and I shiver uncontrollably. The sky lightens for a moment, the clouds pushed aside by the sudden wind and a shaft of dim light settles over the smudge, transforming it into a familiar shape.

"No," I gasp, and all my exhaustion melts away. I limp as quickly as I can, hurrying over the bridge and taking a right, down an access road that leads to a parking lot, down toward the smudge. I stumble a thousand times, as though my legs know I'm staggering toward a nightmare.

Car lights glimmer around the turn and I run towards them, waving frantically, no longer caring who finds me. The car slows as it approaches, one headlight flickering faintly, and then comes to a halt in front of me, the lights blinding, preventing me from seeing who is inside. While I flinch from the light, the car growls to life and swings around me, the driver a dark blur, and the car is gone, up the road and out of sight before my vision rights itself. I stand staring after it in disbelief, wondering who the hell would drive away after seeing a teenage girl in pajamas flailing around on a deserted road in the snow.

A chill settles over me that has nothing to do with the weather. I look to the river, toward the smudge I've been making for, and I notice with a sickening sense of inevitability that it has shifted; the current is slowly plucking it from the safe harbor of the rocks. I forget everything, the pain in my body, the pounding of my head, the ominous driver, and I run full tilt, a last surge of adrenaline giving me new life.

I emerge into the empty parking lot, marking where the outcropping is, and pitch into the thin fence of trees separating the riverbank from the lot. Miraculously, I don't trip over anything, but come to a screeching halt in the pebbles that mark the edge of the water. The smudge is fully visible now, only a hundred yards away, and every part of me is screaming.

A leg is hanging out in space, tugged by the current.

Plunging into the freezing water chest deep, I push forward drunkenly, reaching out to grab the leg before it is pulled away. When I reach it, it is just in time; the rest of the body has nearly been dragged into the deeper section, soon to be lost to the river.

With a choked sob, I pull on it, the weight nearly towing me under-water. After a moment, it gives, the current releasing its hold, and she floats toward me complacently.

Even as I recognize the sodden coat, I am denying it.

I cradle the body to me and turn it over, revealing her death mask, the blue lips and wide staring eyes frozen in an expression of anguish.

My knees give way and I sink, clinging to her. Clinging to my only friend.

"Nicole," I whisper, and everything goes dark.

The moment the water hits my throat I gag, arms flailing to bring me back to the surface as my feet sink in the muck of the Shenandoah. Ni-cole's body drifts subtly toward the current and I grab for her, pulling her back toward me by her arm. I am oddly disconnected as I tug her along beside me, struggling back toward the riverbank. Deep mud around my ankles snatches and grasps, trying to drag us both back.

I crumple on the pebbled bank, hauling Nicole up one last inch until she is resting face up on the ground, gazing unseeing at the heavily falling snow. I just stare at her for a moment, too shocked for anything else, and watch sickly as a snowflake settles on her open eye.

She doesn't blink.

I swing around just in time, heaving acid and bile, my entire body revolting against what I have just seen, the wooden frigidity of Nicole's arm, the taste of dirty water on my tongue.

When I finally stop, gasping, curling around myself like a wounded animal, my mind starts functioning again, and I force myself up and over to Nicole. Even though I know it is useless, that it is far too late, I begin CPR, pounding on her chest with as much strength as I can muster.

I cannot bring myself to breathe into her mouth.

Moments pass and I sag in defeat, finally acknowledging what all my senses have long known.

Nicole is dead.

Dead.

The racking sobs that grip me are painful, huge gulps of frozen air rending my insides, ripping me open. I lie there on the bank next to my dead friend, utterly spent.

There is no reason to hurry now.

After a while, I begin to recognize the signs of my body shutting down. I am tempted to let it.

There is a soft rumble and I imagine the earth is opening up to take us in; hard clumps of dirt will strike my face and everything will finally be quiet. The rumble grows louder, recognizable.

With dizzying effort, I lift my head and register the gleam of lights through the trees. As though in a dream, I am suddenly on my feet, grabbing at the scraping bark of winter-dead branches, propelling myself forward, toward the light.

You're supposed to go toward the light.

When the trees give out, I fall, my legs refusing to support me. My hands are in front of me now, fingers digging into the snow to reach the hard surface of the asphalt beneath, pulling me on toward the light.

"Wait," I shout, but it is no more than a breath, a dry rasp that dissolves into the snow.

The rumbling pauses and there is a muffled thump. Crunching sounds, slow at first and then faster. I pull myself forward one more time and my face sinks into white. It doesn't even feel cold anymore.

"I'm going to save you," a disembodied voice says above me. I feel warmth on my face. "I got you, I got you," the voice continues, and I am rising, rising, the white all around me. My eyes crack open, lashes tearing, frozen together. A concerned face looks down at me, chin covered in stubble, dark brown eyes wild with anxiety.

I am laid on a soft surface and tucked under something heavy. It is warm, hot, blistering. Tears fill up my eyes, but they don't freeze. There is another thump and then the rumbling is all around me, the man's voice soothing and hurried at the same time.

"I'm going to get you to the hospital right now. You just hang on," he promises and picks up a radio attached to the dash, speaking forcefully as the car begins to move.

"Shanholtz here, headed to the hospital. Got a hypothermic girl in the backseat..."

"Stop," I beg, the sound of my voice like rusty nails. "Stop, stop, stop!"

We stop moving and the man turns around to look at me. "What, what is it?"

"S-she's there...she's s-still there," I manage, and lift my arm enough to point toward the frozen bank where Nicole still waits. "Please."

He hesitates a moment and then cranks a dial on the dash, blowing out more blessed, burning heat before he jumps back out of the vehicle, the sound of his steps faint. Minutes pass and I am becoming more aware of how badly my entire body hurts. Thick needles of fire pierce every inch of my skin, striking clear to the bone, and I shiver uncontrollably.

The car door swings open and the man jumps back inside, picking up the radio again as he forces the car up the hill and out onto the road.

"Shanholtz again. There's another girl on the right bank under the Shenandoah Bridge. Dead. Notify the authorities," he barks, his voice calm and crisp.

"Thank you," I whisper, and close my eyes for good.

# CHAPTER TEN

"I DON'T KNOW WHAT ELSE TO tell you," I say wearily, my throat dry and aching. The shivering has stopped now, and I am wrapped in a pile of heated blankets, an IV pumping fluids in my arm, and a warm air humidifier by my hospital bed. The cold is still there, and I am terrified that it will never leave me, that underneath everything, my bones have iced over.

"It's quite common for patients with severe hypothermia to have memory loss and confusion, Detective. It's only been an hour, and she needs rest," my savior says stoutly, stepping closer to me. He hasn't left my side since he found me, and seems to have developed a keen sense of responsibility for me. If it hadn't been for his dedication to his job patrolling National Park property, I would've frozen to death by morning.

"I know that, Shanholtz, but we've got a dead girl here, and…"

Shanholtz gasps in protest and the police officer who has been questioning me since I regained consciousness pauses, shooting me a chagrined look.

"Sorry. I know you've been through a lot, Miss MacKenna, but we really need to figure out exactly what happened."

With a sigh, I rearrange myself, feeling the stiffness in my neck thanks to the over-fluffed hospital pillows. I look over at the detective, a tall, middle-aged man with the frame of a former football player gone to seed. One leathery-skinned hand rests on the rail of the bed, the yellowing fingernails betraying a predilection for cigarettes. He scratches his short, full beard with the other hand, mud colored eyes fixed on me in frustration.

"Detective Radcliffe, I've told you everything. Several times. Nicole called me a little after one, told me she confronted Phillip about Miranda and he flipped out. She told me she was calling from the rafting center and to come pick her up at the river access. She wasn't there, and I couldn't get my car back up the road, so I headed back toward town and

I…saw her from the bridge. I wasn't thinking straight…I just wanted to get her out of the water. And then Ranger Shanholtz found me. That's everything." Inside I am laughing hysterically at my dispassionate summary of the past few hours. Tonight will play over and over again in my nightmares for the rest of my life.

"And you said you saw a car? You think it might have been this Phillip," Radcliffe says skeptically. "How sure are you?"

I look at Radcliffe directly, meeting his eyes. Even though I didn't recognize the car, even if I had been too out of it to make a real identification, I am not lying when I answer him.

"I'm sure."

"She said that already," Shanholtz replies hotly, taking a step toward Radcliffe. "Maybe you should start checking out what she's told you instead of harassing her while she's trying to recover."

Radcliffe's lips tighten and he opens his mouth to argue, but takes another look at me and just shakes his head. I must look pretty bad.

"Know your place, Shanholtz. This is a police investigation, not a park matter." His phone squawks abruptly and he turns away to answer, nodding at whatever news he hears before ending the call. With another glance at me, he yanks back the curtain that hides my bed from the bustle of the emergency ward, his shoes squeaking on the tile floor. "They found the girl's car at the gas station. I'll be back later. Rest up, Miss MacKenna."

When the officer is gone, Shanholtz's shoulders relax slightly and he turns to me, his warm brown eyes surveying me with concern.

"How are you feeling, Derry?" he asks quietly.

Shanholtz is a study in shades of brown with russet hair, coffee colored eyes, and the standard National Parks Service uniform in beige. His cheeks crinkle tightly as he smiles down at me, softly rounded features making his weathered features appealing, friendly. He told me he has a daughter my age. I guess that's where the protective streak comes from.

"Better," I say, giving him my best effort at a smile. He takes one of the chemical heat packs waiting on the counter and breaks it open, placing it gently behind my neck, where the stiffness has turned into a steel rod. "Thanks," I whisper, tears coming to my eyes yet again. I've either been crying or unconscious the entire time he's known me.

"Don't worry, kid. They're going to check into things. They'll find out what happened to your friend. Radcliffe can be kind of…brusque, but he's a good cop," he assures me. I just nod and then close my eyes against the stabbing pain in my temples. "You get some rest. I'll be waiting right outside until your mom gets here." He pats my free hand gently and steps out, closing the curtain behind him.

Tears leak from under my eyelids. Nicole's frozen face paints my vision, the gaping mouth, frosted skin, glassy eyes. Her voice rattles inside my head, her frantic plea, her terror.

'Hurry,' she begged me.

I wasn't fast enough.

I must fall asleep again, because I next open my eyes to find my mother standing over me, her face streaked with tears.

"Mom?"

She bites down on her lips and nods, reaching out to stroke my cheek. "I've failed you."

"What?" I ask, gradually waking up.

"Don't ever do this to me again," she whispers, her voice wobbly. The cold in my bones loses a little of its biting edge.

"Nicole…" I start and then the sobs come again, deep choking gasps that riddle my aching muscles with pain.

"I know, baby. I know. I'm so sorry. Hush…hush. You're safe now, it's over." She murmurs softly to me, her words nonsensical and reassuring, holding me while my body rids itself of the guilt and grief. After a while, I am quiet again, and exhaustion pulls me under once more.

My mom's arms around me jerk and I blink myself awake. Fluorescent light drives into my skull with appalling force as the curtain is yet again yanked aside, revealing Nicole's mother, her face drawn in pallor, eyes hollow.

"Beverly, I'm so sorry," Mom says, standing. Nicole's mom nods absently, her eyes fixed on me.

"I killed my daughter," she says bleakly, taking a step toward me. Mom gives her a wary look and draws closer to me.

"Beverly, I'm sorry," she repeats, her voice becoming firmer, "but Derry's been through a lot."

Beverly laughs, a strangled, croaking sound. "You still have *your* daughter."

I struggle to sit up, ignoring Mom's restraining hand. "Mrs. Sharp, I'm so sorry. I tried to get to her in time, but I didn't know…"

"And you couldn't call me? You didn't call the police?" she shrieks, her tone shrill and unyielding. "You let her die, you stupid girl!"

"I'm tired of dealing with grieving people," a nurse says soothingly, appearing behind Nicole's mother and taking her by the arm, gently tugging her away from me. "Come on now, Mrs. Sharp. You're upset and saying things you don't mean. We need to let this girl get some rest now."

"Let her rest, let her rest. I hope you never *rest* again," Beverly snarls, spinning out of the nurse's hold and stalking down the hall, her shoulders shaking violently.

"Oh god," I whisper, guilt crashing over me, knowing she is right. "Oh god."

"Sweetie, stop it. None of this was your fault. She's just upset and needs to blame someone. She'll get over it, I promise," Mom says, stroking my hair and trying to calm me.

But I know Mom is wrong. In all the confusion of my rescue I haven't had time to really think about how I handled the situation. It's not just that I didn't get to Nicole in time; I made a terrible mistake by going to get her in the first place. I should've called the cops. When she didn't show up to meet me, I should've called. If I hadn't left my damn cell phone in the car like the worst kind of idiot, I could have called.

Shame descends on me in a blistering flood, coagulating in the pit of my stomach like a dirty sponge, radiating nausea and the sick realization that I cannot go back, I can't fix this hollow place where a life should be.

I wonder how I am going to live with myself after tonight.

I bite down hard on my lower lip, not caring when I taste the salt and copper of blood on my tongue. My throat is stiff with sorrow and I can't swallow; my jaw aches with the effort and my eyes are hot with unshed tears.

I have never truly understood what it is to make a mistake. Last year, when I was working in my mom's store alone one afternoon, an older man overpaid for his purchase by fifty dollars. I was busy putting the cash register in order and didn't notice until the man was gone. I looked for him out in the street, and when I couldn't find him, checked to see if he had left a number or address in our correspondence book, but there was nothing. I told mom about it, but she shrugged it off, saying that if he came back we would refund it, but that sort of thing happened all the time, not to worry about it. I stayed up all night thinking about that man going to buy groceries or pick up his prescriptions and finding his money short, being humiliated or worse, unable to purchase his heart medication or something. Because of my inattention, my carelessness. He never came back, even though I kept his fifty dollar bill in an envelope at the bottom of the register for months. Even now, when I think of him, my stomach twinges with the guilt.

But that was not a mistake. Forgetting to turn off the coffee pot, telling a lie and getting caught, failing an exam; these are not mistakes.

Letting my best friend die is a mistake. A devastating, catastrophic mistake that can't be rectified. I can't hold onto her life the way I held on to that fifty dollar bill, putting it in reserve in hope of returning it to her someday. I can't apologize, or make amends, or do anything that will ease the overwhelming wrongness of what I have done. For the rest of my life I will feel the empty space next to me where Nicole should be, I will hear the hollow whisper of her conversation when I speak, I will see the irrevocable mortality in her eyes in my own reflection. I will hear her words, the desperation in her voice when she begged, "Come get me, Derry. I'm scared."

I push my fist against my teeth, biting down hard to keep from howling. For the rest of my life, her shadow will haunt me, forever recriminating, forever asking why I didn't save her.

I feel my mother's hands on me, touching my face, trying to pull my fist away, but it is no more intrusive than a quiet voice in another room. The ache in my throat is unbearable now and I can hear a thin, reedy keen resonating in my chest, trapped beneath the weight of my guilt.

I am still screaming silently when the nurse puts the tranquilizer in my IV and I am tugged underwater again, pulled down and down, Nicole's accusing eyes my anchor.

I am sitting up in bed, trying to keep down the watery scrambled eggs the nurse has just forced on me. Mom is outside my little curtained room talking to the doctor before I am released, and the soft hum of their voices blends with the steady beeping of the machine attached to me with wires and tubes. My hand is one great throb of pain, as though the IV needle has found its home in the marrow of my bones rather than the veins just below the surface. I try to stretch my fingers, but they resist, wrapped together with an invisible string that forces me to keep still.

My mother's voice rises slightly and a new baritone rumble joins the conversation for a moment before the curtain is pulled aside to allow a new visitor.

"I'm angry with myself," Jake says quietly, standing at the bottom of the bed, his hands behind his back. Fear spikes in my chest at the sight of him, but after a moment it fades and I am left surprised and disturbingly pleased to see him.

"What are you doing here?" I croak, my voice still thin and scratchy from the night before.

"The cops called my dad this morning to tell him about Nicole. I'm so sorry, Derry." Jake's shoulders twitch and I can see how he is restraining his movements, as though he knows one false move will edge me over into terror.

His chestnut hair is tousled and his t-shirt is on inside out. I realize that he must have rushed over here as soon as he heard the news, without taking the time to dress correctly or worry about his appearance. The thought that it might be concern for me that spurred his flight weaves a warm tingle through me, a velvet burn.

Irritated by my irrational response, I close my eyes and hope that he'll go away without confusing me any further. Instead, I hear the soft tread of his footsteps as he approaches. His fingertips brush my arm and my eyes fly open.

"Did you have anything to do with Nicole's death?" I ask, watching him carefully, reaching out with all my senses to evaluate his response.

Black fury flashes in his eyes, leaving them glassy and unfocused, like a camera flash has hit him at the wrong angle. He pulls his hands to his side, clenching the fists as he struggles to maintain control. Finally he relaxes and looks down at me with a sad expression.

"I deserve that," he admits before shaking his head, eyes locked onto mine with earnest sincerity. "I had nothing to do with Nicole's death," he says clearly. My skin remains quiet and I breathe a sigh of relief. I didn't really think it was Jake, but given his history of violence, I had to be sure.

"Good," I whisper, abruptly exhausted. I lean back against the elevated mattress, overwhelmed by the discomfort in my body. Every muscle aches and I am so stiff I don't know if I'll be able to walk.

"How are you feeling?" he asks and I give a bitter laugh. He flushes and gives me an apologetic smile. "Sorry. That was a stupid question."

My mother's voice rises in parting and she joins us in my room. "I'm afraid to take you home," she says brightly, holding a sheaf of papers that I assume detail how to care for a recovering hypothermic patient.

"When can we leave?" I ask patiently, ignoring her first statement.

"As soon as they get that nasty IV out of you." She turns her falsely cheerful smile on Jake. "It was so nice of you to check on her, Jake. Derry will need her friends; she's been through a lot."

I suppress the hysterical laugh bubbling up from the knot in my throat. The thought of Jake being my comforting new friend gives me a giddy sensation of unreality, both appealing and disquieting at the same time.

"Where's Cole?" I ask, wondering why Jake is here without his brother, the one that could reasonably be considered, if not a friend, at least an ally.

Jake's face is stony as he returns his gaze to me. "He couldn't make it," he replies shortly. My skin buzzes uncomfortably.

"My father told me to tell you to call him if you need anything," Jake says, turning back to my mom. She glances away to hide the satisfied smile that pulls at her lips before thanking Jake and telling him to come visit me later, when I'm feeling better. Before I have the chance to contradict her, Jake is gone, throwing one last inscrutable look my way. My arm is still warm where his fingers brushed.

# CHAPTER ELEVEN

THE NEXT FEW DAYS ARE a blur. Mom brings me home and promptly quarantines me in my room, not allowing me to go outside or return to school for fear that I will somehow relapse. I don't bother arguing with her. I find I don't have the energy to do anything but lie in bed, staring at the ceiling, replaying that whole night over and over again in my head.

Every now and then I hear the front door open and close, indistinguishable conversations taking place beneath me. My mother comes up every so often to check on me and bring me food, but I only get out of bed to use the bathroom, preferring to remain cocooned in my nest of blankets, shutting out the rest of the world until the thought of Nicole doesn't hurt so much.

On the evening of the third day since I came home, Mom enters my room, placing a steaming mug of tea on the bedside table before standing over me, hands on her hips, clucking disapprovingly.

"I'm afraid you're broken," she says bracingly, gritting her teeth to make an entirely unconvincing smile.

"What?" I ask wearily. She sighs and passes a hand over her face. I look at her more carefully and am surprised to see strain written all over her features. Her eyes are red and puffy, dark rings around them so deep she looks bruised. Everything about her seems to droop and a stab of guilt pricks at me. Resentful, I push it aside, unwilling to add any more to the sea I'm already drowning in.

"I said it's time to get up. The viewing is tonight, and you need to be there."

Her words are like a slap to the face. I shoot her a dirty look and bury my head in my pillow, trying to muffle the sound of her voice.

"I've already seen her," I retort, knowing if I ever actually get out of bed, out of the house, see other people, I'll be forced to acknowledge the fact that the world hasn't stopped spinning, that time didn't just stop the moment I saw the shadow from the bridge.

"Honey, I know this has been awful for you. But you have to get up. You can't just stop living because of what happened. You need to start moving on," Mom says gently, cradling my head in her hand before she stiffens and her voice resumes its usual brisk tones. "Get up, get a shower, and meet me downstairs in half an hour. No more wallowing," she commands before exiting the room, the sound of her footsteps in the hall determined and sharp.

I lay there for another ten minutes, refusing to process what she has asked of me, refusing to even consider complying. Finally, more out of a habit of obedience than an active decision to do so, I roll out of bed and stumble into the hall bathroom, turning the hot water on full blast in the shower, still trying to reach the frozen core that hasn't budged since I found Nicole.

Twenty minutes later I am downstairs, dressed in black, my still damp hair twisted into a sloppy coil at the nape of my neck. Mom shakes her head when she sees me, but gives her best attempt at an encouraging smile and herds me out the door before I can change my mind.

There is only one funeral parlor in town, just a few minutes from the high school. At one point it was a huge old Victorian home, no doubt some pastel color frosted with all the usual frills and gables, but now it is stripped of all fancy and painted in weather-stained ivory with black shutters. The huge wraparound porch is enclosed and filled to the brim with people waiting in line to get inside. I shudder, wondering if they are all here for Nicole. I can't help but think of how alone she felt, how desperate she was to find a friend and wonder where these people were then.

"I don't think I can do this," I whisper, more to myself than to Mom. She reaches over and squeezes my hand.

"You can, sweetie. And you need to. C'mon. Let's get through this," she insists, maintaining her firm grip on my hand and tugging me forward. Unless I want to make a scene I have no choice but to follow her, so I grumble under my breath and trudge alongside, each step more uncertain than the last.

We join the crowd at the back of the receiving line after establishing that yes, everyone is here for Nicole's viewing. I look around at the faces of those in line and smother a sense of disgust. They are nothing but ghouls. They are buzzards, here to pick at what's left of Nicole to feed their own sense of self-importance. Just ahead of me I see Tasha chatting animatedly with one of her clones and a scorching bitterness pulses at the back of my throat. My skin hums discordantly, and the insincerity hovering around me like a poisonous fog is suffocating.

Tasha spots me and her eyes gleam with wicked satisfaction. She waves her hand and gestures for me to join her. I glare back at her in astonishment, wondering how she could possibly think I'd be so stupid. When I don't respond she frowns and mutters something to her companion before pushing her way through the crowd to reach me. Mom's hand is steady on my back, clearly stating her intent to make me suffer through this no matter what.

"I'm pretending to care so I can get attention," she says breathlessly, halting beside me as though it is completely natural. I continue to glare at her and her smile falters, eyes darting back and forth anxiously.

"Who's your friend, Derry?" Mom asks gently. I glance at her and then at Tasha, ignoring the friendly, sympathetic smile she wears and remember the vicious glint in her eyes when she tormented Nicole, how easy it was for her to destroy my friend without a second thought.

"She's not my friend," I reply coldly and turn my back on Tasha, irritation flaring when Mom hisses her disapproval.

"Derry, really," she says, fingernails pressing into my back.

"She's the one who started all the rumors about Nicole on Facebook. She made Nicole's life miserable," I answer, my voice devoid of all emotion. Angry red colors Tasha's face as she glances around to see how many people overheard. Everyone around us has stopped talking and is watching our exchange with unabashed curiosity. Several adults look at Tasha with disapproval, but most of the onlookers are our classmates, and they are moving their eyes back and forth between us like watching a tennis match.

"That's so not true," Tasha says loudly, avoiding my eyes and whatever unwelcome truth they hold for her. Why she is bothering to deny it now when for months she had no problem letting everyone know what she thought about Nicole is beyond me, but it's clear from the expressions of those around us that everyone knows the truth.

"Yes it is, Tasha. Everyone knows. I'm not sure what you're doing here," a smooth, cool voice says behind me, and fierce nausea erupts in my stomach, threatening to bubble over and turn me into a slobbering mess on the floor. Mom's hand on my back steadies me, but nothing has prepared me for my reaction to the sound of that voice.

"Whatever. I was just going to pay my respects, but…" Tasha mutters defensively before pushing through the line to get to the exit. Any relief I might have felt in her departure is drowned out by Nicole's voice replaying my ear.

"I was right about him," she had said.

"Are you okay?" Phillip asks, stepping into my line of vision. He is as beautiful as ever, blond hair shining even under the dim lighting, vivid green eyes focused on me with concern. I wonder how I never noticed the cruel tilt to his mouth before, how the top lip is just a hair too thin, too severe.

Unable to answer, I just nod and watch him carefully, wondering if he is thinking of the way I looked in the road the night Nicole died.

"Hello, I'm Derry's mother, Salinda MacKenna," my mother says, extending a hand for Phillip to shake. When his hand clasps hers, I have to control a violent impulse to smack it away, to prevent him from touching her, to prevent him from contaminating her.

He turns to look at me again, eyes searching mine for an answer to an unasked question. My stomach churns and I can feel a fine trembling dancing over my skin that has more to do with fury than fear. His clear green gaze meets mine and certainty settles under my skin, leaving me quiet.

Phillip killed Nicole.

"I heard about what happened to you, that you found her. I'm so sorry," he says, his tone holding just the right blend of sympathy and unhappy disbelief. I find that my lips curl up to give him a grateful smile.

"Thanks. The whole thing has been pretty upsetting," I say smoothly even as I wonder where the words are coming from. I am disconnected from my own mind, as though the practical part of me has now taken over, shunting my emotions to one side until there is time to deal with them.

"I'm sure. If you need anything at all, I'm here for you," Phillip says, his voice kind, but he can't put false warmth into his eyes. They are reptilian and detached.

"That's so nice, isn't it hon?" Mom asks anxiously. I realize that she must be able to feel the tension in my back, like a bowstring ready to snap.

"I know this isn't the time, but I'd like to talk to you soon." Phillip lowers his voice and steps closer to me. I bite down on my lip to keep from cringing.

"About…well, the police asked me a couple questions, and I just wanted to clear something up." He stops, waiting for a response, but I am absolutely incapable of speech.

"Maybe another time," my mom says, disapproval tightening her voice. For a second, I glimpse a snarl on Phillip's well-shaped lips, but the impression passes and he smiles apologetically and steps back.

"Of course. Sorry. I'll see you at school, Derry," he promises.

"Looking forward to it," I reply quietly, that impassive voice in my head coming to the rescue again. He nods and turns away, back to the group he was standing with a bit behind us.

My shoulders slump from the effort of maintaining control during our conversation and the rest of the wait to get inside passes without incident. I barely notice where I am until I am next in line to see Nicole, the white coffin suddenly huge, vast, taking up the entire room and sucking all the oxygen from my lungs.

"Go ahead honey, I'm right behind you," Mom whispers, giving me a little shove. I stagger forward and fight the primal scream that is clamoring in my throat as I look at her, frozen again, unmoving, all the life drained from her smiling face.

They have clothed her in a blue silk dress I've never seen before, and her hair is back to being lank and dull, resistant to the mortician's well-meaning efforts to curl or shape it. Her lips are unnaturally pink and pushed awkwardly into mimicry of a smile. My face is suddenly wet and I angrily brush the tears away, absurdly furious that they have tried to mask the true expression Nicole's face had held. This complacent smile, these closed eyes and over-blushed cheeks are a selfish attempt to diminish Nicole's last moments, to deny the panic she must have felt before the water claimed her. Beneath those tightly closed lids I know her eyes are still stark with terror, still urging me to hurry, to make it in time.

"I don't think Nicole's death was an accident," a bass rumble says behind me and I turn abruptly to see Detective Radcliffe talking to Nicole's mother, his hat in hand. She nods and presses a tissue to her face, allowing her husband to put an arm around her. He is stony-faced and silent, never making eye contact with any of the mourners who offer him sympathy. There is no life to him, as though he is a living, breathing statue, caught by the sun and turned to stone. Tearing my eyes away, I wonder what

Radcliffe really said, but am more interested in his deeply held conviction. Without another glance at the shell that was once my friend, I walk over to Beverly, who gives me a hateful glare as I approach.

"I am to blame for my daughter's death," she says spitefully, her voice low and mean. I don't know what she really said, but it must have been shocking because Radcliffe gives her a startled look and glances at me with sympathy.

"Now, Mrs. Sharp. There's nothing this young lady could have done. It was an accident," he says placatingly, but Nicole's mom doesn't take her eyes off me. Her husband stares straight ahead, unseeing.

"I thought she was so much better," she whispers miserably, finally dropping her gaze.　　Guilt hardens inside me, shifting and morphing into something less familiar. A cold, clean sense of purpose, knowledge of what must be done to ease this woman's suffering. There is little I can do for Nicole now when I have failed her so ruinously, but I can at least spare her mother the pain of thinking that Nicole took her own life.

"She was better, Mrs. Sharp. Nicole didn't do this to herself. She would never have killed herself. She wouldn't do that to you," I say with as much conviction as possible. Beverly looks up at me, eyes narrowed and unconvinced. She dismisses me with a wave of her hand and pointedly looks past me to the next person in line. My face burns with the rejection.

"Miss MacKenna, it's good to see you out, though I wish it were under better circumstances," Radcliffe says, distracting me from my dark thoughts.

"Thanks," I mumble unthinkingly before focusing my attention on him, remembering what I had heard him say. "Can I talk to you for a second?"

"I was going to ask you the same question," he says, drawing me aside to a small nook with couches. There is a group of students from the high school occupying them, but a sharp nod from Radcliffe sends them scurrying.

"We're going to need to you to come down to the station tomorrow to sign an official statement. We've held off as your mother requested because of your trauma, but we really need to get things wrapped up now."

"What about Phillip? Has he been questioned?" I demand quietly, my voice uncompromising as a rock. My rage is powerful, and I can almost feel it stretching long fingers toward the detective, wrapping around his mind to yank out the truth. He frowns at me uncertainly and begins to speak.

"We asked him whether or not he met with Nicole and he says he didn't. Said that she wanted to meet him at the bridge where Miranda died, but he wasn't comfortable with it and refused her. He said he was home asleep the whole night. His mother and father confirmed it. Says he's sorry you were under the wrong impression. Said Nicole has been pestering him for weeks, she was obsessed with him." Radcliffe breaks off, looking bewildered, no doubt wondering why he is being so candid with me.

For once, I don't feel guilty. Every question from here on is for Nicole, to put her to rest. I don't care if it's unethical anymore.

My initial reaction is to forcefully deny what Phillip has said, to call him a liar, but something stops me, a certainty that I will diminish my credibility if I point accusing fingers just now. I shift gears, getting into what I really want to know.

"What killed her? Was it the fall? Did she drown? Or was it something else?" I demand quickly and quietly, knowing I have only moments before someone notices us sitting here in the corner and disrupts my chance at the officer. I have no doubt he'll avoid me afterwards.

Still looking puzzled, he answers haltingly. "The fall alone from the suspected bridge couldn't have killed her. The water was too deep from all the snowmelt, and the wound on her head doesn't look like it came from a rock. There was something embedded, some kind of organic material. But she did drown. She was still alive when she hit the water."

His words sink in for a moment before I really understand them. My resolve flags, cracking like glass under too much pressure, but I ruthlessly quell it, forcing the weakness back to be agonized over later.

"Did she have any other injuries?" I ask, noting with dismay that my mother is fast approaching, a scowl on her face.

Radcliffe frowns at me and rubs his beard. "You know I shouldn't be telling you all this. Yes. Her neck was broken and the wound on her head was extensive."

"From before or after the fall?"

He shrugs, glancing up as my mother comes to stand next to me, eyes dark with disapproval. "No way of telling just yet. The cut bled before she died is all we know. And the broken neck wouldn't have taken much more to kill her without treatment…" Radcliffe breaks off as my mother gasps. Disappointment is hard enough to chew in my mouth as I watch him slowly come to his senses, realizing on some level something very strange has just happened.

"What are you thinking, telling her things like that? She's been through enough," my mother growls defensively, thwarting any further attempts on my part to obtain any more information.

Radcliffe stares at me with hard, suspicious eyes. "Sorry ma'am. She… asked," he says lamely, at a loss to understand why he has just given me the kind of information the public never hears about. Suddenly I need to get out of here, away from his sharpening glare, away from the whispers and surreptitious glances from my classmates.

"I need to go home," I tell Mom, the panic in my voice genuine. She glances around for a moment as though looking for someone and then nods.

"Okay Sweetie. Let's go." Helping me stand, she shoots another stern look at the officer before herding me through the crowd.

"Tomorrow morning, Miss MacKenna," Radcliffe reminds me, his voice carrying through the din of conversations around us with alarming precision. I face forward and give no sign I heard him.

By the time we get outside, I am holding back tears again, thinking of Nicole being awake, aware when she hit the water. Somehow, up till now I had cherished the idea she didn't know what was happening, that she didn't feel the icy grasp of the current pulling her under. I no longer have that luxury.

"I'm very interested in your daughter," a male voice trumpets from our left and my mom drops my hand like a stone, turning swiftly to meet the speaker.

"Geoffrey. I wondered if I'd see you here," she answers, her own voice practically a simper. Stunned, I look to see to whom she's talking and get my first glimpse of Cole and Jake's father.

Geoffrey Wise is tall and broad-shouldered, a tailored black suit draped elegantly over his lean frame. He is attractive, though not classically handsome like his son Jake and without Cole's chiseled features. He is like a slightly blurred photograph of each of them superimposed over one another, as though all the clarity he lacked was bestowed on his children. Salt-and-pepper hair is brushed back from his face, and faint lines crease between his eyes, giving his expression a severity at odds with the welcoming smile he has trained on my mother. A sense of power hangs over him like a cloak, and I feel a pull toward him, a thin wire between us that snaps tight with awareness. He smiles at my mother and turns his compelling gaze on me.

"So this is Derry. I'm glad to finally meet you," he says, voice settling over me like a warm coat, reassuring and familiar. Crawling insect wings flutter beneath my skin and I throw off the calming influence of his voice and view him with more attention. He watches me with predatory interest, not sexual or lascivious, but with the greedy air of one seeing an item of worth hidden at a flea market.

He is like Cole, like Jake. Like me.

Talented.

Instead of answering him, I glance at Mom, waiting for the introduction. Without knowing what he is capable of, I am reluctant to speak directly to him.

"Honey, this is Mayor Wise. Jake's father," she informs me. I nod as though this is new information to me and give him a wary smile.

"I've heard a lot about you, Derry," he says, smile broad and enigmatic. "I'm so very sorry for what you've been through; your mother has told me what good friends you and Nicole were. I hope you'll let us know if there's anything we can do." He gestures to his right as Jake emerges from the dark sedan at the curb, eyes fixed on me.

"That's very kind of you, Geoffrey. I'm sure we will," Mom answers, when it is clear I am not going to respond. Warning bells are going off in my brain, telling me I cannot win any verbal exchange with this man. An instinctual, bone-deep dislike of the mayor winds through me as I watch him put an arm around his son, their features more clearly similar up close. The sun has gone down, but Jake's hair is still luminous, his skin clear and smooth, the streetlamps kind to his features. The edges of his mouth turn up slightly, shyly.

"My father wants us to date," he says, leaning forward slightly. With an effort, I manage not to flinch.

"Hi, Jake." I realize I am holding myself tense, as though expecting a blow.

"I missed you," another voice chimes in, low and sweet in its honesty. Cole climbs out of the car and hurries toward me, arms outstretched. A loud rushing sounds in my ears and then I am in his arms, tears falling heedlessly on his black wool pea coat.

"Shh, shh, it's okay, it'll be okay," he whispers, stroking my head and holding me tight against him. For the first time since Nicole's phone call,

I feel safe, unassailable. I tune out the sounds of my mother and his father talking, the chatter of people leaving the funeral home, the slosh of passing cars tossing aside wet snow. All that remains is the soft, steady thrum of Cole's heartbeat under my cheek and the quiet hum of his voice in my ear.

"Derry, I didn't realize you knew Cole so well," his father says, tone disapproving. With one last squeeze, Cole releases me and I find that I am steadier on my feet, less afraid, as though he has drawn fear and grief from me like venom from a snake bite. I brush the wetness from my face, wondering if I have permanent tear tracks tattooed down my cheek by now.

"Cole's a good friend," I say firmly, realizing that any anger I still harbored about his reaction to our kiss is irrelevant now. Justice for Nicole is more important, and I could use his support.

Cole's eyes gleam appreciatively at my endorsement and he hangs an arm over my shoulder. Mom looks at us benevolently and I realize that she must like the idea of having both the mayor's sons interested in me, in whatever capacity.

With a swiftness that is immobilizing in its unexpectedness, Jake wrenches Cole's arm away from me and places himself between us, his eyes twin black holes of unexpressed fury.

"Jake, don't be rude," his father commands, and the power of his voice hits me like a baseball bat. I am not the intended recipient, but I still feel as though I ought to apologize for something.

Jake breathes heavily for a moment, jaw clenched tight enough to bleed his face white. His eyes cut to me and whatever he sees there seems to deflate him more effectively than his father's words.

"Sorry," he whispers, and I know he is. He turns around and marches crisply back to the car, leaning with his hands on the roof, face turned away.

"Well…ah, we've got to be going," my mother says, bewildered by the turn of events. Cole takes my hand in his and squeezes reassuringly.

"I'll stop by tonight, okay?" he asks uncertainly and I understand he is aware of my recent avoidance of him. I manage a weak smile and nod. He squeezes my hand again and then walks over to Jake and whispers something to him. After a moment, Jake and Cole join the line to get into the funeral home and I breathe a sigh of relief, ill-equipped to cope with any more drama from the brothers.

"Salinda, I'm sorry about that. I think Derry has had quite an effect on my boys," Geoffrey says smoothly, his gaze fixed on me with an intensity that is incredibly disturbing. Everything about this man screams "danger!" to me, and I have learned to trust my instincts.

"It's been a long day, Geoffrey. I'm going to take Derry home now," Mom says wearily, patting me absently on the shoulder. After another moment, Geoffrey shifts his attention to my mother, turning up the wattage on the smile considerably. Mom blinks and actually bats her eyelashes. With a sense of doom, I tug at her arm and she finally starts moving.

"Of course. May I call later and see how you're both doing?" he asks, his voice rubbing against my mind like silk. I shudder and focus on the cold wind that slaps me in the face, the damp heaviness that permeates the air just before a big snow giving it weight.

"Please. Goodnight, Geoffrey," Mom says and we cross the street to get to the overflow parking lot where our rental car waits. Mom's Torino was hauled up from the riverbank sometime yesterday, but the alignment was off, so she got a loaner while the mechanic fixes it. The fact that she still hasn't punished me for stealing her car and damaging it is some testament to how much she actually worried about me. I find it oddly comforting.

When we finally reach home I go back to my room and flop down on my bed, exhausted to the point of delirium and too rattled to be left alone with my own thoughts.

Miranda's journal is still sitting on my desk, its binding somehow darker than I remember, and I imagine it soaking up Nicole's blood, locking her secrets inside, waiting for me.

Getting slowly out of bed, my body protesting with every shift of muscle, I drag myself over to the desk and sit down in front of the book, fingers resting lightly on the surface. I have no choice now. I promised Nicole I would read it.

I have to keep at least one promise to her.

Undoing the button clasp on the front, I let the book fall open to the first page and begin reading.

*September 30*
*I don't understand Phillip. He was so sweet to me at first; he gave me presents every time he took me out, he carried my books for me, intro-*

*duced me to his friends. He was nice to Nicole. He seemed so perfect. I don't know what has happened to make him change.*

*It's like I don't exist for him when other people aren't around, and then he suddenly becomes that sweet, attentive boyfriend again. The minute we're alone, he drops it. It doesn't make sense and it hurts, it makes me feel like I've done something wrong.*

*October 2*

*He told me he doesn't want me seeing Nicole anymore; that she's not welcome to sit with us at lunch. I asked him why, and he said, 'you belong to me now.' Like that answered my question. I don't get him at all, it's like he's a different person.*

*I didn't listen to him, and I started to go sit with Nicole at lunch today. Before I got to her table, Phillip came up behind me and twisted my arm around my back so hard it brought tears to my eyes. I asked him what the hell he was doing and he said 'don't disobey me. Don't make me look like a fool,' and then dragged me off to his table. As soon as we sat down, he changed, acted all sweet and concerned. He asked me what was wrong, and everyone was looking at me, and I swear there was this...light in his eyes. I lied and said nothing was wrong. I don't know why I did that.*

*October 4*

*I'm going to break up with Phillip tomorrow. I think he's trying to abuse me somehow. It's not physical. Apart from the day he dragged me away from Nicole, he hasn't touched me, except in front of other people. But the things he says to me when we're alone.*

*He called me at three this morning. I was barely awake and he said so many crazy things. He called me his toy and he said he would play with me until I broke. When I saw him at school, he acted like nothing happened. I asked him about the call and he said he didn't call me; he had no idea what I was talking about. And then he acted all worried about me the rest of the day, telling people not to upset me, that I was feeling fragile. He told people at lunch that Nicole and I had a fight, and she wouldn't be coming around anymore.*

*I don't know why I didn't say anything. He just had this look on his face when he talked about Nicole. I think he might hurt her.*

I put the journal down and close my eyes, giving the words

time to reconfigure on the pages beneath my fingers. After
a moment I look through the entries again and find that my
initial impression of the truth isn't far from what she actually
wrote. It is the next entry where things begin to change.

*October 8*
*I have to watch what I write in here. He found the journal in my bag
this afternoon and read it. He was angry. He said I had to stop writing
mean, untrue things about him. He told me not to bother hiding it, he'd
find it. He'd know if I was bad, he said.*
*He says if I misbehave he'll take it out on Nicole.*
*I didn't know people like him existed. It's like he's this empty shell,
and the only thing that fills him up is my misery. It's food and drink to
him. I can't get away from him. I know that he'll just do something to
Nicole. I wish I could tell someone, I feel so alone. I wish Jake wasn't
acting so weird. Half the time he's too angry to talk to me and then
other half he just follows me around like a lost dog. I looked out my
window last night and he was just standing there in the shadows on the
sidewalk, watching me.*

Slow tears twist down my cheeks as Miranda's loneliness and misery
leaks through the pages, blurring my vision and replacing her unmeant
honesty with shallow words that barely scratch the surface of her true
feelings. With increasing depression, I turn the page to find the entries I
have already seen, the truth behind the words lost now except to memory. That Miranda didn't feel safe enough even to write in her journal
what Shockey had done to her, how Phillip treated her when he found
out, how lost and violated she was, breaks my heart.

Anger, fierce and pure, dries my tears and bolsters my grim determination to glean all I can from this journal, to allow Miranda to share her
pain with someone else, even if it is too late to help her. I move on to
the next entry, gritting my teeth in expectation of the emotional assault.

*October 15*
*Everything is numb. I am hollow. They shoved their hands in me and
dragged it all out with their greedy fingers. Everyone has a piece of me
now, everyone but me.*
*I have to carve myself up, shape myself into something new. I don't*

exist anymore. Someone new has to be here. They look at me with accusing eyes, Jake, Nicole, like I should be the same person, but how can they know, they can't know that everything I ever was has been stolen. HE has it, HE has all of me and HE will take whatever's left when I'm done carving up the leftovers. I don't even bleed right...I have to push down so hard to get the blood. I must not have much left. I think it must still be there, a deep puddle on the seat, all that blood. It wouldn't stop, I think the tap is broken.

October 21

I wanted to tell Nicole today. She stopped by my locker and just looked at me. I knew she was going to cry, she makes this face when she's going to, like she's swallowed a lemon. I wanted to tell her, I wanted her to make HIM stop, wanted her to know about Shockey, but then HE came up behind me and put his fingers around my neck and I knew HE would snap my neck right there if I said a word.

HE told me I couldn't tell anyone what Shockey did because HE would look like a fool. I belong to HIM now, and it's my fault I got dirty.

I don't know anymore, I can't remember what I used to be like, how I used to feel. I am this person, an empty person, and I think I'm broken. Maybe HE will let me go soon.

October 24

He put a gun to my head tonight. He took me to a movie with his friends and after he dropped them off he took me to the place where Shockey raped me and he opened the glove compartment. He pulled out the brown paper bag and told me to open it if I was so curious. I told him I didn't need to, I didn't care, but he made me. It was a gun, I don't know what kind, but it was heavy and cold. He picked it up and put it to my head. It didn't really bother me, I think it would have been better if he'd just shot me.

But he said the crazy things again. He said he was almost done with me, and that if I ever told anyone about him he would use the gun on Nicole, he would kill her and he would make sure that I watched. I cried then. I didn't think I still could.

I promised I would stay quiet, I swore it, and he said he didn't believe me, that he would watch me and if he ever saw me even speak to Nicole he would kill her. I believe him, I think it would be easy for him. I *don't know why he hasn't killed me.*

*Then he put the gun away and took me home, he acted sweet again, like he used to. Told me I was his girl, his lovely girl. He said I have a beautiful soul and he's so lucky to have me.*

*He took it. He took my soul.*

*October 30*

*I am going to tell Jake. I can't tell Nicole, but if I tell Jake, he'll keep her safe from HIM. Jake doesn't scare me anymore, nothing can scare me anymore. I'm going to tell him everything. He can stop Shockey, he can make all of it stop. I'm going to tell him tonight.*

*I don't care what he thinks of me anymore, what anyone thinks of me. I just want her safe.*

It is the last entry.

I drop the book and curl myself into a ball, sobbing so hard I can barely draw breath and making this strangled moan that hurts my ears. I don't know how long it goes on, but the tears keep coming. I have never cried like this before, not over my dad leaving, not over some of the horrible things I've learned about people, not even over Nicole's death. It feels as though all the sorrow, all the despair that was contained in those pages is finally being released through me, that Miranda is the one sobbing uncontrollably, not me.

I take a shuddering gasp and drag myself back from the bleak words, willing my hands to be steady as they take the journal again, closing the cover respectfully, as though pulling a sheet over a naked corpse.

Another sob chokes me, but I clench my jaw to prevent its release, somehow convinced that holding that last cry inside will keep me connected to Miranda, to Nicole, to what must be done. With an effort, I swallow it, feeling it shift from the futile weakness it represented to something else, something hard and hot, a knot of flame that lodges itself in my chest and pulses, telling me to do something, anything.

Below, I hear a knocking at the door and know that Cole is here. With another glance at the journal, I make a decision to tell him everything; of all people he can understand why I have to find out what happened to Miranda and Nicole, why I owe it to them. The flame in my chest flares as though satisfied and dwindles to a smolder. I will reserve the fire for the moment I need it most, but keep that same burning sense of purpose firm in my mind. Nothing matters now but finding justice for my friend Nicole, and for the damaged girl who could have been my friend had she lived.

# CHAPTER TWELVE

"I'M AFRAID OF MY BROTHER," Cole says in greeting, dropping into the chair at my desk with a weary sigh. I stare at him, taking in the slightly disheveled state of his clothes and the slowly darkening bruise on the right side of his jaw.

"Did Jake do that?" I ask, pointing at the mark. Cole starts, putting his hand up to his jaw and then frowns, shrugging off the obvious evidence that he's gotten into it with his brother.

"It's no big deal," he says, rolling his shoulders uncomfortably. "I can handle Jake."

"You're the one who told me to be careful around him," I remind him, wondering how two such different people could be related. Cole is all sharp edges and soft center, a deceptive outward package with all the trappings of the classic misunderstood bad-boy. Looking at him now, his sapphire-blue eyes trained on mine defiantly, jaw clenched, I can feel something more is there, swimming just under the surface, waiting for me to ask the right question. Something I can't see clearly just yet.

"Look, I wanted to apologize. I should've come to see you in the hospital," he says. I just raise my eyebrow at him, waiting for the explanation. When he doesn't continue, but just glares at me, daring me to ask why, I retaliate by leaning back on my bed, studying my nails with deliberate interest.

The silence lengthens and I can practically feel the frustration coming off him in waves until he breaks into an admiring laugh.

"You're good at interrogation, you know that?"

I smile and glance over him, for the first time in days feeling something other than guilt or depression. I had planned on telling Cole everything, my suspicions and plans, but being so close to him, knowing his eyes are on me, hearing his voice, being just a short gesture away from touching him, I am suddenly giddy. It's like being deprived of breath for too long and taking that first long, slow sip of air.

"It's been mentioned before. So what's the deal? Why did Jake come see me and not you?" I ask, suddenly serious. Even through my pain over finding Nicole I had registered hurt at his absence.

Cole grimaces and climbs up onto the bed next to me. My heart thuds in my chest as he takes my hand in his, holding it on his thigh.

"I'm going to tell you some stuff about me, about my family, so you'll understand what's going on a little better. And I want to tell you, not just because of your ability, but because I'm worried about you."

My brows draw together in confusion and I open my mouth to speak, but Cole just squeezes my hand and shakes his head.

"No, just let me get this out. Then we'll talk."

I search his eyes for some sense of what he's about to tell me, but finally subside, nodding to let him know I'm ready.

"I think you figured out at the funeral home that my dad is like us. Talented." I nod in confirmation and he continues, looking down at our entwined hands. "So was my dad's brother. My uncle could make people happy, like giving them a shot of serotonin just by smiling. Kind of the opposite of what I do."

He pauses and glances up at me, looking for something. I just stare back at him, still confused as to why he's telling me this. With a shake of his head he lets my hand go and walks over to stand at the window, looking out at the slowly melting snow.

"I didn't know any of this. Not until I moved here. My whole life, I thought I was some kind of freak of nature, an accident. I never knew my father, and Mom never really talked about him, except to say that he wasn't the kind of man she'd want me to be. All I knew was that he got my mom pregnant and then ditched her. I know now that he was married to Jake's mother at the time. She was pregnant with Jake when my mom was pregnant with me."

I curl my lip in disgust, feeling my earlier instinctual dislike of Geoffrey Wise cement. Cole glances back at me and gives a bitter laugh.

"Yeah, I know. Great guy, right? Anyway, she never had contact with him and neither did I. Until she died." He sits back in the chair and leans forward on his knees, one leg bouncing agitatedly, as though he simply cannot keep still.

"It was after…after the neighbor died," he whispers, and I can almost see the tortured boy he had been, standing in front of the collapsed body, empty beer bottles clinking noisily as they rolled across the floor away from the impact. There is a catch in his breath before he continues.

"We didn't have any other family, so I was staying with one of my mom's friends while social services tried to figure out what to do with me. And then he came and said he was my father and I had to come live with him."

"He knew about your mom?" I ask, prodding him gently.

Cole nods, a faraway look in his eyes. "He knew where we were all the time. Just never bothered to come by. Anyway, of course my social worker was thrilled that he came forward, and was even happier about the fact that he was wealthy and a mayor and everything. So I left with him by the end of the week."

"Where did you live before?" I wonder out loud, curious about what kind of changes he had been through.

"Not far from here, just over in Frederick. Half an hour away and he never came to see us." Cole's voice is quiet, controlled, but a vague sense of unease creeps up my spine and I know his restraint is weakening.

"Cole, you don't have to tell me this if you don't want to," I tell him, seeing the rigidity of his back, his too-straight posture.

He glances back at me as though he's forgotten I was there. "Sorry." He takes a deep breath and the slowly increasing disquiet I felt fades to nothing. "Strong emotion makes it harder to control," he admits.

"You never told me what you were so upset about the first time I saw you."

Laughing under his breath, relieved in the change of subject, Cole wipes a hand over his face. "It seems so stupid now. I told you I was expelled, right? Well I was trying to get back into school. I had a meeting with the principal that morning. He told me I would never set foot in his school again. It really pissed me off."

"I can see why. Seems pretty unfair," I commiserate.

"Yeah, well. They have some kind of zero tolerance policy for violence, and I guess hitting a teacher, even accidentally, is a big violation. It doesn't matter anyway. I'll be done with my equivalency exams before Jake graduates."

Seeking to preserve the relative peace, I keep the drama talk to a minimum. "I've already passed mine. Equivalency exams," I clarify when he raises an eyebrow. "Technically I don't need to go to school. I just wanted to see what it was like, before it was too late."

The blue chips of his eyes soften as he walks back over to perch next to me on the bed. "And what do you think now?" he asks kindly.

I am alarmed and embarrassed to find that my eyes are pricking with tears. "I think maybe my mom was right. Maybe I should've just stayed home, worked in the store. Maybe people like me aren't meant to mix with everyone else," I whisper, revealing a fear I hadn't dared admit to myself.

"I think you should do whatever makes you happy. It sounds to me like you haven't had much opportunity." Cole puts an arm around me, pulling me close. I don't resist, noting even through my clumsy attempts to stem the tide of tears, I fit perfectly into the curve of his body, my shoulder tucked snug against his chest, hips tight against his like matching puzzle pieces. A warm tingling flows through me that has nothing to do with our conversation.

"How long have you known about what you can do? I mean, I didn't really get what was going on until I was around thirteen or so. Was it the same for you?" he asks quietly, his fingers tracing circles around my elbow. I feel all my blood rush to where his fingertips brush my skin and it is suddenly difficult to focus on what I want to say.

"No." I clear my throat and force my attention back on his question. "I mean, not really. I don't know exactly when it started. I've been this way as long as I remember."

"Even when you were a kid? That must have been tough. I mean, they say kids are perceptive, but I guess in your case it was more than that." Cole tucks my head under his chin and I can feel his breath shifting my hair.

"You could say that. My dad certainly didn't appreciate it," I say without thinking and then stiffen, trying to pull away from Cole. He tightens his grip and holds onto me until I relax again.

"How is that?" he asks in the same quiet, undemanding tone. Gently, he eases himself back on the bed, tugging me with him, until we lay together, his hand absently twisting my hair.

Off-balance, I answer honestly, telling him something I haven't admitted to anyone, not even Nicole. "It's my fault he left us. He didn't want to be my father anymore."

I feel Cole's lips brush my forehead and something inside me stretches and expands, reaching out for him. The tenuous, golden thread I felt between us the first time we talked is there again, strengthening and drawing us closer. In a rush, I tell him the rest, knowing somehow this connection is important, vital.

"He was already weird about me. When I was taken out of school because of an honesty incident, he stopped spending as much time with me. He never wanted to be alone with me, and he barely spoke around me anymore. My mom and he were fighting all the time, and one night she was tucking me in and told me to ask Dad if he loved somebody else, and to tell her exactly what I heard him say."

Cole draws in a sharp breath but doesn't interrupt; he just keeps stroking my hair, the sharp, citrusy scent of his cologne filling my senses.

"I was eight, and I didn't really understand what she wanted, but I said I'd do it. So the next morning I walked right up to him at breakfast and said 'mommy wants to know do you love somebody else?'" I cringe, remembering the fury that had flooded his face, the almost purple tinge to his skin when he looked up from me to glare at my mother.

"He answered. I think whatever he said was probably bad enough, but I heard what he really meant. He said, 'I don't love you.' And then he left. And never came back."

My throat closes over and I can't speak anymore, all the confused hurt of being unwanted barreling through me all over again. Drawing in a shuddering breath, I turn my face into Cole's chest, trying to smother that dismal, forlorn place where memories of my father live.

"God, Derry. I'm so sorry," he whispers, tightening his embrace until all I can feel are his arms around me, the press of his body against mine. I drag my head up and meet his eyes, dark pools of sympathy and apology for something he hasn't done. "No wonder you were so angry at me for accusing you of being manipulative. That's the last thing you'd be after being used like that. I'm sorry," he says again, and I feel the truth in his words, the tender weight of them settling around me like a soft blanket.

"I forgive you," I whisper, finally letting the bitter taste of rejection I've held onto for weeks dissolve into nothing. He moves closer, his eyes locked on mine, asking permission. My lips part slightly and he closes the gap with his mouth.

This time there is no uncertainty to our kiss, no second thoughts or reproach. For a moment, our lips simply rest against each other, our breath mingling in a perfume of peppermint and honey, and then his hands are tangled in my hair, pulling me closer, as though he can fuse us together forever from the heat of the kiss.

Colors swirl behind my eyes and an intoxicating lightness spreads from our joined lips into my chest, weaving golden strands around the inflexible, frozen thing that has formed there, melting away some of the isolation. My own arms are wrapped around him, twisting his body until he is on top of me, his skin blazing to the touch, making me feel as though I'll never be cold again.

When we finally part, both of us are gasping for air and every inch of me is trembling, aching for more. His eyes are dark and hungry as he gazes down at me, our bodies still pressed together in painful awareness.

"That was…" he murmurs, breaking off to press his lips to mine again. I feel that he is shaking too, and I glow with pride that he is as lost as I am. He releases me again and buries his mouth in the nape of my neck, sending delicious tremors through me until I squeeze him tighter with desperate need.

With a shaky sigh, he draws away, sitting up and pulling me onto his lap, still unwilling to completely break contact. "I'm going to need a bucket of ice, or a cold shower or something," he finally says, a rough laugh in his voice.

A ridiculous urge to giggle rolls over me and I take a deep breath to halt it. "Do you still believe that was me manipulating you?" I ask playfully, nearly drunk with the heat still pulsing through me.

Cole kisses my jaw just below my ear and laughs softly. "I think I was an idiot. Please tell me we can do that again."

For a while, we don't speak, but I learn the curves of his face, marveling that he is not made of sharp angles at all, but smooth contours and delicate skin. His hands drift over my back and hips, memorizing my shape and discovering how to steal my breath.

A knock thunders on the bedroom door and we break apart, giving each other sheepish looks as my mother swings the door open gangbusters style and stands there, hands on hips, a censorious expression on her face.

"My daughter can't get laid if I can't," she says sharply, and I choke on a wild laugh, biting my lower lip to keep from getting hysterical. She narrows her eyes at me and then flushes, guessing at what I must have heard. Clearing her throat to mask her somewhat lessened righteous rage, she gives me a knowing look. "Just keep the door open, okay?"

"Sure thing, Mom," I gasp, nearly losing it when Cole turns to me in bewilderment. Mom nods and disappears, giving me the freedom to lose myself in laughter for a moment.

"What's so funny? What did she really say?" Cole is asking, amusement spreading across his features, making everything in my room a little brighter. I just shake my head and wave the question away. When I finally get myself under control we are both grinning madly and everything has changed between us.

"So you're my girlfriend now, right?" he demands, suddenly serious, his deep blue eyes searching mine. I give him a teasing nudge with my elbow and he relaxes, smiling again.

"Why don't we just start with going on a date?" I suggest and he laughs, putting an arm around me again as he leans against the wall.

"Yeah, okay. But only if it means we get to do this again," he adds.

"Sounds good." I shift closer to him, amazed how different I feel now. The sorrow over Nicole and what I learned about Miranda is still there, the determination to take action still intense, but I don't feel alone anymore. I don't feel like this is only my battle, and a warm rush of gratitude flows through me.

"Look, we still need to talk about some stuff," I say, knowing beyond a doubt that telling Cole everything is a good idea.

He sighs and nods, dropping a kiss on my forehead. "Yeah, I know. I got kind of sidetracked, but I did come here with a purpose."

I open my mouth to interrupt, to tell him what I meant, but Cole doesn't notice and starts talking about his father again. Remembering how concerned he was when he first arrived, I listen, knowing he needs to get this off his chest before I can ask for his help.

"So I was telling you about my dad. The day he brought me home, he sat me down and told me that he knew I was talented and wanted to know what I could do. I was pissed at him, but kind of relieved at the same time, you know? Knowing it came from somewhere, it wasn't just me." His tone is lighter now, freer, and I suspect that our new closeness has made it easier for him to talk to me.

"Anyway, I told him. And then he told me about his ability." Cole's expression darkens, his lips pulling tight and thin. "He has…I guess you'd call it persuasion. It's really subtle and he's good at it. You don't know what he's doing until you're trapped in some action you didn't mean to take, and then there's this resistance; like pushing against a car that's slowly rolling down a hill. You know it's inevitable, that you can't hold it back forever, but once you realize what's happening, that's he's manipulating you, it's so hard not to fight back."

The strain in Cole's voice is painful, and I wonder how many times he has pushed back against his father. I know I got a taste of Geoffrey Wise's talent today, but then again, he wasn't really trying to convince me to do anything. A greasy, dirty feeling is tangled up in my gut at the thought of being made to do something against my will. Cole looks at me and I can see the haunted expression in his eyes. Taking his hand in mine, I kiss his fingers and rest my cheek on his palm. He sighs deeply and smiles at me, making my heart constrict and swell all at once.

"The reason I'm telling you all this is because my dad is interested in you now."

I swallow nervously and bite my lower lip, thinking that I really can't handle any more problems just now. Cole must read some of this in my expression because he shakes his head mournfully, sorry to add to my burdens.

"I'm sorry, Derry. It's mainly because of Jake. He's been…kind of fixated on you for the past few weeks. He talks about you all the time at home. He and Dad are really close, and Dad has a way of making you tell him things anyway. It's why I didn't come to see you in the hospital. Dad used his persuasion on me, made me stay home so I wouldn't be in Jake's way. He only let me come to the viewing tonight because he thought it would look bad for him if I didn't.

"From the way Jake talked about you, he had suspected, but when he saw you today, he knew, right away, that you're like us. I barely got out of the house once he realized I was the one you had become friends with, not Jake." Cole shifts uncomfortably and I tense, expecting some dire revelation.

"He wants to meet with you. Basically so he can figure out how to use you. It's not an excuse, but that's pretty much why I got so paranoid about our first kiss. It's been a while since I didn't have to question my motives for doing something unexpected. I should've known better with you," he insists, his eyes bright with sincerity. "And now I'm warning you. Stay away from him. I don't want you getting mixed up with my dad, or Jake. They're dangerous."

He sighs and seems to deflate slightly, as though he has finally released a last gasp of toxic air. When he meets my eyes again, his own are diffident, as though awaiting a verdict he's not sure will be in his favor.

In answer I brush a silky strand of hair out of his eyes and lay a gentle kiss on his mouth. "Okay," I reply, and his whole body relaxes. "You're the only Wise…or Durant, I'll deal with. Why isn't your last name Wise? That's bugged me for a while," I ask, hoping I'm not being insensitive.

"You're kind of crazy, you know that?" Cole asks incredulously, his lips twitching with amusement. "I tell you that my father is a scheming, cold-blooded bastard who wants to co-opt you for his own nefarious purposes and you want to know about my last name?"

I shrug, wondering what he expected me to say instead. He shakes his head and raises his hands palms out in defeat.

"My mom hated my dad. She didn't want me to have any part of him. So I took her name instead. Dad tried to make me change it when I moved in with him, but I held out. It's all I have left of her. I won't let it go."

"My dad's last name is Romero. When I was old enough to realize he wasn't coming back, I changed my name back to my mother's," I reveal. Cole squeezes my hand and we are quiet for a while, but there is solidarity to our silence, making it lighter, restful.

I glance across the room and my gaze locks on the journal again, guilt pinching at the brief bubble of happiness I had with Cole. Sighing, I return to what matters, what has to be accomplished before I can allow myself any more blissful interludes like this again.

"Cole, I need to tell you some things too. Please just…wait till I'm done to say anything. It's going to sound pretty out there, but it's all true."

He watches me carefully, his eyes veiled with concern. Gesturing for me to begin, he turns around so he is completely facing me, his knees brushing against mine, a reassuring contact.

So I tell him everything. I tell him about my conversations with Nicole, her theories about Phillip. I tell him how my skin is permanently electrified when Phillip's around, how I never hear his hidden truth, how I can never tell if he is lying. I tell him about reading Miranda's journal for the first time. My voice becomes hard and brusque when I tell him about Shockey.

And then, with his arms around me, keeping me warm, I tell him about Nicole's phone call, how I ran out into the night so stupidly, how I let her die. I tell him about the car I saw and how I know in my bones that it was Phillip.

My voice is nothing more than a whisper when I tell him about the burning knot in my chest, that I have to destroy Phillip and Shockey, I have to give some measure of peace to the memory of the lives they ruined so maliciously.

When I am finished, the fire in my chest is hotter, uncomfortable. I let myself be distracted. Guilt scalds the back of my tongue.

"God," Cole finally says, his eyes soft and vulnerable. "I'm so sorry, Derry. I had no idea you were dealing with all that." He tilts his head and sighs. "Poor Nicole. I should've checked on her, tried to find out how she was doing. I just got so wrapped up in how unfair my life was...maybe if I had been around…"

"Don't. It might have helped some, but trust me, Nicole was determined to confront Phillip one way or another. I should've realized it sooner, too. I just didn't think…I guess I didn't really think it was him. When I read what happened to Miranda in her journal, I thought Nicole was wrong. I thought Miranda did kill herself." I rub my eyes, abruptly feeling so exhausted I can barely keep them open. "But I know better now. There is no doubt in my mind that he killed Nicole."

Cole sees how tired I am and eases himself off the bed, grabbing his jacket from where he dropped it on the floor. "Promise me you won't make the same mistake. Promise me you won't do this alone. Let me help," he begs. Despite my weariness, I manage a smile.

"I promise. I was going to ask for your help anyway."

Cole nods and holds his arms open. I jump off the bed and lean into him, listening to the slow, steady march of his heartbeat, my own pulse striving to match.

"You have it. Get some rest. I'll call you tomorrow," he promises. He pulls me closer and kisses me, stirring and soothing me at the same time. We say goodnight and I watch out my window as he walks down the driveway to his motorcycle. He climbs astride and pauses before putting on his helmet, looking up at the faint glow that spills across the yard from my light. Raising a hand, he smiles, knowing I see him.

I stand watching out the window long after he leaves.

# CHAPTER THIRTEEN

I CAN FEEL HIS EYES ON the back of my neck, fingers stretching out to run one long nail down the center, slitting the skin just enough to leave a thin trail of red. When he reaches my spine, I go rigid, paralyzed, knowing without a doubt he has cut the cord that allows me control over my own body. I shift my eyes to look at him and my mouth goes dry in horror as he attaches nearly transparent threads to my wrists, around my knees and ankles. His emerald eyes are vivid, harsh as a smile creases his plastic face, teeth so shiny they are reflective. Squinting, I can almost see something there, like images caught in a mirror, pounding at the glass to get out.

He comes closer, holding a thick tree branch in his hand, and begins to sway it back and forth, easily and gracefully at first and then more sadistically, callously until I realize my limbs are swinging around grotesquely, no longer connected to my body. The grisly dance intensifies, reeling out of control and in a flash of light I can see them, the pale redheaded girl and the pinched, accusing face of the one I let down. They are clawing at the glass wall of his mouth, mutely screaming until they unravel and nothing is left but their eyes, staring ahead, begging.

I come awake with a bolt, my heart pounding and my arms and legs aching. The covers are tangled around me, the bottom sheet pulled almost completely off the bed. For a moment I still cannot move, waiting for his direction, waiting for Phillip to lift his hand and cut the strings.

Gradually the panic eases and I pull my knees up against my chest, hugging my legs close and leaning my head against them. When my breathing finally slows and I can think again, I realize this is the first nightmare I've had in weeks. Remembering the earlier ones featuring Cole before I really knew him, I wonder how my subconscious could ever have given him the role of the villain. Even now, I remember the unnaturally green eyes blazing down at me, so unlike Cole's own profound blue. It was always Phillip who tormented me; I just couldn't recognize it then.

The clock tells me it's just after nine a.m., but the light coming in through my blinds is dim and grey. Shedding the muddle of sheets and blanket, I lurch out of bed and look outside. Everything is gloomy and hushed, the sky the color of wet asphalt, menacing and heavy with the threat of rain. The phone rings and I pick it up absently, still looking out at the moody clouds.

"I'm uncomfortable talking to you," a familiar rumbling voice says in greeting.

"Hello, Detective Radcliffe." My own tone is less than enthusiastic.

"Did you have plans to come down to the station sometime today?" he asks a little too politely.

"Yes. I just woke up. Mom and I will be there in a bit."

"Well, come down as soon as you can. Someone will be here to take your statement. Shouldn't take too long," he assures me and then says goodbye, keeping our conversation as succinct as possible. I have serious doubts he will be the one to debrief me.

"Mom, can you take me down to the station?" I call down the stairs, hearing my mother puttering around in the kitchen.

"I'm ready for things to go back to normal," she answers.

"Repeat, please!" I yell, finding my patience is already running thin this morning.

"Give me fifteen minutes," she replies, a streak of annoyance in her tone. As long as she's lived with me, put up with my little quirk, used it to her advantage, I know she still resents that she is not exempt. She almost always makes me ask her to repeat her first statement, though she knows better by now. Usually I just brush it off, but today, maybe because of my disturbed night, I am on edge.

By the time we are in the car, I have a pounding headache, the kind you only get once or twice a year but can last for days. Even the overcast sky is too bright for me, like staring into a spotlight, and the classic rock station on the radio is close to making my ears bleed.

"You look nice," my mother says placatingly, giving me a warm smile. I glance down at my well-worn jeans and black turtleneck, wondering what she's talking about. I barely looked at my closet when I got dressed.

"Thanks," I mutter, unconvinced despite my quiet skin. Mom tosses me an outrageously cheery smile and I frown, knowing something is up. "What's going on? You seem really…pleased."

Her eyes flit over to me nervously before she shrugs nonchalantly and rolls her eyes. "Nothing. I'm just glad to see you getting out."

My skin twitches at the untruth. "Mom," I say dryly, knowing she will cave.

Her lips purse tightly in annoyance before she answers. "Well, if you must know, Geoffrey called last night and asked me to dinner."

I stop breathing for a moment, panic clutching my lungs. "Why?" I ask sharply, earning an offended look from Mom.

"Shocking though it may be to you, Derry, I believe he finds me attractive. He said I needed cheering up. You won't mind if I go out for an evening sometime this week?" she asks casually, her mind clearly not on me.

A stab of hurt runs through me. For the past couple days she's been unusually thoughtful, checking in to see how I'm feeling, making my favorite meals. Telling me she loves me.

I can feel that sweetness melt away with her words, hot water dumped on an ice cube. I guess the guilt and worry she has been feeling since I got home from the hospital is past its sell-by date.

"Yeah. I'll be fine," I mumble, noticing all too clearly how she barely registers what I say. Back to normal it is.

She comes into the station with me, but sits out in the lobby while a patrolman takes my statement. I don't change anything, leaving the accusations against Phillip standing, hoping that it will prevent them from just sweeping Nicole's death under the rug the way they did with Miranda's. I don't see Radcliffe anywhere.

Just as I am leaving, a flash of teeth catches the corner of my eye. With a sense of the inevitable, I turn around and see Phillip exiting an office at the left side of the long, open room that serves as the heart of the station. He is watching me, a disturbingly broad grin stretching his features. Even from a distance I can see that his eyes are cold, emotionless. He nods at me and his eyes sharpen into the nightmare version of Phillip from the night before, but the moment passes and he turns to shake hands with Detective Radcliffe as he comes out of the conference room. A man and a woman follow, obviously Phillip's parents, their features oddly bland when compared with the crisp good looks of their son. The man glances my way and frowns, turning to Phillip to whisper something in his ear. Phillip looks at me again and nods once, the smile gone.

Turning sharply, I head out to the lobby, wanting to be out of the building before Phillip and his parents catch up. That's a conversation I don't want to have right now.

We return home and I spend a few hours trying to catch up on some of the homework I've missed. Amazing how thoughtful my teachers have been about providing me with lots of complicated assignments to distract me while I'm traumatized. I finish most of them by the time Mom yells up at me to put on something nice, it's almost time to leave for the funeral. I sit staring at my laptop, wishing I was still sick enough to give me an excuse not to attend. The thought of seeing Nicole's parents again, being forced to witness her body being finally interred makes it difficult to breathe.

Putting off reality for as long as possible, I surf the Internet for a bit, not really looking at anything in particular, hardly registering the pages my cursor drifts over. Before I realize what I've done, I have opened up the *Daily Holler's* website, which I haven't done in weeks. Looking at the archive for the past week, I am uncomfortably aware of how many stories must have been written about me finding Nicole. I glance down at the links until I find Householder's byline and open up the article.

### PRETTY SURE NICOLE SHARP WAS MURDERED

I held my tongue when the other girl was found in the river, but two girls dying so similarly in such a short time can't be a coincidence. I talked to my source at the coroner's office, and he said that it was unlikely that Nicole's neck would have broken in the way it did from a fall off the bridge. There were splinters of wood in the head wound, probably from a pine tree. I talked to the detective in charge of the investigation and he's suspicious too. He called in the state police to do forensics, and though he wouldn't tell me much, it was clear that based on where Nicole's body was found, the current would not have carried her from the bridge from which she was supposed to have fallen. Though he wouldn't say more, I definitely got the impression that the police believe that her body was dumped where she was found and that she was attacked elsewhere. I keep trying to get in touch with Derry MacKenna, but her mom has been blocking me.

I stare at the screen, stunned at the information. Suddenly Phillip's presence at the police station and his parents' hostile glares makes more sense. A punch of relief hits my chest. The task of bringing Phillip to justice seems a little less impossible now; instead of having to convince the police of the possibility of his guilt, I'll at least have fertile grounds for any evidence I can find.

Looking over the real article, I am not surprised that Householder didn't mention his suspicions, although he did mention the inclusion of a state police forensics team. I think back to Phillip's expression at the station, trying to remember if he had looked at all worried.

I don't think he did.

Glancing at the clock, I shut down my computer and start getting dressed, all the while mulling over the possibilities the article has opened up for me. Making a mental note to pay Householder a visit to get more details, I pull on a 50's era knee-length black silk dress. For the first time in a week, I actually take care with my hair, pulling it into a clean chignon, making sure that no stray hairs escape. The mirror presents me with a severe reflection, the image of someone harder, more resolute than I'm used to. Taking heart from the thought, I go downstairs and join my mother, gritting my teeth against the evening ahead.

The funeral is brief and nondenominational. It is the first funeral I've ever been to.

I always thought people had funerals in churches, but apparently Nicole and her parents weren't religious. Instead we are packed into a slightly larger room than the viewing parlor in the same funeral home. Once again, I am stunned by the number of people who attend. Mom and I are squished against the wall, forced to stand since all the chairs were claimed by the time we made it to the room. Phillip is here, sitting near the back with his parents. He looked at me once when I first came in, giving me a polite nod before assiduously returning his attention to the funeral director's welcoming statement.

Ranger Shanholtz stands near the back, giving me an encouraging smile when he catches my eye.

Cole and Jake are sitting in the second row with their father, all very solemn looking in black suits and slicked back hair. The resemblance between them is unsettling.

"And so we will miss our beloved Nicole, who was a friend to many

in our community. It is always a tragic loss when someone so young passes, but those who remain should find comfort in our memories of this
bright, smiling girl."

My skin has been buzzing through the entire ceremony, the funeral director's well-intentioned but insincere remarks ringing hollow and
over-rehearsed. I don't understand why someone who knew Nicole
wasn't chosen to speak, someone that could have done her justice.

Not me, not those who failed her.

There is a short smattering of applause and the funeral director steps
down to make room for Nicole's father as he drags his steps up to the
podium, his face drawn with exhaustion and deeply etched sorrow. I bite
my lower lip to hold back the tears threatening to overtake me as I remember how Nicole once said that she would never kill herself. That it
would destroy her parents.

Mr. Sharp stands quietly, breathing deeply for a moment before he
begins.

"I don't think I'll survive this," he whispers, though only I hear the
heartbreaking truth in his words. He clears his throat before he continues, voice gaining firmness. "Her mother and I want to thank all of you
for your continued support through this…difficult time. We know that
Nicole," he says, voice wavering uncertainly before he takes another deep
breath. "Nicole would have been glad to know how much she will be
missed."

Out of the corner of my eye I watch Phillip's reaction to the father
of the girl I know he murdered. Phillip's face is a mask of sympathy; the
slight frown, downturned lips, the sober bearing is all a perfect mimicry
of a mourner. But under my vigilant gaze, the muscles of his face are
shifting and stretching beneath the mask, as though it is only with great
effort he can hold his pose.

The intensity of my scrutiny is rewarded when Mr. Sharp breaks in his
speech, obviously overcome by grief, and is led away by the ever present
funeral director. My eyes are locked on Phillip and I imagine I am the
only one who catches the fleeting smile, the crinkle of amusement at the
corners of his eyes.

Phillip is laughing inside.

"I'm worried you'll embarrass me," Mom whispers harshly, pulling my
attention away.

"What?" I ask quietly. She huffs a sigh and grabs my arm.

"I said you're shaking like crazy. Do you need to step out?" she repeats and I glance down at my hands which are trembling so violently even my mother's hand is shaking where she touches me. I take a deep breath, forcing myself to calm down, to focus on what needs to be done. The shaking subsides and Mom releases me, her cheeks red with embarrassment, though as far as I can tell no one has noticed. Clenching my jaw in irritation, I focus on the rest of the service, listening absently to the funeral director describing how to get to the graveyard where Nicole will be buried. Finally it ends and people begin to shuffle out the door, most of them headed for home. Only close friends and family will be at the gravesite.

That doesn't include me. Nicole's mother requested I not attend the burial.

I catch Beverly Sharp's eye as she moves down the center aisle supported by her husband and a slightly older man I don't recognize. Probably an uncle or cousin.

Her gaze locks with mine and instead of the hatred and blame I have come to expect, there is only confusion. Pity surges through me as I watch her pass, wondering even if I manage to prove Phillip murdered Nicole if it will be of any help to her mother. I simply don't know.

By the time we make it outside, I am sweating with the effort of appearing normal. I have heard so many unknowingly honest comments in the crowd that it is a wonder that I haven't struck out at the voices around me, trying to silence them with my fists since I cannot escape them in my head.

Mom leaves me at the curb while she goes to get the car. People walk around me as though I am encased in an invisible bubble that prevents them from touching me, but they watch me as they pass, curiosity and condemnation in their eyes.

I am the girl who let Nicole die, after all.

A familiar voice carries to my ears and I turn to see Simon Householder pursuing Cole's father down the sidewalk, peppering him with question after question about the oddity of two dead teenage girls who were friends with his son.

When he sees that other people are pausing to watch the exchange, Geoffrey Wise stops and turns to face the crowd, effectively ignoring Simon even while purportedly answering his questions.

"I don't want anyone to know about Jake's involvement with Miranda's death," he says, nodding solemnly, his voice heavy with sorrow but still resonating loudly enough for everyone to hear.

"Our town will always feel the loss of these two young women keenly, and I can promise safety measures on the bridge in question are being investigated as we speak. But as to the involvement of my family with either death, I can only feel disgust that anyone would try to sensationalize these unfortunate events. I believe the families have suffered quite enough, don't you?" he asks, raising his hands out to his captive audience. Everyone within hearing distance claps, shooting dirty glances at Simon. Even I have to concentrate hard not to join in the approval of the mayor's statement. Uneasiness snakes its clammy way down my throat and coils in my stomach as I push off the impulse. Almost as if he can sense my resistance, Geoffrey Wise turns his regal head in my direction, the barest hint of a smile twitching at his lips. Dipping his head to me in silent tribute, he turns and ushers his reluctant sons into the black sedan at the curb.

The crowd disperses quickly after the car pulls away, and I am able to push my way over to Simon, who stares resentfully at the road.

"Simon," I call out, and he snaps his attention around, eyes gleaming with expectation when he spots me.

"I know details about Nicole's death," he says in greeting and I feel my pulse race in reaction to this hidden truth.

"Can we talk?" I ask him, glancing around warily for my mother's car. I know I have only moments before she arrives.

"You going to give me a scoop, young lady?" he demands, putting his pad and pencil away in his overstuffed pocket.

I give him a wry smile. "Only if you return the favor," I stipulate, amused by the mercenary glint in his eyes.

"I forgot how sharp you were, Miss MacKenna. Alright. Let's meet at the café. Say around eight?"

I hear the approach of the Torino, finally restored after its close call by the river. "No, I can't tonight. Mom will never let me back out. How about before school tomorrow? If you can give me a lift afterward."

"Fine. Meet me there at seven."

I nod in affirmation before I slip away, back to where Mom left me waiting. When I glance back, Simon has disappeared, no doubt aware that his continued presence is probably a bad idea. I get into the car without comment and we make the drive home in silence, Mom probably imagining her upcoming date, and me silently resolving to get the truth out of

Simon and find something with which I can go after Phillip.

I worry neither of us will be satisfied.

# CHAPTER FOURTEEN

THE CAFÉ IS BUSTLING THIS morning, a long line waiting at the register for coffee and bagels; almost every table is taken with people still encased in coats and ski jackets shoveling down piping hot food as fast as they can. Simon waits for me at a table near the back, two stacked plates in front of him, the food itself obscured by the bucket of syrup he's poured over everything. I signal to the waitress as I take the seat across from him and order a hot chocolate and blueberry muffin.

"I've got diabetes," Simon mumbles in between bites. I frown, thinking that having that much syrup has got to be bad for someone with diabetes and I consider saying something, but then dismiss the urge. He's not a stupid man. He knows what he's eating is bad for him.

"Good morning," I say, shedding my bulky coat and scarf. Outside the wind is howling and fierce, chips of ice blown around in mini-tornados above the snow drifts. It is the coldest winter on record for the area.

Simon stuffs another heaping forkful in his mouth and gives me a measured look. "Alright, Derry, I've got little time to waste, so why don't you just ask me whatever it is you want to know," he says around the mouthful of food.

I smile in appreciation of his attitude. "Fine. What do you know about Nicole's death that hasn't been printed?" I ask, figuring I don't need to waste time dancing around the issue.

He coughs and goes slightly purple as he chokes on a clump of pancakes. Taking a deep drink of his coffee and rubbing his chest, Simon stalls for time, obviously trying to think of what he can get out of me in return for the information.

Finally he puts down the coffee and the fork and pushes his plate away. "I'll answer your questions if you can give me something to work with."

"I can tell you what Nicole was doing out there that night," I offer quietly, glancing around to make sure no one is eavesdropping. Thankfully, we are ignored; the other patrons are far too focused on their own plates to care what an old reporter and a teenage girl are doing in a corner booth together.

Simon's eyebrows shoot up. "Is that so? Alright then. Here's what I know." He leans forward, keeping his voice low. "Nicole did not jump off the old railroad bridge. She didn't jump off of anything. The coroner says that her head was struck on something sharp and wooden. Looks like pine. From the angle needed to break her neck, he suggested a tree with a broken limb. To have done that kind of damage, she would have had to have been knocked into the tree with a lot of force. Something she couldn't have done without help."

I digest this information, which isn't entirely new, but the confirmation and detail helps to paint a picture. She struggled with Phillip first.

"What else? What about her neck?" I demand, refusing to get sidetracked.

Simon nods and gives me a knowing look. "Coroner said the neck was an odd break. It would have paralyzed her and stunted her breathing, but if she had gotten immediate help she might have survived. Would have been paralyzed, but she might have made it."

Nausea drips down into my stomach, settling uneasily on the hot chocolate I've already drunk. An image flashes before my eyes; Nicole fighting with Phillip and him throwing her on an outthrust tree limb, snapping her neck with the force.

A loud crash resonates through the room and I shake the impression off, glancing around to see a waitress stooping to clean up a dropped tray and several dirty plates. I just watch her for a moment, taking in the bright flush to her cheeks as she gingerly picks up the chunks of broken dishes, her eyes darting around as though daring anyone to say something. I don't know why this is so fascinating to me. I don't know why it is so hard for me to turn back to the conversation.

Simon clears his throat and taps the table to get my attention. "Derry? What are you thinking?" he asks curiously, as though he really cares what I think about the situation.

"Are they treating her…death like an accident, or like a murder?"

He gives me a cynical look. "Now do you really think the police share that kind of detail with me? A lowly reporter?"

I return his look with interest. "But they'll give you every detail about her injuries? Come on, what do you know?"

With an amused grunt, Simon shifts his bulk and glances at his watch. "I think we've concluded the free ride portion of the meal. Your turn," he says, pulling out his ever-present notebook and pen. For a moment I am puzzled. Since I realized people seem to be compelled to answer me honestly when I really want to know something, I have become accustomed to getting answers without much work. Why Simon is able to resist is beyond me, but I feel abruptly certain that he has given me all of this information not because he had to, but because he wanted to.

I narrow my eyes and concentrate, trying to pick up a trace of the peculiar connection I get with Cole and Jake, and even their father, but there is nothing. Only the lengthening pause that hangs between us like an accusation.

"Any time now, sweetheart. We're on a clock, you know," he reminds me. Seeing that I have less than twenty minutes before school I admit defeat and tell him about Nicole's certainty that Phillip murdered Miranda. Off the record, of course.

"What exactly was she basing this on?" Simon asks when I'm done.

"Partly a feeling. But mostly Miranda's journal," I admit, knowing how thin everything sounds out loud.

But Simon perks up at the mention of the journal. "Journal? The police never found one. How did Nicole get it?"

Seeing that I've caught his interest finally, I give him a beatific smile and get to my feet, putting a few dollars down for a tip. "Now do you think anyone would share that kind of detail with me? A lowly reporter?" I return his earlier words wrapped in sarcasm. Simon tightens his mouth in irritation, but after a moment his lips loosen in a grudging smile.

"Fine, Derry. I suppose you'll give me that information when I can tell you more about the investigation?"

I mime delighted surprise. "What a wonderful idea, Mr. Householder. You give me a call when you know something."

He laughs as he throws a twenty down to cover his ridiculously unhealthy meal. "I told you, call me Simon. And yes, I'll call you if I learn anything else. You'll make a fair reporter one of these days, Derry."

I am absurdly pleased by his comment, and cover my blush with the scarf I wind around my face as a shield against the spitting snow. Simon leads me outside and down the street to the train station parking lot where his car waits. He unlocks a tan Malibu and I can't help the laugh that escapes me.

"What?" he demands, dropping heavily into the driver's seat.

"Where did you get this car? From a police auction?" I joke.

He gives me a stunned look as we pull cautiously onto the road toward the high school. "How did you guess?"

"It's got former unmarked police car written all over it."

With a chuckle, he pats the steering wheel affectionately. "It's good for stakeouts."

By the time he drops me off at the front of the school, I feel as though we have cemented our odd little friendship. He waves, pulling away from the curb, and I can see him shaking his head as he drives away.

As I turn to walk up the stairs, all my mirth drains away and my feet are heavy with reluctance. This is the my first day back since Nicole died, and suddenly the thought of maneuvering the hallways alone, the empty seat in history, the deserted alcove where we ate lunch is too much, and I halt on the steps, nearly choking on the wave of desolation that descends over me.

I am still standing there when I hear the crunch of shoes on snow behind me come to a stop, and a hand rests lightly on my shoulder. Turning, half expecting to see Cole, I am surprised when Ruth's sympathetic face confronts me.

"I am worried about Phillip," she says, her real greeting lost.

I haven't really talked much with her since the day I ate lunch with Phillip and the rest of his friends. We nodded at one another in the hallway and exchanged pleasantries, but we moved in different circles once I was firmly established as Nicole's friend.

She squeezes my shoulder and gives me a sad smile. "I'm glad to see you're back. I'm so sorry about Nicole and what happened to you. Let me know if I can do anything," she says, and I know she is sincere. Despite her apparent loyalties to Phillip, I remember that I liked her the first time we talked, and am relieved that at least someone is genuinely sorry about Nicole's death.

"Thanks. I got your card," I reply, remembering that she had been one of the few to send me a note while I was in the hospital. Phillip sent one too.

I shredded it and threw it in the trash.

"Oh, good. I wanted to visit, but I wasn't sure if you wanted company or not," she says and my skin hums lightly. I don't mind; I can't imagine wanting to visit someone I barely know in the hospital. But the sentiment is nice.

"I was pretty out of it most of the time anyway." I take a deep breath and begin ascending the stairs, knowing I can no longer put off the moment I have to resume my school life without Nicole. Ruth comes with me, quietly companionable, her presence a welcome support whether she knows it or not.

We reach the doors before she speaks again. "I know you and Nicole had your own lunch routine, but…it would be nice if you came to sit with me today. I mean, I know Phillip won't mind, and…" she breaks off when she sees my face. "Sorry, I mean, just if you wanted to…"

Forcing a smile I just nod. "Thanks, Ruth. Maybe."

Her answering smile is relieved. "Okay. Well, let me know if I can do anything," she repeats and enters the school, leaving me behind on the snow-dusted welcome mat. With a deep, fortifying breath I follow, ignoring the wet squeak my boots make on the pristine linoleum as I plunge into the flowing stream of students headed to lockers and classrooms.

I get quite a few looks, and hear a number of unwelcome truths as people pass me in the hall. I can feel tears pricking at my eyes and bite my lower lip to keep from showing weakness. I have no idea what people are really saying to me; it could be condolences or insults and I'll never know the difference. All I hear are the hidden truths that whisper only to me.

The door to history is closed when I reach it, and for a moment I seem to see a pinched-faced girl waiting for me, an impatient glint in her eyes, but I blink and the image is gone, the hall is empty.

I take a deep, shuddering breath and enter the room, ignoring the dozen sets of eyes that immediately lock on me, following my every movement. Pausing at Mrs. Sullivan's desk to hand her my official excuse, I glance at Nicole's seat and then freeze, my heart spiking and stalling before it resumes a quickened pace.

Phillip is sitting in her chair.

He catches my eyes and smiles, the smile of a tiger just before it strikes with a crushing blow, the smirk of a wolf before he lunges, the grin of a shark before it snaps its jaws closed over its prey. He smiles and it seems to me that his green eyes glow with anticipation and something else. Something akin to hunger.

"I always liked Nicole," Mrs. Sullivan says and I snap my attention back to her as she signs the excuse and hands it back. "Let me know if you need help getting caught up," she continues and I just nod, completely incapable of speech. There are no other seats available but my usual desk and the one Phillip is supposed to occupy. I have no choice but to take my seat, feeling the electricity light under my skin in the presence of the grinning liar next to me.

"I thought it might be easier for you if you didn't have to think of Nicole's empty seat," Phillip whispers, his eyes wide and innocent-looking. My skin is on fire and a wild rage bubbles just beneath the surface. It takes every ounce of control I have not to reach out and claw the loathsome grin off his face.

When I don't respond, he smirks and turns his attention to the front of the class, where Mrs. Sullivan is passing out some papers. I barely glance at the sheet when it is passed back to me and the guy in the back row has to come get his from me when I forget to hand it to him.

"You'll be starting your major project today. You and your partner will choose one of the events listed and present an oral report two weeks from today. Take some time now to talk it over and come up with some ideas. We'll go over the details in a bit," Mrs. Sullivan announces. I sit staring at the sheet in confusion for a moment, trying to figure out who I'm supposed to work with now that Nicole isn't here.

And then I remember. Nicole was never my partner.

Phillip is.

I turn to see him watching me, his reptilian gaze a cold stroke down my spine.

"Hey there, partner. You know, I'm glad we'll be working together. Maybe it'll give us a chance to talk," he says, false concern marking his face. It's eerie in a way, as though he is only pretending to be human, that he has practiced and nearly mastered expressions of emotion, but is just slightly off, a mirror image instead of reality.

A smile that has no joy stretches my lips. "Lucky us," I mutter, disgust thickening my voice. Phillip scoots his chair over to me, putting his assignment sheet on my desk. His hand rests on top of it and I am tempted to slam my fist down on the fragile fingers.

"Listen, I feel like there's been a misunderstanding somewhere. Did you know that I've been called into the police station twice to answer questions about where I was the night Nicole died?" he demands in a low, furious voice. For the first time I think I'm getting a real reaction from him. He's definitely not happy about being questioned.

"Gosh, I'm sorry to hear that, Phillip," I say, dropping my chin on my hand and fixing my eyes on him as though fascinated by what he has to say. Strangely, I feel no fear facing this creature, this thing that killed my best friend and no doubt wouldn't mind seeing me dead in a ditch somewhere. All I have is that hot spiral of wrath in my chest, and it makes me reckless.

Phillip's gaze narrows and a flicker of fury touches his eyes, gone quick enough that I'm not sure it was there at all.

"I bet." His voice is dry and he gives me a calculating look, as though he is just now beginning to revise his impression of me. "They said that someone had reported that I was on the scene where Nicole was found. That someone had made accusations against me."

I give him my best 'I'm just a dumb chick that you should underestimate' look, one I tend to employ when interviewing fat old politicians. "Who would do such a thing?" I gasp, putting a hand to my chest. "Unless…you don't think it was me, do you? What would make you think that?"

This time there is no mistaking the flare of rage in his eyes and for a moment my bravado falters. This rage is different than mine, different from the uncontrolled ferocity I have seen in Jake's eyes. It is the first wisp of smoke over the horizon that signals a forest fire. It is deep and simmering and absolutely terrifying.

I pull away, straightening in my chair so that I am not so close to him. A pleased smirk crosses his lips before he settles back in his own chair. "I don't think you want to play this game with me, Derry," he says smoothly, no trace of emotion in his voice.

I watch him for a moment and then nod. "No, I don't think I do," I whisper, finally dropping my gaze, uncomfortable with the alien intensity in Phillip's eyes. Shame colors my cheeks and I realize I have just lost some kind of battle. I am failing Nicole yet again.

"Well. Let's forget about it for now. I'm sure you're still too upset to talk about any of this. Maybe you should take some time to think things over before you make any other statements to the police," he says comfortably, his tone patronizing. I wonder if this is how he used to talk to Miranda.

Mrs. Sullivan is drifting through the class, talking to each pair, marking down choices as she passes. She arrives at my desk and looks at Phillip and then me, eyebrow raised.

"I think Phillip is a bit of a sociopath," she says and Phillip nods, looking down at the assignment sheet.

"Yeah, we'd like to do our report on the execution of Anne Boleyn," he says in answer to whatever she's asked. Mrs. Sullivan glances at me for confirmation, but I just nod vacantly, thinking about the piece of information she has unknowingly given me.

When I look at Phillip again it is with new eyes. Why this has never occurred to me before I can't imagine, except that no one really expects anyone they know to be a murdering sociopath. But now it is as though every blank has been filled, every question answered.

Phillip is a sociopath.

Or maybe a psychopath. I make a note to research the difference later.

From what I have learned from movies and books, however, sociopaths are without real emotion, or at least the kind that a normal person can understand. There was a movie I saw once about a con artist who was called a chameleon because he was never the same person, just a reflection of the people around him. He lied all the time and everyone believed him because he didn't have the same kind of tells that most people have; the twitch of an eye, tightening of the mouth, those little signs that indicate someone is trying too hard. This character lied so easily because he was a lie. There was no real person underneath the façade, just the man's ambition.

Phillip is watching me carefully, and I wonder if he can read the epiphany on my face. For the first time, I feel I understand what I'm up against, why my skin is always buzzing around him, why I have never heard a hidden truth from him.

He is a lie. There is nothing true or honest about him, and the face he presents to the world is just a mask that covers a black hole of cruelty. I feel a tiny smile pull at my lips, and I grab on to the first thread of reality I have found about Phillip and cling to it with dogged determination. Somehow this is the key to bringing him down. I just have to figure out how to use it.

I return Phillip's look, the fiery knot in my chest smoldering in satisfaction. We won't be giving this stupid report together.

Phillip will be in jail long before the assignment is due.

# CHAPTER FIFTEEN

I SPEND MY LUNCH IN THE computer lab. Only two other people are here, two boys I don't recognize who are writing some kind of program for computer class. We ignore each other and I am able to concentrate on my task.

I have no idea where to start, so I just type *sociopath* in the Google search bar. There are a lot of results, but after scanning some obviously homemade web pages and a lot of false information, I find a medical site which appears to be largely factual, focused on anti-social personality disorders. There are hardly any sentences that I have to read twice.

Immediately I know I am right about Phillip. The signs that indicate a sociopath are pretty varied, and there are a couple different classifications, but lack of remorse, lack of empathy, aggressive behavior, and a stunted moral code seem to sum up Phillip pretty well.

The website says that sociopaths care about nothing but themselves and their own wish fulfillment. If anything gets in the way of that or they believe themselves to be in danger of anything from humiliation to physical peril, sociopaths are prone to violence or abuse; sometimes emotional, sometimes physical. They are charming, manipulative, and tend to surround themselves with weak personalities they can dominate.

I think about Miranda, how she initially pulled away from Phillip; but once she was vulnerable because of the rape, she was defenseless against him. Given the information about sociopaths, it is not unreasonable to assume if she planned to leave him or tell someone about how he was treating her, Phillip would be moved to murder. The site states that an Amoral Sociopath, which seems to fit the bill with Phillip, can take pleasure in violence and even murder. These are the people who pluck the wings off of flies, who dissect their neighbors' pets, who will one day grow up to be serial killers.

What is most discouraging in the midst of so much confirmation is the repeated indication of high intelligence among sociopaths. Evidently, high-functioning sociopaths, the kind that live next door and have jobs and mortgages, the kind no one would believe is a killer because 'he was always so pleasant,' are almost always of above-average intelligence and very good at covering their tracks.

Given how little actual proof I have been able to turn up about Phillip thus far, this news is disheartening. Particularly since he obviously knows I am onto him. He's smart enough to know he needs to clean up after himself, and I despair of finding anything to pin to him more than my own instinct.

The tone sounds and I drag myself to class, thinking furiously of how to trap Phillip in a confession when my abilities don't seem to work on him.

No one pays any attention to me in my third period class, which comes as a welcome relief. Toward the end of class, I hear a muffled giggling and turn around to see Tasha whispering behind her hand to the girl next to her, eyes focused on me with resentment. With a sigh, I turn forward again, acknowledging that with Nicole no longer in the picture as the perfect victim, Tasha and her cronies will probably turn their attention to me. A savage glee seizes me and I almost wish they would. I could humiliate them far more effectively than they could ever manage since they will have only their feeble imaginations for material, while I have access to all their hidden secrets. When I glance back at Tasha again, my gaze is full of challenge, a giddy sort of volatility that trembles with the need to exact revenge for Nicole's suffering at her hands.

Tasha flinches when she next looks my way, and I can see the hesitation in her eyes, practically hear her remembering when I exposed her boyfriend's affair. She ducks her head and breaks eye contact. I win.

My victory is fleeting and shallow. As I trudge down the hall toward the journalism room, dread threads its way into my veins, slowing me down, dragging my steps. There is a bitter taste on my tongue, a sour bite that seems to reach down into my gut with noxious fingers as I put my hand on the door, knowing the man who brutally raped Miranda is waiting inside, his palms sweaty and too milk-soft, eyes shifting restlessly over the unsuspecting girls in his classroom. For a moment I am nearly faint and my fear of Shockey is as real as the moment I first read Miranda's journal.

"I'm failing my English class," a soothing, familiar male voice breaks into my panic and I turn to see Shane; silly, smiling, safe Shane standing next to me, holding his hand out as though he wants to offer comfort but isn't sure how.

"Shane, hey," I croak, stuffing the distress and dizziness down until I am able to focus clearly. "Sorry, am I in your way?"

He rolls his eyes and wraps his arms around me in a bear hug, smushing my face against the soft cotton of his t-shirt. "I'm so glad you're back, hot stuff. I'm tired of flirting with Megan. She's mean," he laughs, and I feel his sincerity in the silence of my skin. For a moment I just let him hold me, content to bask in his overwhelming masculinity. His hand begins to make little expeditions hither and yon, brushing the top of my butt.

"Whoa there cowboy. I'm not *that* much nicer than Megan," I finally object, gently pulling away. I can't help a laugh at his unrepentant grin. "You are such a hound," I accuse, punching his shoulder lightly.

Shane shrugs and opens the door for me and I am able to walk in, my anxiety dialed back in the secure presence of this big, overprotective male.

"Seriously though, how are you doing?" he asks, his face taking on an unnaturally somber expression. I sigh and shake my head.

"Better. But still…" I say helplessly.

Shane just nods and slings an arm around my shoulders. "Yeah, I know. I'm really sorry about Nicole. I know you guys were friends. I'm here if you need anything, okay?"

My eyes prick with moisture and I blink to keep away the unwelcome tears. "Thanks, Shane."

He gives me another squeeze and then releases me so he can open the door into the lab. I pause and look around, but Shockey isn't in his usual place at his desk. Knowing I am being a coward, my shoulders sag in relief. Maybe he's not here today and I won't have to face him just yet.

I take my seat in front of my usual computer and close my eyes for a moment, allowing my nerves to settle.

"I feel bad about being mean to you." Megan's voice is soft and gentle, unlike anything I've heard from her before. I spin around to see her sitting in her chair, looking strangely vulnerable. Shane drops into his seat, looking back and forth between us with surprise and eagerness. I guess Megan said something less snide than usual.

"Thanks, Megan," I say, hoping that I'm making the right assumption. Apparently I am because she nods and gives me a genuine look of sympathy.

"It's weird, isn't it Shane? Seeing her sit there?" Megan asks, turning to look at Shane, who just shrugs and turns around to boot up his computer.

Frowning, I lean forward. "What do you mean?"

"I don't know. It's just…with Nicole gone I can't help thinking about Miranda. That was her computer when she was on the paper," Megan answers, gesturing toward my station. My hands feel suddenly cold and I inch away from the desk that has been my home since starting this class.

"I guess I never realized she was in journalism," I say slowly, wondering if this might account for some of the rage Jake has always displayed seeing me here.

"Well, not this year…I mean before…" Megan sighs and rubs her hands over her face. "She quit before school started this year. I think she didn't want to have to work with Jake," she explains. I nod, understanding why Miranda might not want to be stuck in an enclosed space with Jake every day while dating someone else.

"I see," I say, looking at the computer as though it has teeth. I am beginning to feel like I cannot get away from Miranda, from things she's touched, things that brought her misery.

"Sorry. I didn't mean to bring all that up. It just felt kind of weird. I don't know," Megan shrugs and blows out her breath in a huff. "Anyway, I'm glad you're okay." She abruptly swings back around to face her own computer, staring with furious intensity at the screen as it loads. I am oddly touched by her admission and wonder how much of her dislike of me has been founded on where I've been sitting, feeling I was taking Miranda's place.

"Thanks," I say quietly and let the matter drop, not wanting to embarrass her further. Her shoulders relax slightly and some of the tension drains from the room.

The door creaks open and Jake walks in.

Though I keep my eyes trained on the floor, I feel him watching me, waiting for some opening. I am careful not to give it to him. With the uncomfortable knowledge everyone in the room is looking at me, I turn back around to face my own computer and go through the motions of starting it up, as though nothing out of the ordinary is going on.

"I hate that you're so scared of me," Jake says quietly, finally moving to take his own seat. Out of the corner of my eye I see Shane ease back and realize he was on the verge of jumping out of his seat. No doubt to keep Jake away from me. In the weeks before Nicole's death, Jake and I had played an uneasy game of civility punctuated by random outbursts of hostility that usually ended with Jake stalking out of the room. More than once, Shane had come between us, clearly not understanding the tension's source, but nonetheless determined to keep me safe.

There is a defeated slump to Jake's shoulders as he falls into his chair and guilt stabs at me momentarily. No matter how edgy I am around him, I can feel a gossamer strand connecting us in a way I don't fully understand. The bond I have with Cole is stronger, as though our time together has fused the strands into something more durable, less flimsy. But even with our backs facing each other, I can still sense Jake, feel the delicate filament that tangles us together unwillingly.

The door opens again and Cathy enters the room, her skin startlingly pale, streaked with traces of smudged mascara and blush ruined by tears. Her hands tremble as they turn the knob to close the door as quietly as possible, as though she is afraid any sound of her presence will bring on an attack. My heart picks up its pace and the fiery knot in my chest seems to pulse angrily, fearfully.

"Hey, Cathy, are you okay?" Shane asks, his brow creased in worry. Cathy simply nods and stumbles over to her chair, stubbornly ignoring the apprehensive looks everyone is casting her way. Jake frowns and walks over to put a hand on her shoulder.

Cathy jerks violently and draws in a sharp breath, her jaw shaking so hard I can hear her teeth clack together.

"Sorry," Jake spits out, confusion and rejection darkening his features with the inevitable anger. An agonized expression disfigures her face as she stares up at him, her eyes shimmering with moisture.

Before anyone can say anything else, the door swings open yet again and Shockey saunters in, his hair looking slightly mussed. With dawning comprehension, I see that his fly is partially unzipped. Sick certainty grips me and rage and terror fight for dominance as I raise my eyes to look at him. Shockey's eyes dart around the room, lingering over Cathy's huddled figure before coming to rest on me.

"I just had Cathy," he says and a tremendous rushing fills my ears, drowning out every other sound; every other word now submerged beneath the incredible rage that spreads through me, setting even my fingertips on fire. I can hear the stuttered gasps of Cathy's breaths, the moist sound of Shockey's hands rubbing together, the wet smack of his lips. Hatred for the man in front of me is like a thick plug in my throat, a violation in and of itself.

"Derry? Are you alright?" the rapist asks me, his rodent eyes narrowing as they take in my white knuckles and curled lip. I am incapable of speech but meet his eyes with my own, thinking of Miranda's shame and the barely audible whimpers from across the room. He flinches at my glare and looks away quickly.

"Well. Back to work everyone. The next edition is due out next week." Shockey practically flees the room and Cathy shudders before turning to her computer, humiliation hovering like a pernicious cloud around her.

"What is it Derry? You looked like you were going to murder him," Shane says, his voice tight with unresolved concern.

All eyes shift to me, but my focus is on Cathy as she turns her wide, pleading eyes to lock with mine. Somehow she knows that I know, and she begs me silently to keep quiet. I give her a nod and promise myself that before the day is out Shockey will be behind bars and, with any luck, getting a taste of his own medicine.

Something in my expression seems to calm Cathy and she gives me the ghost of a smile before turning back around, shutting out the world around her.

"Nothing," I whisper. "After today, nothing."

After a bit, when everyone is working on their stories, I take out my cell and send a text to Cole, asking him if he can get into the building when school lets out in an hour.

After a minute I get a reply.

*I'm in the middle of a fight with my father.*

I blink so that his real message is legible.

*Prbly. Y?*

*Shockey goes down today,* I reply, my fingers tapping the touch screen hard enough to make a clicking sound.

There is a long moment before he responds.

*What do u have in mind?*

*B outside journalism rm at 3:45. Come in if things get nasty. Do ur thing.*

*What r u doing? R u in danger?????*

*Going 2 get him 2 confess. U r just in case.*

Another long pause ensues and I bite my lip, worrying he won't agree and I'll have to come up with some other plan. Finally he replies, and I can practically hear his misgivings.

*Not happy about this. R u sure?*

*Am doing this no matter what.*

*I'll b there.*

Smiling grimly, I tuck the phone away, thinking about how I can arrange things to work in my favor. I know that once I start asking him questions, Shockey will answer me, but I'm not sure how long it will take to get a full confession. Given how easily someone as stubborn as Radcliffe caved, I have no doubt my ability will work on a pathetic worm like Shockey. But if he resists, if it takes too long, he might panic and run, and then I'll never get another chance.

Proving what he did to Miranda will be next to impossible without his confession. The evidence, if there is any left, is probably too old and circumstantial to be worth anything. But if I can get him on tape admitting to the rape, maybe Cathy will corroborate with her own experience. I can't see him squirming out of that.

There is no fear for myself. I trust Cole to intervene if things get physical, though I tend to think Shockey will be too freaked out to come near me. Besides, one look from Cole and Shockey will be on his hands and knees blubbering in terror. He won't be much of a threat then.

I look down at my phone again and flip through the programs until I find the voice recorder. I've used this application so many times, although never without my interviewee's consent. It's considered unethical and in many cases illegal to record someone without their permission.

Somehow, I really don't care right now.

Another thought strikes me and I send a quick text to Mom, telling her that Cole is picking me up. The last thing I need is to have her wandering the hallways looking for me. It's going to be unpleasant enough explaining everything after the fact.

The idea swims across my mind that I am putting myself at serious risk, not just by confronting a known rapist, but by using my ability to bring him to the attention of the authorities. Getting all the dirt and then smoothing it out for an article is different from handing over a recording of me pushing for a confession to the police. No doubt they will question why Shockey is willing to admit what he's done to a high school journalist without any obvious threat, but I can't worry about that just now. Not if I'm going to get justice for Miranda and Cathy.

I put my phone away and stare at my empty computer screen, unable to focus on anything but the questions I will ask, planning the best approach for a quick confession. I am so wound up with nervous energy

I nearly fall out of my chair when Jake rolls over to me, his stormy blue eyes searching mine anxiously.

"I'm worried about Cathy," he says under his breath. I look at him in surprise, realizing for the first time I am hearing him reveal something other than his conflicted feelings about our bizarre relationship.

"What was that?" I ask, leaning forward without my usual hesitation. His eyes register surprise for a moment but it fades as he glances over toward the corner where Cathy is frantically typing, her head dipped so low her hair brushes the keyboard. Everything about her screams submissive.

I am painfully reminded of the Miranda of my nightmares, the fragile wisp that faded to nothing under Phillip's green gaze. I imagine her shoulders must have bowed in the same way; her eyes would have been lowered, ashamed. A fierce protectiveness washes over me and I have to grip down hard to keep myself from rushing out right now to attack Shockey.

Beside me Jake gasps and I glance down to see I haven't gripped the chair as I thought, but my hand clasps his, our fingers wrapped together like a promise.

Quickly I jerk my hand free, but I can see the triumph in Jake's eyes before he hardens his expression. I wait for him to comment, to push, but he just darts a look at Cathy again and lowers his voice.

"Something's wrong. I usually run into her at her locker and we walk to class together, but she wasn't there. She's obviously been crying." He hesitates and then continues, a tint of fury coloring his tone. "Is it just me, or did she seem scared of Shockey?"

I am impressed at his perception, how quickly he connected the dots. As far as I've been able to tell, he is usually too preoccupied with himself to discern the feelings of others. But now as anger leaks from his pores like a vapor, it is concern that dominates his expression. It is unnervingly appealing.

Forcing myself to focus, I give him an appraising look. "What makes you say that?"

"I don't know…she kind of…shrank when he came in." Jake shrugs, clearly uncomfortable with being so open. "I could just feel it."

Since he is so good at causing fear, he should be familiar with the signs, I think wryly, but I don't say it out loud. There is a tenuous rapport between us I am unwilling to shatter just now.

"Could be," I admit warily, keeping my real thoughts to myself. Although I am pleased to see him thinking of someone else, I am not ready to tell him all my plans just yet. Cole is far more reliable, and I don't dare jeopardize my chance to ensnare Shockey.

Back to form, Jake gives me a frustrated glare and tightens his lips. "Whatever. Sorry to have bothered you," he growls, the flash of black in his eyes unmistakable.

Even as I congratulate myself for not giving into my momentary desire to confide in him, disappointment is a stone in my chest at the stiffness in his posture, the easy descent into brittle temper. He is so strong and so weak at the same time and a pang of regret stabs through me before I pull away, returning to my computer and the task ahead. After a moment he gives an irritated grunt and moves back to his side of the room, sinking the room into an uneasy silence once more.

The rest of the period passes slowly, each second inching along with an unbearable pressure and a mounting feeling of doubt. I question my plan over and over, terrified that I am taking the wrong step, that somehow I will make things worse. But each time I move to text Cole to halt the plan, I glance over at Cathy's desolate form and feel the despair surrounding her in a dark aura.

I have no choice. I can't let this happen again.

I should have stopped him before now. Cathy should never have been hurt.

I let the guilt add fuel to the fiery core in my chest, converting it into a stronger substance, tempering it with steel and grit until a fierce blade of resolve takes shape, giving me the nerve to ignore my own trepidation and do what must be done.

When the tone sounds to announce the end of the school day, I remain in my seat, pretending to take my time shutting things down, looking around on the floor for an imaginary pencil, anything that gives me an excuse to linger. Cathy is first out the door, and Jake follows her almost instantaneously. Shane hangs around for a bit, watching me with a blend of amusement and concern, but he finally gives up and leaves. Megan gives me a tentative wave and follows Shane out. I wonder for a moment if I might make a friend there and a blossom of hope sprouts in my mind before I shut it down, knowing I have no right to it until I have fulfilled my promise to Nicole.

I hear the muffled explosions of students laughing and talking as they exit the main classroom, the distant slam of lockers, the buzz of excited adolescence vibrating in the floors. Finally, it is quiet. I turn on the recorder on my phone and place it out of sight beside the computer, trusting that it will work the way it's supposed to, that it won't fail me when it matters most.

Glancing at the clock on the wall, I see it is almost three forty-five and I take a deep breath, trying to squelch my writhing stomach, the dizzy swirling in my head.

The doorknob turns. The squeaking protest of the hinges is like a scream to my suddenly hypersensitive ears. My heart pounds hard against my ribs, the loudest thing I've ever heard.

"I can smell your fear," Shockey says quietly, tilting his head as though asking me a question. I take a shaky breath and force myself to smile and speak in an even voice.

"Why was Cathy so upset today?" I ask, putting as much force behind the question as I can. Shockey blinks in surprise and then answers, his lips moving slowly, precisely, as though the words are being carved from his mouth with a scalpel.

"She didn't like when I put my hand up her shirt." He sucks in a breath and gives me a bewildered look, one I have come to recognize so well. My panic begins to subside and I stand, training my eyes on him mercilessly.

"Why did you do that, Mr. Shockey?"

"Because I like to touch young girls. I like to hurt them." He is breathing hard now and backing towards the door. Alarmed, I stalk toward him, pushing him in the opposite direction, toward the wall.

"Did you touch Miranda, too? Did you hurt her?" I demand, amazed at how calm I sound, how perfectly in control.

He clenches his jaw, as though to trap the damning words inside, but he can't help himself and he answers, panic leaking into his eyes.

"Yes."

"What did you do to Miranda, Mr. Shockey?"

"I…I made her touch me…I…why am I saying this?" His voice trembles wildly and I can hear hysteria creep into his tone.

"What did you do to Miranda?" I repeat, relentless, knowing I have to get it out of him before he breaks.

"I raped her, I raped her, I took her in my car and I put my hand over her mouth and promised her if she ever told on me I would come to her house and do it again."

The air is filled with the animal sounds of his terror, and he stares wildly at me as though I am a demon sent to torture him. Maybe I am.

"When did you rape Miranda?" I urge, knowing I have to get as much detail as possible if this is going to hold up.

"In October, a few weeks before she died…she was walking home from school and I took her in my car to the campsite over the bridge and I raped her. I did it twice and then I left her there." He is openly weeping now, slowly sinking down to his knees against the wall.

"Did you kill her?" I ask before it's too late, knowing I have only moments before he breaks away.

"No, no I didn't kill her! Please…" he pleads, extending a hand toward me. I jerk away and despite the disgust roiling through me, satisfaction flares in my chest and I feel as though I can breathe a little easier.

"You're going to jail, Shockey. You sick bastard," I growl and spit on the floor in front of him. He cowers there, everything about him flaccid and worthless, defeated, ruined.

I take a step back, moving toward my phone, readying myself to flee before he gathers his wits.

I am too slow.

He strikes like a snake, without warning, in a flash of violence so intense my head spins, knocking me off balance. His hands are around my neck, vice-like, iron wedges driving into my throat with incredible force. I claw at him, frenzied, black spots dancing around my vision as I struggle for air, knowing with doomed certainty how stupid I've been, how my rage made me careless, dismissive of the instinct of every cornered beast to strike out, to maim the thing that has forced it to the edge.

"Cole," I gasp, realizing that he should have come in already, but the door remains closed. I kick at Shockey's legs, his knees, connecting hard enough that he grunts, but he doesn't let go. Suddenly we are on the floor and his body weighs me down, heavier than I imagined, hips grinding me into the rough carpet as though he can push me through the concrete into the ground. Oblivion is hovering, waiting to drag me under, stealing my fight and I grapple with renewed vigor, ignoring the burning in my throat, the slice of his too-long nails digging into my skin. My knee strikes against his groin, but barely disrupts him, too weak to do any real damage.

Instead he laughs and removes a hand from my throat to fumble at the buttons of my jeans, forcing a new, deeper punch of terror through me.

"I'll kill you, you freaky little bitch," he growls, the venom of his spit dropping on my face like acid. The world is dark around the edges and I flail uselessly, trying to reach something I can hit him with. I have only seconds left and desperation takes away any rational thought process until I am only a vessel of instinct, a last gasp, a final strike.

I feel his hardness pressing against me and every nerve revolts, giving me one last surge of strength. Ignoring the protest of my battered neck, I twist with excruciating effort until I can see his snarling face and stab my thumb into his eye, pushing into the pulpy mass, feeling the bile rise in my throat, strangling me. He howls with pain and wrath and jerks his hand away from my pants to pull my thumb away. His grip on my throat loosens slightly and I turn my head to bite down hard on his arm, feeling the pop as his skin breaks, the brackish copper of his blood filling my mouth.

He releases me long enough to grab my head and slams it hard against the floor, white lights flashing across my vision, stunning me. Sucking in a deep breath, I scream, but the sound is barely more than a harsh rasp. It seems to infuriate him, and he gives an animalistic growl, his eyes no longer resembling anything human.

He does something to my ribs with his elbow that leaves me wheezing with agony before he strikes my face so hard I hear my neck crack and then his hands are on my throat again and I know this is it. I am already suffocating and my hips buck uselessly beneath his bulk.

The door bangs open, crashing into Shockey's legs with devastating force. He screams as something in his knee snaps with sickening clarity and then suddenly he is off me, hanging in midair, face nearly purple with visceral hate. I drag myself backward, trying to get away, and then I see him, I see Jake, gripping the back of Shockey's neck and holding him several feet above the floor with no more effort than clutching a basketball. Shockey's eyes go wide with awareness and with a savage roar Jake flings him across the room to slam against the desk of computers and crash to the floor. Shockey twitches and frantically tries to get to his feet, but Jake is on him in an instant, pulling him up by his head and then smashing it against the desk with enough force to crack his jaw. Shockey slumps to the floor, bleeding and unconscious.

I try to get up, but my vision goes hazy and I sink back to my knees, watching with a sense of unreality as Jake raises his fist like a sledgehammer and poises it to come down on Shockey's limp frame.

Some part of me waits quietly, knowing that if I do nothing, this blow will kill Shockey and he will never hurt anyone again. He deserves to die. I believe it with my whole being.

I struggle to my feet and fling my arms around Jake's waist, pulling him back, ignoring the brutal slash of pain in my side, and he collapses on top of me, knocking preciously bought air out of my lungs.

"Don't, Jake," I whisper. "You'll kill him. Don't do it, please, please…" I beg, my voice little more than a whisper. He shrugs off my hold with pathetically little effort and gets to his feet, ignoring me and readying for the strike again.

"No! Please, Jake, for me, please stop."

Jake turns slightly and I nearly scream in terror again, seeing the un-controlled gale of rage in his glare, his irises wholly black with inhuman fury. My fear must register with him somehow and he blinks, lowering his arm slightly.

"Please, Jake, you've done enough. I need your help, I'm hurt," I soothe, reaching out for him, wincing as pain wracks every inch of me. For a nev-er-ending moment he vibrates with the force of his battle to regain con-trol, his eyes locked on mine like an anchor, the frail connection between us twining tighter, more potent, until all I can feel is the space separating us like a shivering pane of glass that splinters and falls as he takes one step toward me, then another. I sag, my body shutting down with exhaustion and shock, and he is there, catching me, wrapping me in his arms and covering my face with his kisses, his gentle words, the fluttering tremor of his pulse no more than the brush of a feather across my skin.

My vision swims and lurches and it is dark, and the pain follows me.

# CHAPTER SIXTEEN

VOICES MURMUR OVERHEAD AND SOMETHING warm strokes my face, but the ground beneath me is hard and unforgiving. I blink, my vision coming into focus before everything goes grey and upside down. I collapse to the side and vomit uncontrollably, great heaves that seem to shred my organs and break bones with their intensity. When there is nothing left but the acidic burn on my tongue, someone rolls me back over, lying my aching head on something soft before putting hands on my sides, pushing slightly, testing.

A tremor races over me and I whimper, hating the sound even as it escapes. Compelling myself to emerge from the safety of my shock-protected mind, I force my eyes open and swallow the nausea that threatens to tear me apart.

"I almost killed a man," Jake says, dropping to his knees beside me.

"Thank god, you're finally awake. I think you've got a concussion or something; you keep passing out."

I raise a hand to my head and gently prod the back of my skull, wincing at the tender lump at the base. "Can you help me sit up?" My voice chafes the back of my throat, which is throbbing hotly.

"I don't think I'd better. We're waiting for the EMTs. I think your head is in bad shape," Jake says, his voice as gentle as I've ever heard it. His cloudy blue eyes stare down at me with a murky blend of worry and adoration. Panic itches along my skin, and suddenly I can't stand to be touched, as though his fingers are sinking through the skin like a hot knife through butter.

"Too close," I whisper and after a moment he seems to understand, pulling away slightly so that I don't feel so penned in. For once, he doesn't seem irritated with me.

"Is that better?" he asks solicitously, his eyes steady on mine. I nod and then close my eyes against the pain.

"Thank you. You saved me." Opening my eyes, I reach out and take his hand, giving a grateful squeeze. His eyes blaze with emotion and he just nods, looking away after a moment and taking a deep, balancing breath.

Having no idea how long I've been out or what's happened since, I glance around the room as much as possible without moving. To my right, I can see Shockey and my vision nearly goes black with terror, but after a moment I register he is still unconscious, blood trickling from the side of his mouth. I almost ask if he is dead, but I remember what Jake first said and breathe easier. The computers on the desk above Shockey are a mess, on their sides, the keyboards drooping listlessly over the lip of the table. The desks along the front wall of the room are fine, untouched, and I pray my phone is still there.

"Jake. My phone is over there, behind my computer. Can you get it?"

He disappears and I can hear him fumbling around with the equipment before he drops back down next to me, holding the phone out. I take it carefully and look at the screen, blinking against the stab of light that seems to pierce through the soft tissue of my brain. The recorder is long since turned off, but I flip through the files until I find the one I need.

I hit play and my own voice comes out clearly, starting the conversation that led to me lying battered and bruised on the floor. I mean to turn it off before it can get too far, but Jake hears the mention of Miranda and goes stiff, staring down at me incredulously. The recording plays through about half of my fight with Shockey before cutting off.

Jake looks down at the phone for a moment and takes a deep breath. Without a word, he stands and takes a step toward Shockey's inert body and I know without a doubt he is closing in for a killing blow.

"Jake no, you don't need to. He's going to jail, he'll be punished," I croak, desperately trying to get to my feet, ignoring the sick spinning in my head and the spike of pain in my side. Before I manage to do much more than groan, another taller figure steps through the now-propped open door.

"I am going to use this situation for my re-election campaign," a commanding voice booms, halting Jake in his tracks as though he has walked into a wall. Geoffrey Wise towers over me, his designer suit without a crease or wrinkle, hair gelled back into a careful wave, making him look like he's just walked off the factory line.

"Jake, I said come here." The words hit again with a mixture of dominance and an unexpected sense of contentment. Nothing can go wrong if I just listen to that voice.

Jake slowly stirs, his feet dragging as he turns away from the body and toward his father, his movements almost robotic. When Jake is safely out of the way behind his father, Geoffrey turns his attention to me.

"I'm glad to see you're still with us, Derry. You're far too valuable to lose through carelessness." The tone of his voice is right, but words are jarringly callous. Still, my skin is quiet, and I know he means what he says.

That's what worries me.

Glancing around, I realize who is missing. "Where's Cole? He was supposed to be here, that's why I…"

"Yes, yes, well," Geoffrey interrupts, ignoring the rumble of frustration from his son. "Cole got held up by the principal when he tried to sneak onto school grounds. By the time he arrived on the scene, Jake had already taken care of everything, so I told him to go home."

Betrayal and disappointment snake through my gut, almost overtaking the discomfort in my head and ribs. I never imagined Cole wouldn't come for me, that he would let me down. Tears leak from my burning eyes and I close them, too tired to deal with any more drama, too tired to think of all the consequences.

The sounds of rolling wheels and loud voices penetrate the haze of self-pity and I open bleary eyes to see a paramedic drop down next to me, checking my vital signs, prodding the knot on my head, pressing careful hands on my ribs.

"Mayor Wise pays me to steal medical records," the younger of the two says, his eyes soft and comforting despite the venal curve to his lips. The other EMT has finished examining Shockey, who is now making incoherent sounds of waking. My pulse leaps and I begin to shake, sending needles of pain through my chest and head.

"Terry, get him out of here. I think she's having a panic attack," my paramedic says, gently putting an oxygen mask over my face and telling me to breathe.

Things are blurry and fast for a while, and by the time I'm lucid again, I am on a stretcher, a neck brace tucked around me. Two police officers, one of whom took my statement about Nicole just the day before, are wandering around, taking notes and talking to Jake. The familiar officer, whose name I think is Sowers, catches my eye and gives me an encouraging smile.

"The mayor is telling us how to handle the crime scene," he says, giving me an awkward pat on the arm. I don't know what to say in response, sure whatever he's really telling me is not even close to what I heard. I glance around, looking for Jake and his father, but they are nowhere to be seen as I am rolled out of the room and down the hallway.

"I don't want to go to the hospital," I whisper, but no one pays any attention to me and I am loaded unceremoniously into the ambulance.

I thought my head was hurting before, but I have never felt pain like this, bumping unmercifully as the ambulance hurtles over every pothole with the speed of a wild horse. The sirens scream all around me, searing the inside of my skull with the kind of hurt that makes it impossible to think. I am beginning to wish Shockey had succeeded in killing me.

As though thinking his name conjured him, I look to my right and see him lying there, strapped to his own gurney, a paramedic working to stabilize him. Evidently they are afraid he punctured a lung when Jake hurled him across the room.

Even knowing Shockey is incapacitated, that handcuffs chain him to the gurney, I am chill with fear. His eyes are open and fixed on me with such intense hatred I know if he ever gets the chance again, he will murder me.

My paramedic sees what I'm looking at and steps between us, tossing a glare over his shoulder. "I'm so sorry we had to bring him on the same trip; he's banged up even worse than you and we didn't want to wait. I won't let him near you honey," he says reassuringly. Despite what I know about his illicit activities for the mayor, I am comforted. He hasn't left my side once and has kept up a steady train of pleasant chatter to distract me, whether I have been conscious or not.

I give him a weary smile and then close my eyes, but I can still feel the heat of Shockey's hatred eating up all the oxygen until there is nothing left to breathe but the poisonous remains.

By the time we reach the hospital and I am processed, stuck back in the exact same room I occupied in the emergency room only a week before, I have reached a kind of numb acceptance. The nurses are calling it shock, but I know that's not it. I was shocked when I found Nicole, when I dragged her dead body out of a frozen river. Nothing can shock me after that.

My mother arrives before long, her face streaked with tears, a frenzied look in her eyes. Guilt stabs me through when I realize what she must have been through hearing I am in the hospital after nearly dying yet again. The nurses have to hold her back while they finish putting in IVs and getting ice for my throat. Once I'm relatively settled, waiting for them to bring in the portable x-ray machine to check my ribs and neck, Mom is allowed to take a seat next to me, her hand trembling as she takes mine.

"I can't survive losing you," she says quietly, and I know whatever she has really said would mean less to me than these words. So often I feel that she only puts up with me because of my gift and the benefits it brings her. There are many times that I question whether she really loves me or if she resents me for being the tool that destroyed her marriage. But I see in her eyes, feel in the peace under my skin, hear in her accidental honesty she does love me, in her own way.

"I love you too, Mom," I whisper.

"I'll kill that dirty sonofabitch," Mom growls under her breath as the doctor inventories my injuries, which aren't really all that bad considering. My neck is bruised and covered in small lacerations from Shockey's nails, but thankfully he didn't have enough strength to do any permanent damage to my trachea. I am covered in contusions and muscles I didn't know existed are clamoring for attention, including my heavily bruised side, but the most serious injury is a mild concussion.

"Yes, well," the doctor says, looking uncomfortable at the naked fury in my mother's eyes. "We'll want to keep Derry here overnight, just for observation. She'll need someone checking on her vitals periodically and can only sleep in short bursts for the next twenty-four hours."

With a groan I reach up my free hand to rub the bridge of my nose, although it brings me no relief. The last thing I want is to be stuck in this hospital again, particularly when the man responsible for me being here is somewhere down the hall, hooked up to his own life-saving machines.

"Alright," Mom sighs, getting to her feet. She follows the doctor out to sign the admission forms and I am alone for the first time since the fight. The pulse monitor hooked up to my middle finger beeps steadily, and after a while the repetition lulls me into a drowsy state of indifference. When Mom returns I am barely awake, so she sits in the chair next to my bed and in a soft voice tells me about the antiques auction she is going to next week, describing the pieces she's going to try for, who she hopes to sell them to.

Eventually I drop off, only to be woken an hour later to give my statement to Officer Sowers, who is much gentler with his questions than the last time.

"And you say you have all of this on tape?" he asks eagerly.

"Yes, on my phone. I don't know what happened to it," I reply with sudden anxiety.

"It's fine, we have it in evidence. You told us at the scene, though you were a little incoherent." He gives me a kindly smile and I relax, knowing that recording is my ace in the hole.

"Okay. Yeah, he told me about Cathy. And raping Miranda." I pause, swallowing the lump in my throat. It hurts.

"And then he attacked you?"

"Right." I force my attention back on the moment. "Some of the fight is on the recording too."

Sowers gives me a calculating look. "Why do you think he told you all that? I mean, it's pretty unusual for someone to just dump a confession on a kid."

This is where things get tricky. "I don't know really. I just asked, and he answered. People tend to tell me things," I say, knowing I'm being cagey, but seeing no way around it.

Raising a skeptical eyebrow, Sowers resumes his questions, retrieving details from me about the fight and how Jake fit into the picture.

"How did Jake find me in time?" I asked, finally lucid enough to start wondering about his father's presence at the school.

"He said he left his backpack behind and came back for it. Apparently he heard sounds of a struggle and joined in just in time."

I remember Jake rushing after Cathy when the class ended and bless whatever hand of fate made him forget his bag. I have no doubt that I would be dead by now if he hadn't returned, and as much as the debt makes me uncomfortable, I'd rather be alive to repay it.

"Why was the mayor there?"

Sowers shrugs and puts his notebook and pen away. "Apparently Jake called him after calling 911. His dad beat us there."

Unsure of how to respond to this information, I change tactics.

"How's the investigation into Nicole's death going?" I ask, wondering if I might be able to get more out of Sowers than I have from Radcliffe, who has avoided me like the plague since our little conversation at the funeral home.

"You know I can't really talk to you about an ongoing investigation," Sowers chides gently. I turn my bruised face toward him, my eyes full of plea. He sighs and leans forward, speaking quietly. "But between us, not so great. The coroner has removed the accidental death ruling, but unless we can find where Nicole was injured, or link it to someone it's difficult to move forward."

I can hear the frustration in his voice and take heart. "What about Phillip? I've told you all that his car was there moments before I found Nicole; can't you search it or something?"

Sowers just shakes his head. "Your word is not enough for a warrant. There's nothing that ties him to Nicole just now. We'll keep an eye out, but it doesn't look good."

Smiling sadly, I nod, recognizing without more evidence, I'm never going to see Phillip pay for what he did to Nicole and Miranda. "Thanks anyway," I say, my eyes heavy from exhaustion and trauma. I know that in my dreams tonight, I will fight Shockey again and lose.

"You take it easy and quit getting into trouble, you hear? Come down to the station when you're feeling better so you can sign your statement." Sowers gets to his feet, brushing invisible lint from his dark slacks. "And between you and me," he adds softly, his eyes locking onto mine, radiating sincerity. "You watch out for that Phillip."

With a final nod to me, he leaves and the nurse enters to assault me with a penlight, the blinding light curling its way around my eyeballs and drilling into my skull.

"Your mom left just before he got here," the nurse hovering over me says, moving her finger back and forth, clearly asking me to follow it with my eyes. I oblige and submit to her other requests with as much grace as possible, which isn't much considering all I want is to go back to sleep. "She said to tell you she'd be back in the morning."

I thank the nurse and sink back into the pillow, preparing myself for an uncomfortable night. My neck is a raw ache and every breath I take sends fresh agony through my side. Even with the lights out and the curtain drawn, the faint light from the IV monitor elicits a stab of pain from my bruised head. I close my eyes and drift, neither awake nor sleeping but somewhere in between.

My eyes open and I sit halfway up before pain thrusts me down again. Blinking, I look around for whatever has woken me, but the room is drenched in shadow and my sleep-blurred vision makes everything muddled.

Something shifts to my left and I swing my head over, nearly crying out when pain slams into my skull from the movement. A dark figure rises from the chair and I wonder for a moment if my mother has come back, but menace stretches out sticky fingers and wraps around my neck, making my breath shallow and stuttered.

"You know, I bet I could smother you with that pillow before anyone would notice," Phillip says, his voice smooth and calm.

Dread pools in my stomach, frigid and deep. I reach to push the button that will call the nurse, but Phillip's hand is abruptly there, stopping me, turning my wrist so my palm is facing up, the angle a distinct threat. He looks at it, considering, and then begins to bend the wrist backward, winning a harsh gasp from me.

His shark's teeth gleam whitely in the dim light and for a moment I am trapped in the nightmare I've had so many times, with his reptilian green gaze fixed on me hungrily.

Phillip sighs and releases his aggressive grip, taking my hand in his like a lover's. "But then I'd have to explain what I'm doing here after hours and there would be awkward questions..." His eyes tighten with annoyance. "And I hate awkward questions."

"What do you want, Phillip?" I rasp, my throat nearly closed in fear.

"I want you to stop telling the police that I killed Nicole. They've been asking me about Miranda too, and I really don't appreciate it." His plastic face mimics a wounded expression. "I've been so nice to you. I don't know why you're acting like this."

His nonchalant mention of Nicole and Miranda stirs something in me. Fear burns away with mounting anger and I jerk my hand out of his, ignoring the slash along my side from the violence of my rejection.

"You killed Nicole, Phillip. I know it. And you don't scare me, not anymore." My voice is cold and unyielding and a brief flicker of uncertainty races behind his eyes before the bland mask regains control. He releases my hand and takes a step back. I immediately punch the button that will summon help and Phillip gives me a wry smile.

"Please reconsider what you think you know, Derry. I'd hate to see anything happen to you. After all, we're friends, aren't we?" He melts into the darkness and slips past the curtain seconds before it swings back with a burst of light and the nurse appears, her smile tired but friendly.

"I'm cheating on my husband," she says inquiringly. Relief washes over me and I realize just how much fear I was suppressing, no matter how brave a face I had put on for Phillip.

"Can I have some water?" I ask, conceding that there is little point in mentioning Phillip's visit. It was a warning anyway; I haven't pushed him to dire action just yet.

But I'm close.

# CHAPTER SEVENTEEN

"A RE YOU SURE YOU'RE UP for this?" Mom asks again, biting her lip with indecision. I have a flash of déjà vu, remembering how we sat just like this in the car, waiting outside the school on my first day. The same sense of uncertainty, of hidden peril hovers outside the window, misted into the fog that has gripped the town since early this morning.

"Yes, I'm fine," I assure her. On the whole, I'm being honest. My head is much better after three days of bed rest and my side barely twinges when I move now. Mom was reluctant to let me go back to school so soon, especially since I had only been back one day before being assaulted by my teacher. But I prevailed, mainly because I wouldn't shut up about it.

"Call me if anything happens or if you get scared." She hesitates and then gives me a one-armed hug, pulling me in at an awkward angle that stretches my side uncomfortably. I ignore it and take in the embrace. They are too rare to cut short.

"I will, I promise. I'll see you later," I say and jump out of the car before she has the chance to change her mind. After a final wave, I turn and climb the stairs, thinking I have known more sorrow and pain in this school than anywhere I've ever been.

I'm really starting to hate this place.

Once inside I feel as though I'm alone on a stage, a spotlight trained on my every movement. Eyes follow me wherever I go, whispers poking at the tender meat of my brain as I make my way through the crowd. Several people stop to say things to me; based on their sympathetic and encouraging expressions, I assume condolences or words of comfort and so I smile and nod, feeling like a hollow bobble-head doll. My head begins to pound from the harsh glare of the florescent lights bouncing off the reflective surface of the linoleum.

I make it to my first class early, not bothering to stop by my locker. Only a few seats are filled and I take mine, carefully avoiding the looks being thrown my way. Mrs. Sullivan gets up from her desk and strides over to me, casting a suppressing glare at the students who watch me closely from the other side of the room. Abashed, they return to their conversation. I pretend it's not about me.

"I was raped in college," Mrs. Sullivan says, her eyes warm with concern as she takes a seat in the empty desk to my left. I cough to cover my gasp and rub my hands over my eyes, trying to push back the tears that seem to be ever present.

"I'm sorry?" I say resignedly, beyond trying to figure out what was really said.

"I said I think you are very brave. Please, let me know if I can do anything for you. You've been through a rough time since coming here." She pats me gently on the shoulder before returning to the front of the class, nodding at the sudden influx of students.

I clench my jaw and stiffen my limbs as Phillip enters the room, his golden hair brushed back from slightly pink cheeks and emerald eyes. I wonder how I ever found him appealing. He makes my stomach turn now.

His eyes meet mine and he holds my stare as he maneuvers down the aisle, his approach sinuous and predatory. I force myself not to look away, not to show him how terrified he makes me. I haven't seen him since his impromptu hospital visit and I am on edge, waiting for his next move.

Dropping into his former seat behind me, Phillip reaches out a hand and strokes the fading bruise along my cheekbone. "I was so sorry to hear about your little altercation, Derry. You do have a habit of making the wrong people angry."

My breath hisses out of me like a punctured tire and I slap his hand away. "Don't touch me, Phillip. You don't scare me. Your little visit in the hospital just proved how twisted you really are."

He leans forward, pasting a confused expression on his face. "What are you talking about, Derry? I didn't come to see you. I wanted to, but I was afraid it would upset you. I know we've had our differences lately," he murmurs. I whip around, ignoring the stab of pain in my head and fix him with a severe look.

"Don't try that bullshit on me, Phillip. You and I both know you were there, and what you said," I whisper angrily, ignoring the quiet buzz of conversation around us, my whole universe centered on the treacherous glint in his eyes.

The faintest trace of a smirk pulls at his lips before he straightens up, his expression morphing seamlessly into bewildered concern. "Derry, I don't know what you're talking about. I know you've been traumatized recently, but please don't try to shift blame on me. I've been so worried about you," he declares, voice slightly raised, drawing the attention of the rest of the class.

I dart a glance around the room, taking in the avid faces of my classmates. They seem hungry, eager for conflict, and I realize the trap Phillip has set for me.

"You've had a head injury, Derry. It's no wonder you're confused. I just want to be here for you," he continues, his every breath mocking me, every word driving hot needles through my skin.

Though my classmates whisper, I can still hear them and the truths they are holding back, many of which indicate they believe I'm making everything up for attention. The injustice of this sears me from the inside out and for a moment I think I know how Jake feels when the rage overtakes him. The urge to dig my fingers into Phillip's neck, to watch panic flood his eyes as he struggles for breath is nearly overwhelming.

"You liar," I whisper, my voice low and furious. Phillip just raises his eyebrows and shakes his head at me sorrowfully.

"I think all this trauma has really messed with your head, Derry. You should be more careful." He holds my gaze for another moment and then turns away, digging through his bag, clearly dismissing me.

Shaking with rage, I turn around, facing forward, biting the inside of my cheek to keep from screaming. For a moment, I am filled with doubt. Did I imagine his appearance in the hospital? The whole thing was so surreal, almost dreamlike in my memory. The more I think about it, the more I wonder why the nurse hadn't said anything about seeing him. Or that no one had noticed him. Had our conversation just been one of my nightmares, made real from stress and pain?

I shift around to look at him again. He glances up and gives me a smile, his teeth glinting whitely. I narrow my eyes and turn back around. That way lies madness.

I am unable to concentrate on the rest of the class, Phillip's presence behind me making my skin buzz painfully the entire time, reminding me that nothing about him can be trusted.

When the tone finally sounds, I make a beeline for the door, needing to get as far away from him as possible. I nearly make it out the door, but a hand grips my arm in a painful squeeze and I halt, knowing without turning around it is Phillip.

"Derry, I don't want you to be angry with me. We need to work on our project, remember? Why don't we meet up this afternoon at the café by the tracks? I know that's one of your favorite spots," he suggests, eyes cold, like a creature that has never touched emotion, only lives with a view to kill.

"Get your hand off me," I growl, pulling away sharply. "I'm not Miranda. You can't break me." He releases me and I make my escape. I understand the threat. He knows where I like to go, tracks my movements. He can find me when he wants.

Biology is as slow and mind-numbing as usual, but at least no one bothers me. Even Tasha avoids my eyes, and when the period ends I am disappointed. It was peaceful for just a little while.

I head towards the cafeteria with a sense of dread, thinking that maybe I should just go find an empty classroom somewhere to eat. I turn around and start to do just that when I am interrupted.

"I'm sad that Phillip is interested in you," Ruth's voice penetrates my stupor of indecision and I wince. The last thing I want to do is hang out with anyone even remotely connected with Phillip.

"Hey Ruth," I mumble, looking for a way out of this conversation.

"Do you want to sit with me? Phillip said he thought you looked a little lost. He's very worried about you," she explains, gesturing to the back of the cafeteria where Phillip is sitting at a table, watching us. He lifts his hand in a wave and I feel my teeth grind together. He is toying with me. The way he played with Miranda before destroying her.

"No thanks, I..." I break off as Megan drops down at a nearby table and my shoulders slump in relief. "I'm joining Megan. But thanks," I say, hurrying over to the table before Ruth can protest.

Megan looks surprised to see me, but makes room at the table, gesturing me to an empty chair across from her. "I've got a crush on Shane," she says in the most civil tone I've heard her use to date. "How are you doing?"

"Okay. Wishing people would stop asking me that," I return with a smile. She gives me a sheepish grin, shaking her head.

"Yeah, I guess I would too in your position. Let me just say though, that Shockey is a creep and we all knew he was a perv. He deserves whatever he gets," she assures me. I appreciate the gesture, but thinking about his hands on me, the feral light in his eyes when he attacked sends a cold rush through me. I just nod and open my brown paper bag, fishing out the sandwich Mom made for me last night while she was still feeling domestic.

I am quiet through lunch, listening absently to Megan and her friends chatting and making appropriate noises every once in a while. The sandwich is lead in my stomach and the thought of three more hours of pretending everything is fine, ignoring the curious stares and barely whispered commentary is draining. I put my head in my hands and swallow, still feeling the stiffness in my throat from all the inflammation. The urge to call Mom and ask her to come pick me up drowns out the inner voice telling me to brave it out, to show everyone that it doesn't bother me, to show Phillip I'm not weak.

As though reading my thoughts, my phone buzzes in my bag, and I dig through it eagerly, hoping for some escape. A smile spreads across my face when I see the text message from Cole.

*I'm defying my father.*

I blink and the words reform.

*I'm outside the school. Come meet me?*

Without thinking too hard about it, I reply *YES!* and grab my things, standing up hurriedly.

"Where are you headed?" Megan asks curiously, noting my sudden change of mood.

"Gotta go," I answer, dumping the remains of my lunch in the trash and hurrying toward the doors to the student parking lot. I am almost home free when a voice calls out, stopping me in my tracks.

"I hate my brother," Jake says, hastening to my side, frowning. I stifle the surge of annoyance as he puts a hand on my shoulder. Whatever happened between us before, Jake did save my life. That counts for something.

"Hi, Jake. I'm just heading out," I say, taking a step forward, hoping he'll get the hint. He follows me and looks out the door to see Cole waiting on his motorcycle. Jake's face darkens with anger.

"So you're still going with him? Even though he didn't come for you? Have you forgotten who pulled that animal off you?" he growls, his fingers digging painfully into my shoulder.

"Jake, calm down. You're hurting me," I say in a calm voice, trying to talk him down before he loses control. The pressure on my shoulder eases but he doesn't let me go.

"You're mine," he snarls, turning me so I have to face him. The possessiveness in his tone is as alarming as the barely restrained strength of his grip.

"Jake, you're scaring me."

He takes a deep, shuddering breath and releases me, fisting his hands in his hair, face stiff with strain. "I don't know why I do this, I don't know why I want you so much," he finally whispers, his voice heavy with grief. I watch him, fighting the wave of pity that sweeps over me, urging me to put my arms around him.

"I don't understand it either, Jake. I don't want you to feel this way," I say quietly, wishing he could acknowledge the possibility that he is as gifted as his father and brother, learn to control it. But denial is written across his features and he just studies me with frustrated desire.

"I can feel you, all the time." He takes a step closer to me, brushing my bruised cheek gently with his knuckles. "You're in my head when I'm alone, and when I'm near you," he breathes in, inhaling my scent. "You are everywhere, dancing over my skin, churning in my blood. I don't want to hurt you, but you fight me and I just lose it." He fixes pleading eyes on me. "Stop fighting me, Derry. Please."

I am quaking, horrified, because deep down, some part of me wants to stop fighting him. My lips still remember his taste in my mouth, the heat of burnt cinnamon. My skin still trembles with the intense need I felt for him in that first moment, before rationality set in and told me that violence wasn't love, just a lethal attraction that led to nothing but dead ends and closed doors.

"I'm sorry, Jake. I'm so thankful for what you did, and I will always be grateful. But you frighten me, and until you get some control I can't be around you." I keep my voice gentle, soothing, praying that he will understand the words and not just hear the rejection.

"Miranda was scared of me too," he groans miserably, hand dropping away from my face. Forgetting Cole, who has stepped off his bike and is looking impatiently at the doors, I focus on Jake.

"What happened with her Jake? Did you have something to do with her death?" I ask quietly, but with the force of my will behind it. I am beginning to understand how much effort I have to put into the questions I really want answered.

He hesitates, and I can see him trying to deny it, but finally he blows out a breath and answers. "I don't know."

"What happened with her?" I repeat, vitally interested in the truth, believing this might be my best chance of getting it from him.

Jake's stormy blue eyes meet mine briefly before he looks down at the floor, misery diminishing him somehow, shrinking him in my eyes.

"I was so angry, all the time. I didn't used to be this way. Dad always said I was aggressive, but I had it under control. And then I just woke up one morning and everything pissed me off, all the time. Miranda was flirting with this guy at a party…she was wearing a skimpy bathing suit and he was ogling her…" he breaks off, fury charging his eyes, tremors of rage rolling down his arms.

"Jake, please," I whisper, putting my hand on his arm. He stares down at it for a moment and takes a deep breath, steadying himself.

"I lost it. I shoved her, harder than I meant to. I apologized, but she wouldn't hear it. She said if I'd do it once, I'd do it again, and she wasn't waiting around to be beaten on." His voice is almost incredulous, as though stunned that she could've believed such a thing. Denial so strong it adds to his rage.

"She was with Phillip and I knew something was wrong. She walked around like someone was going to hit her all the time, but she wouldn't talk to me. Nicole even told me she was worried, thought I should try to talk to Miranda. But everything I tried, she just shot down."

He shakes his head, remembering. I don't dare interrupt, seeing that he is lost in the memory, not really thinking of what he's saying. The halls are growing quieter around us as students leave the cafeteria for their lockers and the next class. It feels as though we are trapped in a glass bubble, held in stasis until the poison in Jake's mind can be released.

"Then she called me. She said she needed to tell me something, needed my help. She asked me to meet her on the walkway at the old train bridge that night. I came, but I was angry. I felt like she was jerking me around, using me for something."

He is quiet for a moment, and I prompt him, needing to see this story to its end. "What happened when you met her?"

Jake glances up at me, swirling blue depths begging me for something, forgiveness or absolution. "She wasn't on the walkway. She was standing at the edge of the old bridge, the one Dad had blocked off since it's so uneven and there are no supports. So I climbed the fence and came out with her. She just stood there for a while, staring down at the water, like it was whispering to her."

He rubs his face and I can see the reluctance to continue, but he does, little knowing he no longer has a choice.

"I asked her what she wanted, and she asked me if I still loved her." Jake's eyes shine with unshed tears before he blinks them away and shakes his head. "I told her she was a slut and I was glad to be rid of her."

I gasp and recoil instinctively as he reaches out for me, his hands bracing on my arms. "Why? Why did you say that?" I demand, disbelief racing through me even as I feel the truth of his words.

"Because she left me! Because she chose someone else and then let him turn her into this frightened bunny. She didn't want *me*, she just wanted something from me. So I wanted to hurt her. But I didn't touch her, I swear."

Suddenly the need to hurt Jake is more than I can bear, choking my air supply, burning through my skin like acid. He has to know what she wanted to tell him. He should carry that guilt, the way I carry mine.

"She was going to tell you that Shockey raped her. She was going to tell you that Phillip threatened to hurt Nicole, that he had been methodically tormenting her for weeks. He held a damn gun to her head! She needed you, Jake! What did you ever do for her? She was damaged, broken, and that's what you said to her?"

Jake staggers away from me, fresh horror wiping all other emotion from his face as my words sink in. He shakes his head dumbly, staring at me, begging me to take it back, but I just glare at him, feeling the weight of the injustice of Miranda's last moments press against my mind.

"What did you do, Jake? What did you do then, when she needed you most?" I hiss, my rage rivaling his.

"I told her she could jump off the bridge before I'd do a damn thing for her, and I left. I left her there on the bridge. And she was dead in the morning," he sobs, dropping to his knees, wrapping his arms around my hips and burying his face in my stomach. Deep, heaving rasps rack his body as I stare down at him in disgust. Even if he didn't push her off the bridge, he left her there to die. Either by Phillip's hand or her own.

Jake's hands are not clean of her death.

"Let me go, Jake," I say quietly, glad that the halls are empty and no one has come looking for us. Out the doors I can see Cole striding towards us, obviously intent on finding me. Thanks to the reflective glass, I know he can't see the scene playing out so close to him, and I am glad. I don't know how he would react to seeing Jake and me like this. It wouldn't be pretty.

Jake doesn't respond, just keeps his face pressed against me, clutching my hips as a drowning man clings to a rock. After a moment, my anger with him fades and all I can feel is pity. He failed the one he loved. I can relate.

I place a hand on his head and stroke his hair, the silky strands parting under my fingers. Jake gives a deep sigh and his body stills, and I can feel him regaining control.

The door swings open and Cole sees us, his eyes going dark as his gaze settles on his half-brother.

"He's trying to take you away from me," he growls, marching forward, leaking fear like heavy cologne.

"Cole, please," I beg, panic pushing through my mind with all the subtlety of a battering ram. Instantly it disappears as Cole locks it down, pausing to take a calming breath. Jake finally releases me and stands between us, all traces of grief gone in a sudden blaze of anger.

"Get away from her, Jake," Cole warns, stepping toward him, fists clenched. Jake just tightens his jaw and moves closer to me, clearly staking a claim.

Abruptly I am too tired to deal with all the posturing, all the drama. I've been through enough in the past couple weeks to last a lifetime and all I want is a pair of strong arms to hold me, to take my burdens for a little while. "Take me home, Cole."

Both of them look at me, almost as if they've forgotten I'm here, apart from being some piece of meat they can tear between the two of them. Irritation sticks in my gut and I pull away from Jake and start walking past Cole, aiming for his bike. If he won't take me home, I'll drive the damn thing myself.

"I don't belong to either of you, so just drop it. For God's sake, you barely know me," I toss back over my shoulder, pushing my way out into the chill winter air, the breeze kissing my face cleanly. After a moment, the door opens again and Cole runs to catch up with me.

"I'm sorry, Derry. He has that effect on me." I nod my acceptance of his apology and wait patiently for him to start up the bike and hand me a helmet.

"Do you ever drive a car? I mean, we've had six feet of snow in the past month and I've never seen you in something with four wheels."

Cole laughs and squeezes my hands around his waist as he kicks the cycle into gear. "I'll get one if it'll make you happy," he promises and the rest of his words are lost in the wind as the school disappears behind us and our speech is swallowed by the road.

The sky trembles on the edge of nightfall, clinging to the last vestiges of sunlight disappearing over the mountains, shifting a purple-hued sunset into velvety black. It reminds me of some evenings back home in Williamsburg where the dense patches of forest would eat every trace of light until the darkness was tangible, a primeval force that crouched just out of sight, ready to strike.

I huddle on the stone steps outside the store, burrowing into the high collar of my coat and staring down at the leather-bound journal in my gloved hands. Guilt squats inside me, thick and disapproving, the taste acrid on my tongue. Somewhere in the night Phillip is walking around free, smiling his shark's smile, gloating that one more day has passed since he murdered Nicole and no one can touch him.

I read through Miranda's diary again while tending the store this evening. Mom left me in charge while she went on her long awaited date with Cole's father. Nothing I said could convince her to skip it. Even when I told her I wasn't feeling well. She just gave me a skeptical look and said I'd spent enough time in bed.

Cole stayed with me for a while, but had to go to work eventually. Our conversation had been stilted at best, downright uncomfortable at times.

"Why didn't you come like you promised?" I had finally asked, wanting to hear the truth from him rather than his brother.

He sighed and rubbed his face wearily. "My dad. The principal called him when he caught me sneaking in and Dad commanded me to go home and stay there until he got back. I had no choice."

"Is it really that absolute? There's no way of fighting him off?" I had asked, dubious.

Cole just shook his head sadly. "No. Not for me, not for Jake. It hurts when I try to disobey him, like my blood is on fire, boiling inside me. It's incapacitating." He grabbed my hands and gave me an earnest look. "I'm so sorry, Derry. It's all my fault. I should have been more careful coming in, but I was worried and didn't pay attention to my surroundings. I hate that I have to be grateful to Jake, but I'm so glad he got there in time. I swear I tried," he had pleaded, sapphire eyes boring into mine.

"I understand," I told him, but part of me didn't. Part of me still wonders if he could've fought harder. I felt myself withdraw from him slightly in that moment.

With the cold front still gripping Harpers Ferry and the gorgeous snow from the week before melted into soggy piles of grey and brown at the sides of the road, foot traffic was meager and business was slower. I had plenty of time to read Miranda's self-deceiving words, the false picture she painted for herself while pretending that her world wasn't disintegrating in her hands. I thought it might be less painful to read now that I would no longer see the truth behind the words, but the image of a broken red-haired doll clutching a pen stuck in my mind and I cried almost as much as I did the first time.

A frigid wind blasts me and I give up, unlocking the shop and standing behind the door, leaving the lights out, watching across the street for the moment Cole will get off work and come to take me home. He promised tonight we would talk about how to get evidence about Phillip to the police. Cole even swore if it came down to it, he would plant something of Nicole's in Phillip's car, just so a warrant could be issued.

I will do anything at this point. Every moment Phillip walks free is an insult to Nicole and a danger to me.

I lean my head against the icy glass door and watch down the street as a car pulls alongside the curb by the pizza parlor. Something about the way the left light flickers is familiar and I freeze, my entire body on point.

The headlights I saw on the access road the night Nicole died had that slight flicker.

As I watch, breathless, Phillip emerges from the car, his blond hair picking up the faint glow from the dim streetlamps overhead. His profile is in shadow, but I know the way he moves. He glances up the street toward the store before he stuffs his keys in his coat pocket and enters the restaurant.

Suddenly I am sprinting down the street, jerking to a stop outside the pizza place to peer inside. Phillip stands at the counter, talking to the cashier and pointing overhead at the menu on the wall. My heart skitters and leaps in a manic pattern as I back away, glancing about the street to see if anyone else is around.

The night is silent and for once I feel like I'm in the right place at the right time. I stalk over to his car and say a silent prayer, hoping that he didn't bother to lock it. I try the passenger door, but have no luck. In frustration, I squint into the dark interior, looking for any way to open the car and catch my breath as I see the rear door behind the driver's side is unlocked, the button extended past its mates. Tossing a cautious glance over my shoulder I walk around to the other side of the car, hoping if anyone does happen to pass by, nothing will look suspicious.

I stuff the journal inside my coat and gently pry the door open, my pulse racing and making my head spin. Adrenaline is pumping through me and for a moment I feel invincible, powerful. I reach up and flick off the interior light so I won't be given away, and lean into the car, looking for the best place to stash the journal where Phillip won't notice it but will still count as in plain sight. Once Phillip gets back in his car, I'll call Detective Radcliffe and tell him I noticed the journal Nicole had shown me the day she died in his car. That should be enough to get them a search warrant, and I have to believe there is some other evidence in this car that will link Phillip to Nicole's death.

I decide to put it under the back of the driver's seat, sticking out onto the floor just enough that I can claim to have seen it. Shame twists ugly fingers in my gut as I really consider what I am about to do. Two months ago I would never have imagined I would even think of planting evidence of a murder in a classmate's car, but in my fear I have become reckless in my quest for vengeance.

A sharp cry startles me and I pull out of the car just in time to see Phillip racing toward me, the café door slamming home behind him, light spilling out from the doorway to illuminate the unadulterated rage etched on his face. I suck in a breath and turn to run, but he leaps on me and knocks me to the ground, slapping my forehead against the cobblestones.

Everything is dark and fuzzy, black swirls twisting sickly through my vision and I feel myself being lifted and shoved, my shoulder landing against something hard before another blow smashes into my face and the world goes black.

I come to with a start and immediately lunge for the door, the handle standing out with stark clarity in the center of a blur, as though the only thing my bruised brain is capable of focusing on is a way out. Phillip curses viciously before swinging the car off the road violently enough to knock me back again. He shoots out of the car and I scramble for the door, planning to kick him and run. But the door behind me opens instead and his arm is around my neck, pulling me into an unforgiving embrace that cuts off my air and sends dark spots flashing before my eyes.

"You stupid bitch, you couldn't leave well enough alone, could you? I was going to take my time with you, do things clean this time, but you forced my hand. Shit, this is going to be hard to cover up," Phillip snarls, his breathing labored. I strike out at him with everything I have, knowing if I lose consciousness this time I will likely not recover. "You and that freak Nicole just keep pushing me. Calling me a murderer, drawing attention to me. I didn't even kill Miranda and you bitches won't quit! Now I've got get rid of you too, and this is going to be a pain in the ass to clean up." He sounds more annoyed than anything.

My struggle is getting weaker, my arms barely flailing and my kicks failing to accomplish anything. A stone sits where my lungs should be, and I feel my eyes bulging out of my skull, trying to release the terrible pressure in my head. My fingers catch something solid and I dig my nails in, raking them across Phillip's neck, feeling the skin rip and catch beneath my clawed hands.

His arm-lock around my neck tightens and my arms go limp. He is still growling, cursing me, cursing Nicole, but I am drifting on a sea of misery, agonized gasps barely clearing my lips as the darkness descends again and the emerald glow of Phillip's eyes dims and sputters out.

I am cold and cramped, my knees bent at an awkward angle, as though I have been stuffed into a box too small for me. I blink my eyes open but nothing greets my vision apart from darkness so complete it is suffocating. Panic races through me and I reach out only to meet a solid wall inches above my face, solid and metallic. Great gulps of air punch into me and I begin to hyperventilate, sure I have been buried alive, that somehow I am trapped in the ground with Miranda and Nicole, planted in some psychotic version of a garden in Phillip's backyard.

The sound and sense of movement gradually bring me back, and once my breathing subsides, I can hear the rumble of the wheels rolling beneath me and realize I am in the trunk of his car. Somehow I am awake and alive, probably being transported somewhere more secluded so Phillip can murder me in privacy. A sob escapes me, scorching my aching throat, my neck so tender I am sure whatever injuries Shockey left me with have grown more serious after Phillip's handling.

I think of Nicole, lying in this very trunk, paralyzed but still alive, bleeding and broken, knowing she wouldn't escape, that I didn't come for her in time and grief overwhelms me with sharpness that exceeds any discomfort my body suffers. With pain comes some clarity and I push past the panic to try and think, think of anything I can do to save myself.

Groaning with effort, I pat my hands around, feeling the inside of the trunk for a weapon or way out. My efforts meet with nothing and the panic redoubles as I realize I have no idea how long I've been out or how much time I have left before Phillip reaches his destination and comes to finish me. I reach around frantically, finding where the trunk should open, but am unable to locate a catch or release switch. Cursing the idiotic impulse that drove me to break into the car in the first place, I bite my lip to keep from screaming in frustration and command myself to focus.

Two years ago Mom and I were pulled over for a burnt out taillight and we had to get the police officer to show us how to replace the bulb. He didn't give us a ticket, mainly because I think he recognized how incompetent Mom was when it came to cars, but he explained that most cars have panels inside the trunk that hide the wiring for the lights and all we had to do was pull the bulb out through the panel and screw a new one in before reinserting the whole thing.

I shift so I am generally facing the front of the trunk, toward where I believe the taillights must be. Running my hands over the carpeted surface, I feel for anything out of the ordinary, anything that might signal a panel. The car rocks as the wheels pass over an uneven surface and I clutch the edge of the fabric to keep myself from rolling. I feel the material pull slightly, giving against the pressure and I yank harder until a space is cleared enough for me to feel around beneath it.

Seconds pass by in tortured breaths, my body protesting the way I lay, the queasy ache in my head, the throbbing of my neck; but at last I feel something, a dip in the floor I can stick a finger beneath. Stretching, I pull up and feel it give way, and a nest of wires rests beneath my hand. Nearly sobbing in relief, I haul at the wires, not having any way of figuring out what each one is for, just praying that they connect to what I need.

The wires catch on something and I change the angle, curving my wrist so that I can thread them all the way out. After an eternity, a brilliant stab of light pierces the gloom of the trunk and I am nearly blinded by the tiny bulb of the taillight. My face is wet with tears as I blink furiously, trying to adjust my vision.

The enclosure comes into focus, the light weaker than I initially believed, but still enough to illuminate most of the space into which I am crowded. Seeing the finite space in the light does something to my breathing, as though my body is trying to shrink my lungs to fit and it takes me precious moments to regain control, to convince myself there is still air in the trunk. My nostrils burn and there is a chemical smell emanating from the carpet that seems stronger the longer I am in here.

My hands shake, making the light bounce erratically as I search for anything that could be used as a weapon, but I am sorely disappointed. There is a windbreaker shoved into the corner and an empty soda cup from a fast-food restaurant, and nothing else. A howl of frustration nearly escapes me, but I keep quiet, knowing the longer Phillip believes me to be unconscious, the better. I'm not sure where he's taking me or if he even has a plan, but I feel certain he'll be moved to hurry up the inevitable if I draw attention to myself.

Miranda's journal pokes into my bruised side and I reach for it, whimpering at the odd angle. Pulling the book out, I put it on the trunk floor, thinking bitterly I managed to plant the evidence after all. Much good it would do me.

The light slips from my hand and I clutch the roof to keep from being tossed around as the car swerves wildly before accelerating. He has made a decision. My time is growing short.

With my hand on the journal I take a deep breath, wincing at the pain in my side. My head swims and nausea threatens to cause a tumult in my stomach. I briefly consider trying to cut myself on something, to leave a trace of my blood in the hope that someone might eventually check this trunk for evidence. If I can't take Phillip down, at least maybe I'll succeed from beyond the grave.

Even as I think it, I recognize my thoughts are getting away from me, the air is growing denser and harder to swallow; my body is fighting exhaustion and concussion. I have never been hurt this much in so short a time in my life, and it is catching up with me. Forcing myself to take deep, even breaths, I clench my hands into fists and shift around until I think I'll be able to kick when the trunk opens. I know this is my only chance now, to surprise Phillip and maybe get far enough away to call for help. Pushing aside the pain and terror, I tense my body, coiled and ready to strike.

The thundering movement of the wheels below me slows and grows steadier, as though Phillip is suddenly taking more care with his driving. And then I hear it, the most beautiful sound, music so exquisite tears stream down my face, dropping home on the rough fabric beneath my cheek.

A police siren.

The sound is slightly muted in the trunk, but there is no mistaking the banshee wail that slices through the rumbling of the tires, the groan of the road. I pray, silently and fervently, and weep with relief when I feel the car drift to the side, slowing gradually into a halt. I can picture Phillip sitting in the driver's seat, confident I'm unconscious or dead in the trunk, but perhaps there is a tinge of fear in those green eyes, a tightness to his sculpted lips, the taste of uncertainty on his tongue.

As soon as I hear the muffled thump of a car door closing I scream with everything I have, pounding and kicking on the roof of the trunk with frantic force, unexpected strength coursing through me. I scream for Miranda, for the pain she never shared, for the time she lost. I scream for Nicole, for her fury and vengeance, for the loss of something I barely had. I scream until my tortured throat is on fire and still push past it.

The trunk opens.

# CHAPTER EIGHTEEN

"I KNEW THIS KID WAS A psycho," Officer Sowers's voice cries out over me, shock written all over his face. He immediately extends a hand and I grab it, using his weight as leverage to pull myself out of the trunk. I come to my feet trembling, knees nearly giving out beneath me, but the shell-shocked officer steadies me, pulling me around to the side of the car.

"You stay right there, and don't move. You've got a lot of explaining to do," he shouts at Phillip. Sowers turns to me, concern creasing his face. "Derry, are you alright? What happened?"

I glance over at Phillip, fear coursing through me in a painful burst as I take in his murderous expression. He is leaning against the passenger door, hands and legs spread. Humiliation burns in his eyes and I know he is imagining all the ways he will punish me for it.

Something occurs to me, looking at where he is standing. "Officer Sowers," I gasp, my voice raspy and grating. "Phillip has a gun in his glove compartment."

Phillip registers surprise before he lunges for the door handle, his quickness startling, but Sowers releases me and pins Phillip to the car again, his hand pressed into the back of his neck as he growls warnings in his ear.

"Move again, creep. Go ahead." Sowers pulls his radio out of his belt and calls dispatch. "Sowers here. I've got the Bennett kid pulled over on Broken Ridge. He had Derry MacKenna in his trunk." He glances my way again. "I assume you didn't want to be in there?" he asks dryly.

I snort, wondering where Sowers got his sense of humor. "No, I really didn't." Suddenly the opportunity is too perfect, the kind of moment I've been waiting for since the certainty of Phillip's guilt took hold. "Officer, when I was in the trunk, I saw something in there…I think it was a journal Nicole had. She said it was Miranda's."

Sowers gives me an incredulous look before an expression of deep satisfaction settles. "Notify Detective Radcliffe of our location. There may be evidence he needs to see," he says into his radio.

Tears leak onto my cheeks, turning frigid as the cold air hits them, but I don't care. I've done it. Shockey is in the hospital with a collapsed lung, a prolonged stay in a prison infirmary in his future. Phillip will go to jail for kidnapping me. Miranda's journal will tie him to Nicole's death, and I have no doubt that there are fibers and other forensic things in that trunk that will tie the noose. My knees collapse under me and I sag against the car, openly sobbing, relief pumping through me faster than my blood. Sowers gives me a troubled look and then drags Phillip by his collar back to the police cruiser a few feet away. After securing Phillip in handcuffs in the back of the car, Sowers returns to me, eyes surveying me for hidden damage.

He asks me something, but all I can do is laugh. I hear the hysteria in it, the uncontrolled note that has him worried, but the release is exquisite and I revel in it, savoring the lessening of the terrible weight that has held my head down for so long.

I am still laughing weakly when Detective Radcliffe makes it to the scene, followed by an ambulance. Seeing it, I groan and get to my feet, determined to convince the powers that be I have no need of medical attention. The thought of another ride in the back of that tin can while my head is pounding like this sends a shudder through me. I reach up to feel the lump on my forehead where I hit the cobblestones. It's pronounced, but there's no bleeding, so I have hopes that I can just go home and curl up with an ice pack and a Tylenol.

"I am scared of you," Detective Radcliffe says in greeting, walking directly to me, his eyes taking in my bedraggled appearance. "It seems you've gotten yourself in another pickle."

"Not on purpose, Detective."

He snorts and nods his head. "Right. So, Officer Sowers here tells me you found something while you were hanging out in the trunk?" He gestures toward the still open trunk and I walk over with him, gaining more stability with each step. Out of the corner of my eye, I see my paramedic friend from a few days ago move toward me, but Radcliffe waves him off, clearly placing priority on evidence over my health.

We stand in front of the open trunk and I point directly at the journal I had placed in the back. "Nicole showed me that the day she died. She said it was Miranda's and it made her think Phillip had something to do with Miranda's death." I pause, remembering some of Phillip's furious ramblings while he was choking me to death. He had said he hadn't killed Miranda. My stomach twists uneasily. At that point, moments before he planned to kill me, there was no reason for him to lie. He confessed he murdered Nicole, so why hold back about Miranda?

I drag myself back to the moment, deciding to worry about his culpability later. Either way, he is going to jail and everyone will know what a monster he is.

Radcliffe uses his gloves to lift the journal out of the trunk and opens it tenderly, as though afraid to disturb any lingering traces of the girl whose thoughts lay dormant within. He flips through the book cautiously, his eyes widening and mouth turning down in distress as Miranda's shaky mental state and evidence of Phillip's abuse is laid out in black and white. Even though the words on the paper don't really reflect what she felt when she wrote them, there is still enough angst to give a pretty clear picture.

"Sowers, get the kit from my trunk," Radcliffe barks, his eyes drifting over to me with curiosity, as though he is really seeing me for the first time. "You're a deep one, aren't you? What were you doing around Phillip's car anyway?"

I don't even try to make something up. I have a feeling being knocked unconscious and stuffed in a trunk will outweigh my original plans. "Honestly, I was trying to get into his car. I was hoping to find some evidence that would link him to Nicole, to get something that would warrant a search."

Radcliffe nods and a smile quirks the edges of his mouth. "That was stupid. But I get it," he says quietly, eyes washing over me with approval. "Quick thinking with the taillight."

I beam under his praise, the pain in my head growing slightly dimmer. "Thanks. I didn't really think it would work," I admit, still wondering what lucky stroke of fate led a police cruiser to be waiting along whatever off the beaten path Phillip had brought me on. We are on a narrow road sandwiched between a tall fence of trees and a cliff face, the sound of gently moving water tickling the edge of my hearing. I have no idea where we are.

"It might not have if I hadn't had every officer on the force keeping an eye on him," Radcliffe reveals nonchalantly. I stare at him open-mouthed and he releases a reluctant chuckle.

"You're not the only one who thought there was something off about that kid. In questioning…he just seemed too pleased with himself. It didn't sit right. And we knew Nicole's wound couldn't have been self-inflicted…" he trails off, giving me a sharp look. "Now that information is not for the general public, young lady. How do you get people to tell you these things?" he asks as Sowers returns with what looks like a plastic briefcase.

"Just a gift, I guess," I answer, finally allowing the paramedic to drag me to the back of the ambulance where he clucks over my injuries, reminding me that my head has taken one too many knocks in the past few days.

A few minutes later Radcliffe strides toward me, muttering into his radio. "I'm sick at heart over the dead girl," he says quietly, and tears prick my eyes at his unwitting honesty. I feel guilty that I suspected this big-hearted, if gruff, man of being negligent or uncaring. If I had been frustrated knowing that Phillip was walking around free because of lack of evidence, I could only imagine how Radcliffe must have felt, allowing him to leave the police station unhampered.

"I'm sorry that you had to go through all this Miss MacKenna. I know you've had a tough time of it. But you being trapped in that trunk is the best thing that could've happened in this case," he says, putting his big hand on my shoulder for an awkward pat. "There's old blood in the trunk. Looks like he tried to clean it, maybe with bleach, but the Luminol picked it up. My money is on it belonging to Nicole. I owe you thanks, young lady."

He tips his hat to me and tells the paramedic to quit wasting time and get me to the hospital. I beg for them to let me go home, but no one listens and once again I endure the loudest, most bone-jarring ride of my life.

I am arguing with the doctor, who has become familiar enough for me to address on a first name basis when my mother and Geoffrey Wise walk in. Mom immediately races for me, taking my bruised head into her arms and sobbing in great, unintelligible gulps. I can hear the loss of control balancing on a precipice in her voice and know she has been pushed too far. No matter how complicated our relationship, Mom loves me, and me nearly dying three times in one month has pushed her to the limit. I stroke her hair and mutter soothing words, my eyes on Geoffrey and his speculative expression.

"I'm going make you work for me," he says, voice full of sympathy. I bare my teeth at him.

"I should've been there to save you," Jake says, joining us in the over-crowded room, bumping up against the blood pressure monitor before shifting back to the wall. I suppress a sigh and give him a tight smile. I really want to go home and get in my own bed.

"Jake was worried about you, so I told him he could come by. I hope you don't mind," Geoffrey says, watching me greedily. Pretty soon he and I are going to have a long conversation; one where I ask some leading questions and he gives me honest answers.

"Where's Cole?" I demand, ignoring the flash of hurt on Jake's face. Geoffrey's face darkens at the mention of his other son and I wonder what it is about Cole that makes him so antagonistic.

"He had to stay home, unfortunately. I'm sure you'll see him when you're feeling better," he answers. My skin hums with the lie.

The doctor huffs, having had enough of the bizarre family dynamic going on, and shoos everyone but my mother out of the room. He proceeds to tell her although I have collected a new set of bruises to go with my already heavily decorated body, I don't seem too much worse for the wear. Apparently the forehead is not as bad a place to be hit as the back of the head, so my concussion is holding steady at only a seven on the agony scale.

Small favors.

There are raised voices in the hallway and then I hear it, the deeply compelling sound of Geoffrey Wise's words of command. "Go home now, Cole."

My heart picks up its pace, making the machines I'm hooked up to screech in alarm. The weight of Geoffrey's order pushes against me and even Mom stands up and looks as though she is about to walk out.

The curtain parts and Cole steps in, his face red, sweat beaded along his forehead, strain and effort in every movement as he plods toward me, his legs moving slow and stiff as though trapped in sand. He is fighting his father's compulsion.

Fighting for me.

I reach out my hand and take his, entwining our fingers. He takes a shuddering breath and then moves forward uninhibited, as though he has thrown off the knotted rope that was holding him back. Giving me a weary smile, he leans over and presses his lips to mine, the touch gentle and demanding all at once. When he pulls away, I am shaky and short of breath, forgetting everyone else standing around arguing, my eyes fixed on his.

"I love you," he whispers and I feel something wild and hopeful in my chest, a promise being born. Whatever he has really said doesn't matter and I don't want to know. I hold on to this moment and don't let go.

# CHAPTER NINETEEN

"WHAT DO YOU THINK WE are?" I ask Cole, leaning against him, feeling the warmth of his arms surround me. He stands behind my chair, dropping his chin on my head. It has been a week since the night Phillip was arrested and he has been in custody since. Cole has been with me practically every waking moment. He hasn't been to work all week, saying he'd rather stay with me at the store. Mom hasn't started paying him, but I'm pretty sure she'll cave soon. She likes having him around to carry the big stuff to clients' cars.

"What do you mean?" he asks, kissing the nearly faded bruise on my forehead before coming around to sit on the counter. I push back the display of thumb rings Mom has sitting by the cash register in hopes of attracting younger customers and give him a knowing look.

"Exactly what I asked. Why are we the way we are? Why can we do the things we do? Haven't you ever wondered?"

Cole rolls his eyes and smiles. "Of course I've wondered. I asked my dad, but he just mumbled something about superior genetics. I guess it's just never been that important to me." He shrugs and picks up one of the rings to twirl around his finger.

I sigh and watch the older couple across the room study a hope chest Mom picked up at an auction yesterday. The woman is busy examining the inlay on the wood, but her husband watches her, his eyes warm and affectionate, his hand resting gently on her back. She turns and glances up at him and an entire conversation takes place between them, a lifetime of exchanges that lead to the same conclusion; they will do whatever makes the other happy. It's a beautiful sort of normalcy, made extraordinary by its consistent predictability.

A sharp pang of jealousy slices through me and I turn to look at Cole. He smiles at me, his entire face lighting, softening his hard edges, bringing the sapphire gleam in his eyes into focus. The jealousy fades and I find myself once again wondering what on earth I've done to deserve that expression on his face, the sweet intensity of his gaze.

"I know what you're thinking," he says teasingly, brushing my cheek with his lips, breath tickling my ear.

"Oh yeah? What's that?" I ask archly, leaning into him and pulling in his scent, dark citrus and spice.

"You're thinking you'll never get to be normal like them. That because of your talent you'll always be alone, on the fringes."

I pull away and look up at him, startled at his insight. "How did you know that?"

"Because I was thinking it too, just for a second. But you're wrong, Derry. We'll get a taste of normal." He hops off the counter as the couple approaches, their smiles bringing an answering grin to my face. "I'll make sure of it," Cole whispers.

I stand at the overlook where Nicole and I had our conversation the day she died. The last time I spoke with her, laughed with her. All the snow has melted and the bare trees are desolate without their frosting. Everything around me is stark and cold, but I ignore the despondency that threatens to creep into my chest. I have come here every evening since I got out of the hospital, looking for something, thinking maybe I could get a sense of completion, a final answer.

Nicole's mother came to see me at the store today. The sight of her red-rimmed eyes and haggard appearance brought up a surge of guilt that nearly choked me.

"Today is the first day I've gotten out of bed since the funeral," she had said, her voice slightly wobbly.

I glanced at Cole and he nodded at me encouragingly, so I assumed she had said something normal, like *hello*, or *can I talk to you for a moment*.

Cole had come closer to me, prepared to give support, but I sent him away, knowing whatever Beverly had to say to me, I deserved.

Once Cole had disappeared into the back stockroom, she came behind the counter and put an awkward hand on my arm, as though she had forgotten how to touch another human being.

"Derry, I came to tell you that I'm so sorry for the things I said. I would've come before, but to be honest, I was ashamed." My skin was quiet with her sincerity and I shook my head at her, wondering how she could think even for a moment she owed me an apology.

"Mrs. Sharp, I…"

"No dear, don't interrupt. This isn't easy for me." She sighed and then steeled her shoulders, determination finding its way into her expression. "Nicole would be furious with me over how I've treated you. And I was wrong. Yes, you could've handled things better, but you're young, and we don't always make the best decisions when we're young. You did what you thought was best for Nicole, and I know losing her has been…difficult for you."

Tears flowed freely down my face while I just continued to shake my head at her, unable to respond. She squeezed my arm once and let me go, already pulling away.

"I'm sorry if you got into danger with Phillip because of guilt over what I said. I never wanted you to put yourself in harm's way. But I want to thank you for finding out the truth. You can't know what it means to Nicole's father and me, knowing she didn't want to leave us." Beverly drew in a harsh breath and bit her trembling lip, trying to stay in control. "Thank you, and take care of yourself."

She had hurried out the door and down the street before I could protest, leaving me alone with my tumultuous thoughts, robbed of the chance to beg for forgiveness once more.

I look over the water and think of Nicole, of her quick laugh when no one was watching, of the ferocity of her loyalty, the glimpse of real friendship she gave me. Tears slide down my cheeks and I know I am saying goodbye to her. Somehow, I think she would understand.

My gaze shifts and I am looking over at the defunct train bridge where Miranda took her last step. Phillip has confessed to Nicole's murder, although of course he claims it was an accident and he was too afraid to call the police. Not sure how he's explaining my presence in his trunk, but I feel certain he's got a perfectly reasonable defense. I doubt it'll do him much good; Officer Sowers told me in private there was a lot of evidence tying Phillip to Nicole's death.

But he swears he had nothing to do with Miranda, and so far his alibi for that night checks out. Despite Nicole's blind certainty, despite my own disgust for his broken morality, even I must admit it seems he had nothing to do with Miranda's fall.

The loud rushing of the river below calls my attention again and I stare down into its swirling depths, the cold purity strangely appealing; an answer more final and absolute than any I could conceive. Miranda's death is a question I will probably never resolve. A truth I will never grasp. I stare down at the water and wonder what she saw in it, if there had been an answer deep under the surface that called to her, or if she simply slipped and cried out for another chance as the current took her under.

My phone buzzes in my pocket and I pull myself away from dark thoughts to see the calls I've missed. Cole and my mother, both within minutes of one another. Remembering Mom's shattered expression when she saw me in the hospital bed for the third time, I know losing me would have broken her, and I shudder to think of her wandering around angry and guilty like Nicole's mother. Or simply packing my things away in despair the way Miranda's mother did.

A reluctant smile pulls at my lips and I send them both text messages promising I'm on my way home.

Casting a final glance at the river, I whisper, "Goodbye, Nicole. Goodbye, Miranda."

I walk back to the store, to my home, my stride lighter with each step, the burning knot of guilt and rage in my chest only a faint ember now. I fought for them, and now there are people who will fight for me, who will keep me from stumbling off whatever bridge tempts me with long-denied answers.

When we take that icy plunge, we are not the only ones who drown.

# ACKNOWLEDGMENTS

FIRST, LET ME JUST THANK all who took a chance on a self-published author and picked up my book. It's absolutely terrifying to take something you've put so much work into, so much love and effort, and throw it out to sea, hoping that someone will notice and grab hold. So thanks to all the readers, please stick with me and support other indie authors as well.

I've got to thank my parents for being so supportive. They read everything I write and always give me honest, constructive feedback. They are my editors, my biggest cheerleaders, and have put up with me yammering on about all the various characters trying to get space in my head for years now. I love them so much and am beyond lucky to have such a great support system.

I also need to thank my Uncle Frank, super-cop, who checked over my book for inconsistencies and gave me some great advice about making the murder investigation more believable. He is one of many in my family who have been supportive and uncomplaining beta-readers, so thanks!

Thank you to Payton for being such a wonderful cover model, and thanks to her mom Amie for taking the photo. You are two wonderful ladies, and thanks for your support! And a huge thank you to Kim at The Killion Group for creating such a stunning cover design.

Thank you to Bev, who has been tireless in helping me promote my books, and is such a supportive friend and reader. You are awesome, lady!

Also, a big thanks to the people at the information desk in Harpers Ferry for not arresting me when I asked questions about pushing people off a bridge.

Being a self-published author is kind of like staggering around an obstacle course in the dark, and there are many people who help to shed light when I need it. I have been fortunate enough to get wonderful advice and support from fellow authors; truly, there is no one kinder or more supportive than a fellow author! Thanks also to all the bloggers who have hosted my books and recommended them, and all the reviewers who have been so kind. And finally, I have tremendous gratitude and admiration for all the other indie authors out there who have paved the way and keep inspiring others to follow their examples. Keep the lights burning.

# ABOUT THE AUTHOR

MATTIE DUNMAN IS A LIFELONG resident of "Wild & Wonderful" West Virginia, and has dreamed of being a writer since she first held a pen in hand.

A self-published author, Mattie has pursued several useless degrees to support this dream, and is presently lost in the stacks of her local library. She spends most of her free time writing, but also indulges in reading and traveling.

She is the proud owner of an adorably insane American Eskimo named Finn, tyrannical orange tabby Bella, and a sweet calico named Peabody, who take up more of her attention than they probably should.

Mattie loves to hear from readers, so please check her out on Facebook!

Thanks for reading!

www.ingramcontent.com/pod-product-compliance
Lightning Source LLC
Chambersburg PA
CBHW020628110726
47899CB00002B/694